KU-618-952

SPECIAL MESSAGE TO READERS

This book is published under the auspices of

THE ULVERSCROFT FOUNDATION

(registered charity No. 264873 UK)

Established in 1972 to provide funds for research, diagnosis and treatment of eye diseases. Examples of contributions made are: —

A Children's Assessment Unit at Moorfield's Hospital, London.

•

Twin operating theatres at the Western Ophthalmic Hospital, London.

•

A Chair of Ophthalmology at the Royal Australian College of Ophthalmologists.

•

The Ulverscroft Children's Eye Unit at the Great Ormond Street Hospital For Sick Children, London.

You can help further the work of the Foundation by making a donation or leaving a legacy. Every contribution, no matter how small, is received with gratitude. Please write for details to:

**THE ULVERSCROFT FOUNDATION,
The Green, Bradgate Road, Anstey,
Leicester LE7 7FU, England.
Telephone: (0116) 236 4325**

**In Australia write to:
THE ULVERSCROFT FOUNDATION,
c/o The Royal Australian and New Zealand
College of Ophthalmologists,
94-98 Chalmers Street, Surry Hills,
N.S.W. 2010, Australia**

Shirley Smith was born in Yorkshire; for some time she worked as a headmistress in Manchester, and as an inspector in South Yorkshire. She has two daughters, a son and nine grandchildren.

Shirley lives with her husband in Radcliffe-on Trent.

FORGOTTEN AS A DREAM

Ireland, 1815. Life is unbearable for young and beautiful Lizzie Baines when her cruel stepfather sells her to Captain Preston. She runs away and seeks sanctuary with the wealthy Miss Jane Gibson who taught her at Sunday school. Miss Gibson and Miss Bradbury, her companion, take Lizzie to the Hanbury Academy for the Daughters of Gentlefolk in England. And, after two years at Hanbury, Lizzie becomes the paid companion to Lady Gascoine, Miss Gibson's sister. But Lizzie's trouble begins when she meets Lady Gascoine's two sons. She must face much unhappiness before she can find the man of her dreams.

Books by Shirley Smith
Published by The House of Ulverscroft:

DEAR MISS GREY
DANGEROUS LEGACY
TANGLED DESTINY
A PARTICULAR CIRCUMSTANCE

SHIRLEY SMITH

◆

FORGOTTEN AS A DREAM

Complete and Unabridged

ULVERSCROFT
Leicester

First published in Great Britain in 2009 by
Robert Hale Limited
London

First Large Print Edition
published 2010
by arrangement with
Robert Hale Limited
London

The moral right of the author has been asserted

Copyright © 2009 by Shirley Smith
All rights reserved

British Library CIP Data

Smith, Shirley, *1942 –*
    Forgotten as a dream.
    1. Fathers and daughters- -Fiction. 2. Female
    friendship- -Fiction. 3. Aristocracy (Social class)- -
    England- -Fiction. 4. Ireland- -Social conditions- -
    19th century- -Fiction. 5. Love stories.
    6. Large type books.
    I. Title
    823.9′2–dc22

    ISBN 978–1–44480–140–8

Published by
F. A. Thorpe (Publishing)
Anstey, Leicestershire

Set by Words & Graphics Ltd.
Anstey, Leicestershire
Printed and bound in Great Britain by
T. J. International Ltd., Padstow, Cornwall

This book is printed on acid-free paper

This book is dedicated to Nick Sparrow
with sincere thanks for the kind support
he has given.

PROLOGUE

Ireland 1815

They were about to go to bed when Miss Gibson thought she heard a noise outside the front door. 'See who that is, Bradbury,' she said to her companion. 'The servants are nearly all a-bed now, but one never knows . . .'

The recently appointed Mrs Bradbury was shocked and horrified at what was before her. The white-faced young girl who had rung the doorbell stood swaying with exhaustion and was hardly able to state her business. Then her legs buckled slowly as she fainted clean away.

When she came to, she was lying on Miss Gibson's brocade chaise longue, with Jane Gibson, in her dressing gown, wafting *sal volatile* under her nose and holding ready a glass of brandy. 'Whatever can be the matter, Elizabeth? Why are you here and all alone? Do your parents know where you are, my dear? Will no one be worried about you?'

'They have given me to be married to Captain Preston!' Elizabeth blurted out. 'I

1

had to leave. If you refuse me I shall do away with myself. I mean it. I can't be married to a monster who beats me unmercifully . . . And I know not why!' She burst into tears.

'A woman's place is with her husband,' Jane said gravely. 'It is not given to us to put aside those who have joined in holy matrimony. Here, take a little sip of brandy, Elizabeth. Then we must think about getting you home safely.'

'But I am not married yet, nor will be. I would as soon be dead.'

Jane left Elizabeth a moment, to explain to Miss Bradbury that Elizabeth's father Mr Baines and his common-law wife had come into a bit of money and to avoid paying their debts they had fled the district. They had with them his wife's three sons and Elizabeth, the natural daughter of Mr Baines. She had been able to keep in touch with them, even though the visits were irregular, and she had been pleased to observe that the house was tidy and that Elizabeth had put on some weight. She didn't know that Elizabeth had been given in matrimony to Captain Preston. She must be about sixteen.

But when Jane Gibson saw the extent of the livid weals on Elizabeth's body, it was she who needed the brandy. 'Dear God in heaven!' she exclaimed. 'Is this what the monster has done to you, child? I cannot wonder that you have run away. Now let us think, Bradbury. Get the child washed and ready for bed. Light the fire in her bedroom. Put a warming pan in the bed for her. I shall bring upstairs one of my possets and some soothing ointment.'

Miss Bradbury gently peeled off Elizabeth's cloak and washed her carefully. She was put to bed in one of Miss Gibson's own nightgowns and, truth to tell, both ladies thoroughly enjoyed cosseting the pathetic waif who had arrived so unexpectedly on their doorstep. They listened, appalled and almost unbelieving, to the terrible story, sobbed out by the distraught girl. But at last the unhappy Elizabeth was settled and she was asleep before the two women at last were able to seek their own beds.

★   ★   ★

The next day, Miss Gibson was all decision. 'I shall have to take you to London,' she said, noting approvingly that Elizabeth had eaten a fairly good breakfast. 'For you must know, Elizabeth, that there will be people searching for you, here in Ireland, and it wouldn't do for you to be found here and hauled back to the unspeakable Captain Preston. Of course,

I shall have to inform Mr Baines, your father, that you are safe, but in the meantime,' she went on, 'perhaps my sister will be able to offer you a position, which would maintain you and enable you to earn your own living. An abigail, perhaps . . . A companion, even . . . We shall have to see. And in the meantime, we shall keep our plans secret.'

Totally bemused, Elizabeth let the two women make the necessary arrangements and, after receiving confirmation from Jane Gibson's sister, Lady Gascoine, in London, their tickets were secured on the packet to Liverpool. From Liverpool they were to go on the stagecoach to Jane Gibson's widowed sister's London residence. All this took time, for Miss Gibson was an experienced and fastidious traveller, demanding the right seat, the most salubrious of hotels and the very best of service.

When told of his daughter's flight, Mr Baines shrugged his shoulders. He had his money and would take care not to be in Captain Preston's vicinity for some time.

As for James Preston, having slept off his hangover and found that Elizabeth had disappeared completely, he shouted impossible questions to his housekeeper, who was either unwilling or unable to answer them. Baines affected to know nothing and he was not assured of Elizabeth's safety for as long as it took Miss Gibson to get her away to London.

Enraged Preston yelled, 'Well, the trashy jade's gone and bad 'cess to her. Pray God she never comes back. I will not be responsible for the bog-reared bitch or any of her thieving family.

'*But I will have my bride price back, so help me . . .* '

1

Hawton House, in the most fashionable part of the West End, was home to the widowed Lady Gascoine and her two sons, Frederick and Robert. She had generously sent her own carriage to meet her sister Jane and her companions at their last posting inn and, their baggage safely stowed, they made themselves comfortable in the luxurious, beautifully sprung vehicle. It had been a long and tiring journey from Dublin, in spite of the comfortable hotels and Jane Gibson's meticulous planning, and Elizabeth was pleased to be able to lean back against the luxurious squabs and rest.

During their drive to the London townhouse, Miss Gibson managed to convey in a tactful way that Frederick, the elder of the two, was twenty-seven and spent most of his time gaming and racing. He was betrothed to Isabella Mason, a young lady from Norfolk but seemed in no hurry to set a wedding date. The Masons had a country estate of several thousand acres in Norfolk, but the country bored Sir Frederick and in spite of his engagement to Isabella, he was seldom seen out of London.

Robert, who was the younger brother, had once been betrothed to a young lady, Amanda Andrews, whom he'd met in London, but less than a year later she had died of pneumonia.

'Poor young man, he was devastated,' declared Jane Gibson. 'And after three years, he appears still to be unable to recover from his sad loss. Instead he seems to have busied himself in his studies of antique art and sculpture. My sister informs me that although he does not shun society, he is a very private person and has never looked at another young lady since poor Amanda passed away.' She sighed. 'But, as is the way of all mothers, my dear sister favours her first-born and sees no fault in him. She was delighted with his engagement to Miss Mason, but is disappointed that such a handsome and personable fellow is proving so tardy at getting married and providing her with longed-for grandchildren.' Under her silk bonnet, Jane Gibson's eyes grew dark and thoughtful. 'It is so sad for Robert that he lost his only true love so tragically. I am sure they would have been so happy . . . ' She shook herself and continued briskly, 'But Frederick is the real charmer of the family. He is a young man still sowing his wild oats, Bradbury, but one of these fine days I am sure he will come about and settle down. It's not our problem, though, and no doubt he will eventually please his mama by marrying Miss Mason . . . '

Elizabeth was silent. She had nothing to say. She had no idea what 'sowing wild oats' meant. She wasn't even sure what 'a real charmer' was. She didn't think any of the men who had been invited into George Baines's kitchen could ever be described as 'a real charmer'. She thought with revulsion of the rough military officers bawling for more wine, shouting their coarse remarks and attempting to touch her as she scurried round, trying to do whatever Baines and his companions wanted of her. Her mind, which had become almost numbed by what had happened and by the decisive actions of Jane Gibson, returned in devastating flashback to Captain Preston and his sadistic treatment of her. She began to shudder uncontrollably and hugged her thin arms about herself.

Miss Gibson wrapped the rug more closely around her and asked her kindly, 'What is it, child? What ails you? Are you cold? We shall soon be there and Mary always keeps a warm house. It won't be long now.' She lowered her voice a little and said, 'When you are presented to Lady Gascoine, you must hold out your hand and say, 'How do you do, ma'am?' That is all. Do not address any

9

remarks to Lady Gascoine unless she addresses you. Do not stare or fidget. Answer when spoken to, without mumbling, and you will do.'

'Yes, Miss Gibson,' Elizabeth whispered and continued to stare out of the carriage window, almost mesmerized by the passing scenery. Events had piled up on top of one another to such a degree that each new experience seemed totally unreal. The cruel James Preston and her journey in the packet from Dublin, the kindness of the two elderly ladies who now sat chatting in their refined London accents . . . they were part of a kaleidoscope of random impressions which her youthful brain was attempting to assimilate. She was only vaguely aware of the quiet conversation between Miss Gibson and her companion.

'Of course, since Sir William died, Frederick Gascoine is the *nonpareil* of the family. You will hear of nothing else, my dear Bradbury, except 'Frederick this and Frederick that' during our visit. My sister talks of him with more than the usual mother's pride in her offspring. Since Sir William died, Frederick has established himself in a very fast set of young London blades with luxurious apartments in West Kensington, although my younger nephew, Robert has remained quietly in his mama's residence in Hawton Square. But I can tell you that although we may not see Frederick much during our stay with my sister, we shall hear of nothing else. She will talk about him with such pride that there will be room for little else in our conversation. For you must know that according to his mama, he is the best and most fearless rider in London. That he is clever to the point of being a genius, which I know to be false — even by the standards of my own modest governess, he is lamentably stupid. Lady Gascoine will recount to us how much he is admired by the *ton* for his exceptional good looks and dress, which are so unusual as to make him an icon for other young blades. If anyone has the lack of judgement to praise his brother or any of his circle of friends, Lady Gascoine will top it at once with another anecdote about Frederick's superior prowess in any activity you care to name . . . '

Jane Gibson paused to draw breath and Elizabeth heard Miss Bradbury say, 'And does not his mama hold Robert in any affection or esteem?'

'Yes, I am sure she has a mother's love for Robert, but since his father's death, Frederick has been set so high on the pedestal that my sister seems blind to aught else. And then, of course, there was the disappointment at Miss Andrews' untimely death. No, Lady Gascoine has set all her hopes of happiness on the marriage of Frederick and Isabella.'

Miss Bradbury glanced at her and said hesitantly, 'Do I take it then, ma'am, that you are not fond of your eldest nephew?'

'Oh, no,' Jane Gibson said quickly. 'He is as attractive as his mama says and more. I am just so resentful of the way he rules the roost and squanders all the money, now that he has inherited the title. Robert is naturally clever and is interested in how the estate should be managed. His mama finds this tedious and is easily bored by his bookish interests. Consequently, she overlooks his good points and concentrates solely on the flamboyant charm of her eldest.'

'And does Robert have no skills at manly pursuits?'

'Most certainly he does. He is an expert huntsman and first-class shot. He is a member of various sporting clubs in London but he says there is no pleasure in killing merely for recreation. While the other members of Lady Gascoine's house party are playing billiards or gambling over the cards, Robert is to be found solving some tenant farmer's problem or poring over his collection of antique books and cataloguing the artefacts he brought back with him from his Grand Tour.'

The words 'Grand Tour' meant nothing to Elizabeth and she continued to watch the passing scene, too tired to concentrate on what was being said and yet too tense and uneasy for sleep.

'I look forward to meeting all three of them,' Bradbury said, smiling at Jane Gibson.

'All *four* of them,' Jane Gibson corrected her. 'There is also Miss Holmes.'

'Miss Holmes?'

'Yes, Lavinia Holmes. Some distant relative of my late brother-in-law. As a young girl in the 1770s she met a most charming and hardened rake at a ball, who thought that she had expectations of a considerable inheritance. He persuaded her to elope with him but when he found out she was just a poor relation, he abandoned her. She was fetched back but her reputation was ruined. My sister took her in out of pity and now she is a sort of unpaid companion.'

'What is she like?' Bradbury asked curiously. 'Is she young? Is she pretty?'

Jane Gibson laughed. 'Hardly,' she said. 'The romance was years ago. She was no oil painting then and now she is a plain, middle-aged woman. It is easy to see that the adventurous rake was only after her because he thought she was an heiress.'

Elizabeth's eyelids gradually began to droop and she laid her head back against the padded squabs of Lady Gascoine's carriage and slept.

It seemed like only the next moment that the coach turned into the great wrought-iron gates of Hawton House, and swept round the shingled half-moon drive to pull up at the huge front door.

Staggering dazedly out of the coach, Elizabeth blinked round in bewilderment.

She had never seen a building so large and imposing. Why, it was grander and more magnificent than the parish church at Tollyvara! There were two life-sized stone lions facing a wrought-iron lamp standard, flames protected in a glass orb, and these lights were echoed at the top of wide stone steps, leading up to the huge carved door. In the early dusk, the lions, standing back to back, each with their lifelike tails and fierce teeth, made Elizabeth shudder all over again. They looked so real, especially the male one with the huge flowing mane, that she could easily believe those teeth could tear someone to pieces. She thought of the three ragged stepchildren of Baines and how they had tormented her. They would have given her the final blow if they could

. . . She shivered at the thought.

The coachman sprang down and helped the ladies out of the carriage and then beat a smart tattoo on the magnificent front door, which was opened immediately by a very portly butler who motioned to the footman to bring in the luggage. If it was noticed that the young girl, who stumbled wearily up the steps, had very little luggage to bring in, it was not remarked upon. They were ushered into the marble hall by the dignified butler and his flunkeys and this time Elizabeth almost lost her breath at the scene before her. If she'd thought the drive and portico magnificent, they were as nothing compared to the marble hall. High Doric pillars, not of actual marble but of Derbyshire alabaster, flanked the hall and staircase. Set very high up in the walls on top of noble columns were busts of Roman gods and goddesses, the whole designed to echo the appearance of a Roman temple. Elizabeth had absolutely no knowledge of the architectural points of Roman temples, she was conscious only of an overwhelming sensation of awe and her own humble station in relation to the grandeur that surrounded her.

The next half an hour passed in a dream as they were escorted to the south drawing-room, a more intimate little sitting-room than the main saloon and much favoured by Lady Gascoine for entertaining. Once again, Elizabeth was overwhelmed by the magnificence of her surroundings. There was a good fire in the marble fireplace and the reflections on the polished brass fire irons flickered in concert with those of the fire.

On the left of the fireplace was a painting of one of the distant ancestors of Sir William Gascoine. He had been a chief justice and was pictured in red robes trimmed with ermine. On the right of the fireplace was quite a different portrait of Sir William, about thirty, surrounded by gun dogs. He was about to load his gun and at his feet was one of the game birds he had already shot. With his light feathery brush strokes, the artist had echoed the faint stripes on the bird's breast feathers on His Lordship's fashionable striped waistcoat.

In spite of her exhaustion, Elizabeth couldn't help but look at it. Her eyes were drawn to the poor dead creature with its lolling, bloodied neck and already fading plumage. Distressed, she looked away, back to the bright fire.

Her Ladyship was waiting to greet them, and kissed both Miss Bradbury and Miss Gibson very graciously as they entered. In the background, rather like a big, lumpy

16

dragonfly, was Miss Holmes, serious and unsmiling and seemingly totally lacking in any grace or charm.

Elizabeth was gently urged forward by Miss Gibson. She extended her hand in greeting and even attempted a little curtsy to the lady of the house. This was greeted with indulgent smiles by the ladies, but glancing sideways, Elizabeth was very conscious of the unhappy glance of the dowager, Lady Gascoine's companion, and she made an attempt to nod in a friendly manner in her direction. Glasses of cordial and small ratafia were produced as if from nowhere and handed round sombrely by Holmes, but Elizabeth had little appetite and did not attempt to keep up with the conversation of Miss Gibson and her sister.

She merely remained silent and passive until Lady Gascoine said brightly, 'Well now, my dears, Holmes will show you to your rooms. I arranged a bed for the child in your dressing-room, Jane. I'd as lief not be disturbed if she is a restless sleeper. Remember we keep town hours here and will dine at seven.'

Her Ladyship's smile was so kind it took the sting out of her words and Elizabeth obediently followed Miss Gibson and Brad-bury as they went with Holmes to their rooms.

At precisely seven o'clock, there was a muffled and musical reverberation throughout the house as the gong signalled that it was time for dinner. Elizabeth was standing in the middle of the dressing-room to the main guest bedroom, having been told by Jane Gibson not to move, as Bradbury went to her own bedroom for the curling irons. Both women were changed into elegant frocks for dinner and had put aside their velvet evening reticules while they concentrated on Elizabeth. The previous hour had been spent by the two ladies in transforming their protégé from a gauche wild fawn into a pretty and slender nymph. Bradbury had ironed a simple white gown, with a sash of blue velvet, and cast it over the girl's head in a trice. The sash was fastened in a bow round her waist and her long, slim feet were thrust into a brand new pair of slippers. Bradbury was back in an instant and the long lustrous locks were soon curled into fashionable guinea-gold, sausage ringlets.

'There, child, you will do,' Jane Gibson declared as she stood back to admire Bradbury's handiwork. 'One moment, Bradbury. A ribbon,' she ordered, and the tireless Bradbury reappeared with the daintiest and narrowest length of blue satin ribbon and threaded it through Elizabeth's hair.

Even Jane Gibson, not the sort of woman to give way to weak feminine sentiment, was overcome with pleasure at the transformation of her gawky little Elizabeth. Her eyes glowed with emotion as she said again, 'Yes, Bradbury, I think she will do.'

A dainty little beaded reticule was thrust in her hand and Jane Gibson gave Elizabeth a little push and said, 'There, child, you look a picture.' And Elizabeth was forced to agree. At first she didn't recognize the pretty young girl who looked back at her from the cheval mirror and when she did, she gasped and turned and looked wonderingly at Bradbury.

She was forced to walk very carefully, her feet feeling strange in the unaccustomed slippers and her body feeling light and airy in the graceful muslin gown. She had to hold her head up in an entirely new and dignified way now that she had ringlets and ribbons, like a real lady.

They were almost at the bottom of the large staircase when there was a sudden commotion in the marble hall. Footmen appeared from nowhere and the front door burst open to reveal the most handsome man that Elizabeth had ever seen. He brought something of the cold air in with him and his tall figure, dressed in a many caped greatcoat, disturbed the atmosphere so much that she instinctively froze and cowered back against the balusters, never taking her eyes off him.

His hair was reddish gold and he was dressed immaculately in a style much in fashion among the Regency bucks of London and very much favoured by the friends of the Prince Regent. The beautifully shaped locks were slightly longer at the back and, although he was clean shaven, he made a concession to the fashion of the day and sported a pair of side whiskers. She continued to stare at him as he pulled off his driving gloves and tossed the greatcoat to a servant. Then she became aware of his grey eyes gazing curiously into hers and dropped her own, blushing furiously.

'Aunt Jane. Miss Bradbury. What a pleasure. And . . . ?' He looked from one to the other, but his eyes returned to Elizabeth.

'My . . . ward . . . ' Jane Gibson said smoothly. 'Miss Elizabeth Baines. From Ireland.'

Elizabeth had never been called 'Miss' before. Having safely negotiated the last step of the stairs, she dropped a modest curtsy, as Miss Gibson had taught her.

'How do you do, sir?' she whispered shyly. Her soft Irish brogue was very pronounced, but Elizabeth had absolutely no idea how enchanting it sounded to a sophisticated London ear.

'I do very well, my dear,' he murmured and he smiled undisguised pleasure at such an innocent chit. 'I shall do even better when that confounded manservant of mine has organized my dinner clothes and got me to Mama's dining-room in time for dinner.'

The mama in question, statuesque in black velvet, appeared at that moment and began to exclaim and scold at him as if he were still a schoolboy. 'Why, Frederick, whatever are you at to arrive just as dinner is about to be served? My dear boy, you know how miffed Wilkins gets if things have to be kept waiting.'

He kissed her, then shrugged and smiled as he walked in a leisurely fashion up the stairs, accompanied by her gentle chiding.

'Incorrigible boy,' she said fondly to her sister. 'What am I to do with him?' Then she hurried away to tell Wilkins that dinner must be delayed a little, to give Sir Frederick time to change for dinner.

It was a relatively informal meal to welcome the honoured guests. The second son, Robert, joined them and Elizabeth was almost crippled with embarrassment and nerves when once again she had to offer her hand, as she'd been taught by Jane Gibson. At least her curtsy was a little more practised, she thought, and she didn't wobble as she looked up into those cool eyes, that sometimes flashed green like his brother Frederick's and yet were so subtly different. He was just as handsome as his brother, but with a face completely lacking in any signs of dissipation. His hair was more brown than gold, more chestnut colour than auburn. He was tall and slender, but his shoulders were slightly broader than Frederick's and his evening clothes seemed to accentuate his athletic muscular frame. His smile was sardonic but gentle.

For the first time in her young life, Elizabeth gradually began to feel less threatened when in the presence of a man. The feeling was such a novelty that she took a few minutes to absorb this new situation, and then she dared look at him again.

She was utterly nonplussed to realize that he was looking back at her, studying her with just as much interest as Frederick. She noticed that he had good colour for a man who tended to stay indoors quite a bit. She noticed again his aristocratic features, again so like Frederick's and yet more defined and, yes, more humorous, as though he could see a joke in most situations. For some reason she felt sure that Frederick would never give way to laughter. She was glad that it was Robert who was opposite her at the dining table and not Sir Frederick Gascoine. All this she absorbed mentally in a second, before she had to look away from Robert Gascoine and fix her eyes on her plate.

She noticed that Robert was quietly spoken and said little that was not to the point, while Frederick, at the head of the table, never stopped talking, his talk being on fast horses and impossible wagers among his set of racing friends.

'I am persuaded that Richards will have to marry his little heiress forthwith,' he said, almost licking his lips over his friend's huge losses at the racecourse. 'It is the only way he can recover. He is in so deep and his pa has vowed not to honour any more of his debts. He owes over twenty thousand already, but maybe Miss Vance's fortune will set him on his feet again.'

Frederick's mama hung on his every word, occasionally glancing round to see who else in the assembled company had noticed his latest *bon mot* or flash of wit. Elizabeth said nothing. When next she peeped out from under her shyly lowered eyelashes, it was to find out how to use the knife and fork she was holding.

A footman stood behind every chair and the one assigned to Elizabeth was young and graceful. As Elizabeth stared in frozen dismay at the frightening collection of gleaming cutlery, he would lean forward and on the pretext of adjusting a salt cellar, or straightening a spoon, managed to convey in the most tactful way possible the correct pieces for each course. She watched carefully as Lady Gascoine was served first and noted which dishes she chose to eat, how much and how she ate it. Although she was trembling with nerves, she copied Her Ladyship faithfully in what she ate and what she rejected. As each huge serving dish was presented to her, she managed to acquit herself very creditably, whispering an almost inaudible 'No thank you' to the dishes she was refusing and inclining her head slightly at what she would accept.

She was so constrained in the formal atmosphere of these strangers that she was almost too afraid to glance about her until after the pudding plates had been removed and the dessert plates had been circulated. Luscious peaches from the hothouses in Norfolk and ripe black grapes with the bloom still on them were on colourful display. Elizabeth once more followed Lady Gascoine's example and politely refused it. She had no idea how to eat the fruit and was not prepared to show herself up. When she did dare to cast a glance round the table, she caught her guide and mentor, Miss Gibson, looking at her and to Elizabeth's surprise she was smiling at her, openly approving.

At this moment, Robert, as though he had noticed Miss Gibson's smile, also looked at her. With a slightly amused expression, he said quietly, 'I understand that this is your first visit to London, Miss Baines. It must seem very different to you after rural Ireland.'

The 'Miss Baines' didn't sink in at first, and then Elizabeth's throat constricted at being addressed directly and she only managed 'Yes, sir' and 'No, sir' to every one of Robert's open-ended questions, her delicate skin blushing rosy pink each time she had to make a response. No one else said a word to her and she was pleased and relieved when Lady Gascoine at last led the ladies to the drawing-room. Under the pretext of showing her the fine piano at the end of the room, Jane Gibson gently squeezed Elizabeth's elbow and whispered, 'Well done, my dear. You were a credit to Bradbury and me at dinner. We were so proud of you.'

Elizabeth blushed as usual and looked down, clasping her hands nervously round the borrowed reticule, unable to say a word.

During the manly ritual of port and brandy, in the absence of the ladies, Frederick had continued on the theme of his latest horses. 'Purchased a pair of greys in Ireland as it happens, bruth,' he boasted. 'And invincible, I'd say. My groom Kelly is lyrical about them. Only got 'em back last week. Talking of Ireland,' he continued, changing the subject completely, 'what's with Aunt Jane and the little colleen she's introduced to Mama? What's the thinking behind that, I wonder? You don't think our revered aunt has gone a bit soft in the top storey, do you?' Without waiting for an answer, he continued, 'Mama told me before dinner that Aunt Jane seems on a crusade where this chit is concerned. Going to have her educated and launched as a lady's maid or some such. Seems a smokey thing for the old girl to do at her time of life. Taking little thing, though, ain't she?'

Robert had no need to reply because Frederick never listened to anyone's replies anyway. But he had to admit she was a taking little thing and seemed very unsophisticated. Her soft shy brogue completely bowled him over. He had no idea what his aunt's plans were but he hoped Elizabeth's particular charm would never leave her.

She was pretty, too, Robert thought as the two brothers eventually joined the ladies in the drawing-room. She was standing by the piano, he noticed, and was blushing at something Aunt Jane had said, her hands clasped tightly round her little evening bag. Unusually, the lashes fringing her blue eyes were dark and contrasted with the fair hair framing her charming face. Although she had spoken so little, the lilting Irish accent was very noticeable. If his aunt were indeed going to send her to school, he hoped she wouldn't learn to affect the spoiled manners of so many of the educated young ladies he met in London.

At this moment his mama spoke across the room. 'Why not play for us, Robert? I am sure Miss Holmes will oblige us with a song.'

Elizabeth started away from the piano as though she'd been bitten, while the unsmiling Miss Holmes obediently sorted through the music sheets and chose one for him to play. Robert good-humouredly seated himself at the piano and played the introduction. It was from Act 1 of Mozart's *Cosi Fan Tutte* and the plain, middle-aged woman sang it with a surprising passion. She had an unexpectedly powerful soprano voice, which filled Lady Gascoine's large drawing-room with its rich sound. Miss Holmes sang in Italian. Elizabeth listened, rooted to the spot. She had no idea what the words meant but she knew that the strong feeling was absolutely heartfelt.

There was respectful applause when the aria ended and Robert immediately walked towards her and said, 'Miss Holmes has an exceptionable voice, do you not think so, Miss Baines?'

Frederick began impatiently to order one of the footmen to set up a table for cards, and the other ladies settled down to drink cordial and chat, but Elizabeth was trapped where she was. She stared down at her feet and gulped and blushed, managing only a whispered, 'Yes, sir.'

'Miss Baines, are your feet troubling you?' He spoke so softly and seriously that her eyes flew to his, startled by this unusual question. He was smiling, the normally cool and grey eyes sparkling and alive with laughter, and she realized he was funning her.

She was forced to smile in return. Her slim shoulders relaxed and she took a deep breath, suddenly feeling happier than she had done in weeks.

'That is better,' he said. 'You look so pretty when you smile.' He reached across the piano and picked up Miss Holmes's music. 'Did you understand any of the words?' he asked her.

'N . . . No,' she said. 'But I . . . I likes the sounds of them, so I do.' It was her longest speech since she had arrived and she even dared risk another glance at him.

He smiled as though pleased with her reply and stood even closer to her so that he could point to the words 'come scoglio immoto resta'. 'She is singing, as the rock remains unmoved against the winds and the storm, so this spirit is still strong in its faith and its love and she will never be unfaithful to her lover.'

He was so close to her now that she could smell the pleasant manly scent of him and feel the warmth of his breath on her cheek. Apart from violent George Baines and the equally vile Captain Preston, Elizabeth had never been in such close proximity to a man. She was so terrified of this invasion of her private space that she began to tremble uncontrollably and moved away from him at once.

But at that moment, Frederick called across to his brother, 'Are we playing this hand of cards, Robert, or are you going to study music all night?'

Robert Gascoine smiled and said, 'Please excuse me, Miss Baines. I am needed elsewhere.' He put the music back and went to join Frederick at the card table. Miss Holmes seemed about to retire and Jane Gibson whispered that it was time Elizabeth went to bed.

'You have had a very busy day, my dear,'

she said, smiling. 'I shall look in on you later,' she said, 'and see that you are comfortable. Say good night now, Elizabeth.'

Elizabeth obediently said good night and set off up the grand staircase to her room. She was relieved to be alone at last. It was a strain, trying not to disgrace Miss Gibson, and she wished she were not so awkward. For the first time in her young life, Elizabeth realized how truly ignorant she was, both in her reading and in her manners. She sighed as she threw her nightgown over her head and hastily said her prayers. The bed was a warm cocoon and gradually she began to relax and let her mind roam over all the things that had happened to her in the last few days.

She was in that delicious state between sleeping and waking when the door opened and someone came into the room. Thinking it was Miss Gibson, Elizabeth raised her head to look at the visitor but it was Miss Holmes, carrying a candle, which she shielded with her other hand.

'Are you awake, Elizabeth?'

'Yes, ma'am. Miss Gibson has given me some books, but I am too tired to read.' Elizabeth was surprised by this visitation and said nothing more, as the dour Miss Holmes moved closer and sat on the bed.

'So you are to be the new charity girl, are

you? I also have had that honour once, when I first came here. But there's nothing so cold as charity. Remember that, child.'

Elizabeth was at a loss and began to flounder. 'I . . . I do not know what will happen to me . . . Miss Gibson has been . . . has been . . . so kind. She has helped me and taught me to read . . . I owe her everything . . . '

'And you may be sure, she will exact her payment in full.'

'Wh — what do you mean?'

'I mean, child, that nothing is ever for nothing. As the Spanish proverb says, '*Have what you want. Have it and pay for it*'. Jane Gibson is well able to be bountiful. Her father left her well provided for. He bequeathed her a manor house and land in Ireland. She can be charitable to a younger girl. She can afford to do without a husband and remain unmarried. She has no children of her own but she can be kind to other people's children. When she dies, her fortune will go to her nephews and their heirs.'

'I do not . . . do not understand.'

'You will, child. You will. You will be groomed to be a companion to some old woman. Perhaps to take the place of Miss Bradbury. I expect you already know of my own disgraceful fate. Jilted at the altar

31

because I was not what I seemed. Not an heiress with a handsome fortune like your Miss Gibson. Merely a plain Jane with a loving heart.'

At the words 'plain Jane', Elizabeth's own heart contracted and she saw again, in her mind's eye, Kate Molloy and the three cruel boys who had tried to kill her spirit with their taunts of 'plain Jane' and 'ugly duckling'. Impulsively, she put out her hand to touch that of the older woman, feeling a deep compassion for her obvious suffering.

'But . . . you. But you have such nice things. You live in this big house — '

'True. But nothing belongs to me and I belong to no one. I am the unpaid servant. The ugly unmarried poor relation. The dogsbody and whipping boy for the whole household. There is only one person who treats me with any humanity and that is Robert Gascoine. But he has got his own life with his books and his collections. If I die tomorrow, not one of them will remember me for very long. Is that what you want your future to be, girl? Your youth dwindling and dribbling away in comfortable penury for the rest of your days?'

Elizabeth looked up at her, appalled by this sudden outburst, not fully understanding the older woman's emotional outpouring. She saw Miss Holmes's bitter twisted mouth, working with passion, and she was afraid. She wished that Jane Gibson would come upstairs and wondered how long she would be.

Miss Holmes suddenly seemed to collect herself and perhaps thought she had said too much. She withdrew her hand from beneath Elizabeth's and stood up abruptly. 'Well, I will leave you to think on these things.'

Still carrying the candle, she left the room, leaving Elizabeth to the dark and her own thoughts. She lay for some time, unable to sleep, as different emotions whirled around in her brain. The room was warm and she watched the last glowing coals in the grate bringing the brass fire irons to life. She heard Miss Gibson enter on tiptoes and she pretended to be asleep. Jane planted an awkward motherly kiss on Elizabeth's cheek, then crept out with her candle.

All at once Elizabeth was alone. She lay on her back, solitary in the large bed. The moon appeared from nowhere and threw fitful scudding shadows on the walls. Elizabeth thought of the moon shining through the bare windows of the Baines' cottage, with its broken panes stuffed with filthy rags. Every last bit of happiness and excitement of the day ebbed away from her. She felt all the kindness and generosity shown her by Jane

Gibson could not be real. Whatever happened, she would still be Lizzie Baines, forced to endure the casual sadism of her family in Ireland. That is how it would be for ever and ever. She would always be an ugly duckling just as Miss Gibson would always be a rich lady living in her big house.

She lay for a long time with her eyes wide open till the light from the window seemed to shimmer and blur. Then, on an impulse, she went to the window and drew back the curtains to look out across the cobbled mews towards the stables. Everything was still and deserted. She drew a deep breath, trying to calm herself. It was colder in the room now, and as she turned to get back in bed, she passed the connecting door leading into Miss Gibson's bedroom.

Then she heard Jane Gibson say softly, 'Our darling little Lizzie is fast asleep, Bradbury,' before the two women went back downstairs to Lady Gascoine. Strangely comforted, Elizabeth gradually drifted off to sleep.

2

'My dear Jane, what you propose is absolute madness.' Lady Mary Gascoine spoke gently to her sister, but nevertheless she spoke firmly and with great conviction. 'You would be educating the child above her station in life. After all, what would she be at the end of it, except a child from the very lowest of the low of Irish society? The only result of your misplaced desire to have her educated will be the rejection of her own kind and be assured she will not be accepted by polite society either. This will make her nobody's child, trained and educated for a place in life she will never achieve.'

Jane Gibson was equally quiet and equally firm. 'I have to thank you, my dear Mary, for your generous hospitality to us and your kindness to Elizabeth. But I assure you that there is great potential for refinement and intelligence in the girl, which I am deter-mined to encourage. Bradbury and I have discussed the possibility of one of the new seminaries for young ladies which seem to be starting up lately in London and Bath. Elizabeth has the ability to do very well if she were to be twenty-four hours a day in the company of well-brought-up young ladies whose teachers are striving to nurture a sense of decorum and good manners among them.'

Lady Gascoine leaned forward earnestly from the waist to try and press her point. 'But what if she were to fail, my dear? What if she were to emerge from the education you have imposed upon her, only to remain the same low-lived hoyden as she was before? Or supposing the seminary or academy rejects her as being unworthy or uneducable?'

Jane Gibson's thin cheeks flushed bright red. 'Your pardon, Mary. I really must protest at that. Elizabeth Baines is not, definitely not, a low-lived Irish hoyden. She is a sensitive and intelligent young girl who is deserving of all our sympathy and support. Bradbury and I are of the same mind. We have been discussing the idea of Miss Arabella Hanbury's Academy for Young Ladies in Bath and have sent for details of the prospectus.'

Lady Gascoine groaned softly. 'But she is not a young lady. I appeal to you, Miss Bradbury. Cannot you prevail on Jane to think the plan through a little further? What is the point of these unreal expectations? What will be the girl's future when she leaves this . . . this . . . academy in Bath? Will she make a respectable marriage? Will she be able to achieve gainful employment? Become a governess? A seamstress? What? Or will she drift unhappily, educated, but with no particular social role, lacking a portion for marriage and too refined for working life?'

Bradbury answered now, in a low, diffident voice. 'Lady Gascoine, ma'am, I was once that child. When my father perished at sea, I was the eldest of ten children and my dear mama was left with no means of supporting us. The ship's officers had a charity which funded six boys to go to school and naval college. Two of my sisters were found positions in private houses, doing sewing and mending and assisting Maria the nursery maid. Mama and my youngest sister died of typhoid in 1770. I found a place as companion to an elderly lady but when she died, Miss Jane was my benefactress and saviour. She took me in, fed me and clothed me and helped me when no other would. Without her, I would have perished. With respect, ma'am, it is all too easy to pass by on the other side when one sees a fellow human being in distress. It is far harder to address the problem and effect some aid . . . '

Bradbury's soft, respectful voice ceased but she continued to look earnestly at Lady Gascoine, who was still unmoved.

'But you were a gently-brought-up girl,' she

protested. 'Your father was Captain Alexander Bradbury, a distinguished English captain in the Royal Navy, who fought with distinction under Admiral Lord Rodney. Elizabeth Baines is a slum urchin from the bogs of Ireland. There is no comparison.'

Miss Gibson was adamant. Without in any way quarrelling with her esteemed sister, she brought the discussion to a close by kissing Lady Gascoine fondly and saying very pleasantly, 'Dear Mary, we are destined to disagree on this. My mind is made up. I intend to send Elizabeth to school in Bath. Bradbury and I will kit her out this week with all that a young girl requires for the Hanbury Academy. If she proves unworthy of Miss Hanbury's time and effort, I will let you say 'I told you so', but I have a feeling that she will not let us down and will, in fact, be a credit to us.'

The next few days passed in a dream for the bemused Elizabeth, who was taken in hand by her two guardian angels. She didn't know how old she was but she reckoned about sixteen. The prospect of travelling to school appalled her.

The prospectus and list of equipment that Miss Hanbury considered minimum requirement in the way of clothes and toiletries was intimidating. Other necessities such as needlework requisites, drawing and writing materials arrived the next day by special post from the shop. Frequent visits were made to the dressmaker to fit Elizabeth for her new clothes, shawls and slippers and to the various shops to track down the things she needed.

No mention was made in Miss Hanbury's prospectus of standards required in the way of literacy or social deportment. Arabella had spent a lifetime putting a gloss on young ladies who were less than adequate in areas of intellectual and social development. There were many girls sent by busy parents who were in trade, or whose fathers were posted overseas. She saw it as a challenge to help these girls overcome their deficiencies and to leave her establishment one hundred per cent more developed than when they entered it. To Miss Hanbury, the rough-hewn rock of the immature adolescent female was the raw material for her consummate skill as a teacher. To fashion each one into a refined and accomplished young lady was her stated aim and she was tireless in her efforts.

Elizabeth was still a little wary of travelling so far from home, but Miss Gibson and Bradbury were very impressed with the school and so reassuring that she found herself looking forward to it.

She made the journey to Bath in Lady Gascoine's own coach, with both Bradbury and Miss Gibson in attendance, and when they arrived at the academy they were immediately shown into Miss Hanbury's private sitting-room and interviewed by the lady herself. It was not a formal affair, merely an opportunity for Arabella Hanbury to inspect the prospective pupil at first hand and note where improvements could be made. This was not an obvious procedure. Tea and refreshments were served and as Miss Hanbury chatted to the two ladies, she occasionally addressed a remark or a question to the shy Elizabeth. As the tea and cakes were passed round, she noticed unconscious, natural grace of the slender hands, the girl's luxuriant golden hair and pretty face with its refined bone structure and the almost frozen stillness of her posture. As though she had never learned to trust anyone, Miss Hanbury thought.

Elizabeth managed not to spill anything or disgrace herself in any way, but Miss Hanbury decided, on the basis of her experienced observation, that ironing out the pronounced Irish brogue and giving social confidence to the rather gauche young girl would be her priority. Any other accomplishment the girl picked up would be a bonus.

All three of them were more than a little tearful when the time came for Miss Gibson and Bradbury to say their farewells — both promised to write regularly and seemed reluctant to leave her. But with the resilience of youth, Elizabeth soon settled into the school routine and made some friends. All memories of her natural father, Mr Baines, and the man she had been promised to in marriage, Captain Preston, began to fade.

Having mastered the cutlery and use of the china, which was on the table at every meal in the refectory, she began to lose her fear of it and become more confident. Some girls remarked on her golden curls admiringly; one girl in particular, Honoria Wilshaw, begged shyly to be allowed to arrange it in a more modish way. Honoria had three older sisters, who had all had their London coming-out season. She knew all there was to know about the latest fashions in hairstyles. Elizabeth was an apt pupil and in no time at all had mastered the art herself and began to look altogether a more fashionable young miss. She felt that Honoria would be her friend for ever.

Jane Gibson passed all the news of her protégé to Lady Gascoine. Both Jane and Bradbury were delighted with the girl's progress and were ever ready to praise her.

Tuesday
Dear Miss Gibson and Miss Bradbury,
Thank you for the letter and my allowance which I received this morning. Yesterday we went sketching and the art mistress allowed my friend Honoria and me to go into a little wood at the edge of the garden. There were so many small and delicate flowers and Miss Pemberton said that my sketch was excellent and that I might do a watercolour of the same subject. Honoria has also told me that on Friday, Signor Guiseppe, the dancing master, will give us lessons in the waltz! I will let you know how we get on. I must go now,
  With love from,
  Elizabeth Baines

The two maiden ladies were ecstatic at the young Elizabeth's progress. Although she was only a paid companion, Bradbury had become a close friend to Jane Gibson and there were no secrets between them. Miss Gibson treated her as an equal and they both saw in the young Elizabeth the promise and hope of their own youth. That she was both beautiful and innocent in spite of her appalling background gave the women an extra desire to nurture and protect her. She had quickly become their life, their raison d'être, their loved one, the focus of their rather staid and restricted lives. Both women looked forward to Elizabeth's weekly letters and, blissfully unaware of the situation, Elizabeth artlessly confided on paper all her experiences, youthful hopes and fears in this transitional time of her education. The two women were delighted: it almost seemed as if they both had a second chance at life through her. Although past their own youth, they were transported by her happiness and success, as she reported all her girlish dreams and all her activities at Miss Hanbury's Academy.

Twice a year they took her to a townhouse in Bath which they rented for the holidays, marvelling at the progress she was making in her studies. As for Elizabeth, her clothes and equipment were the best that money could buy and her self-esteem soared as the other girls complimented her on the quality of her evening dresses and her finely appointed needlework basket. She never mentioned her previous life in Ireland; her youthful hopes and dreams for the future seemed far stronger and longer-lasting than any of the unhappy past.

She revelled in her opportunities for education and began to love the books in Miss Hanbury's library. She even enjoyed sewing lessons, not that she was any good at embroidery — quite the opposite, in fact, but this deficiency made her all the more popular with her fellow students. She discovered in herself a talent for watercolour painting and this pleased her. Her botany and watercolour lessons with Miss Gibson were given a new dimension on Miss Pemberton's sketching trips. Now she was not only to paint the delicate specimens but to explain their botanical names as well.

The ladies were delighted when in the holidays she demonstrated the deportment exercises she had learned, which involved the usual walking round with a book balanced on the head and also Arabella Hanbury's progressive stretching and relaxation postures, to enable a young lady to endure the stresses of an evening ball without becoming too exhausted or losing her perfect posture. She even achieved some small skill at the pianoforte and could accompany her own naturally sweet, low voice in some of the Irish airs she had learned as a child.

Monday
Dear Miss Gibson and Miss Bradbury,
There was wild excitement yesterday, for the rumour was that Signor Guiseppe judged that we were advanced enough to

learn the waltz. Miss Hanbury has warned us of its dangers and stipulates that if we master this rather fast and dangerous dance, we may only dance it if our parents give permission. He warned us that some ladies find it so taxing and stimulating that they are like to faint with it all. He can be so amusing when he is talking to us. When he was sure I knew the steps, he took me in his arms and demonstrated dancing with a partner. You will be pleased to know that your little Lizzie did not faint or have the vapours and my friends were generous in their praise and congratulations.

We were able to go riding this afternoon, but I am too tired to write any more to you and look forward to seeing you on Friday for the two-week holiday.

My love to you both,
From your devoted Elizabeth

The fees for Miss Hanbury's Academy were not cheap, but Miss Gibson considered it money well spent. They visited four times a year and each time they met with their protégé, they noticed a marked change in her. She never gave a thought now to her previous life; it was as though Baines no longer existed. He never tried to get in touch and she and Miss Gibson decided to let sleeping dogs lie.

She was no longer scrawny but was gracefully slim and had grown two inches taller in two years. Her hair was still gloriously curly but was now dressed in formal ringlets which framed her pretty face. She glowed with hope and confidence and her expression, though shy, was more open.

In the last week at school, Miss Arabella Hanbury described her as one of Hanbury Academy's successes and Jane Gibson was bound to agree. But the last week was marred by a sudden shock.

My dear Elizabeth,
I have rather bad news for you. Although Bradbury and I are rejoicing at the thought of seeing you next week, and making plans for the future, I must tell you that Miss Holmes, my sister's erstwhile friend and companion, has unfortunately had a seizure and died suddenly on Wednesday night. This was a terrible shock to Lady Gascoine, as you may imagine. Doctor Godfrey was called as soon as she felt unwell, but it was too late. She was dead before he arrived. The funeral is tomorrow and although the formalities will have been observed,

by the time you leave Miss Hanbury's, Lady Gascoine will still be affected by her sad loss. Bradbury and I both feel she will need our support at this time, so we will be staying at Hawton House for an indefinite time, to comfort poor Mary in her distress. Bradbury will come to meet you next Friday and I have already informed Miss Hanbury of this.

Until then, Elizabeth, I remain
Yours sincerely,
Jane Gibson

The news was a great surprise to Elizabeth, but coming as it did when she was so distracted with the idea of leaving school, and saying goodbye to her friends, she didn't take it in very clearly. Instead, her thoughts were all of seeing Miss Gibson and Bradbury again and what the future might hold for her. It was 7 November 1805 and in *The Times* newspaper that day was printed a very affecting account of Lord Nelson's last moments. As he was being carried down to the cockpit, severely wounded, he said, 'Don't let me be thrown overboard; tell Hardy to carry me.'

Elizabeth had read nothing of this and would have been almost indifferent to the national hero's fate even if she had read it, because on that particular day, she was about to leave Miss Hanbury's Academy for ever. Her schooldays were over and although she was going in Lady Gascoine's carriage, only Bradbury would be accompanying her. Miss Jane Gibson was obliged to sit with Lady Gascoine and keep her company when her spirits were low after her sad loss.

She did not exactly know how to broach the subject of death so she waited until Bradbury spoke of it herself. Bradbury was matter of fact about it and merely stressed how tactful they all had to be at this time of mourning for the death of Holmes. Elizabeth was too cheerful to take it in properly. She said her goodbyes to Miss Hanbury before stepping into the carriage.

'Goodbye, Miss Baines. Give my regards to dear Miss Gibson and my sincere condolences in her sad loss. Have a pleasant journey. I hope you remember the Hanbury Academy with pleasure and affection, Elizabeth, and may return before too long to renew your acquaintance with us.'

Arabella Hanbury waved a scented handkerchief at the coach, which contained her last departing pupil and the stolid Bradbury. She continued to watch as the two of them set off for London for the last time. She was pleased and relieved that all her girls had now returned to their families for the holiday. Some girls with parents abroad — would be spending the holidays, and later Christmas, with relatives. Some would be travelling long distances to be with their loved ones. They would be back in January. Some, like Elizabeth, would not be returning. Their schooldays were over.

A very beautiful young girl, Miss Hanbury reflected, and one who had worked hard at her studies. She wondered if Miss Gibson would agree to let Elizabeth become a pupil teacher at the academy. She would certainly be an asset, she thought, as she turned and went back into school. A girl with strong intelligence and intellectual independence of mind. She recalled that Miss Gibson had spoken of some earlier difficulties the girl had had, back in Ireland. They must have shaped Elizabeth's character, she decided, because even at eighteen it was very well formed.

The last two years had been successfully spent in moulding Elizabeth into a more refined young lady who would be acceptable in polite society. Perhaps she would be a governess or a lady's companion, even. Why, yes, the companion. Miss Holmes had vacated such a post. The idea of her being Miss Holmes's successor was now quite feasible. Failing that, she would certainly be eligible for a post in Miss Hanbury's own school. One thing was certain, in the friendly and civilized atmosphere of the academy, Elizabeth had completely overcome her previous overwhelming shyness and inhibition. She was attractive and popular, a totally different girl from the one who had so nervously taken tea with her two years ago. Miss Hanbury hoped that Elizabeth would one day make a successful marriage to some decent and worthy man.

Arabella Hanbury sighed with sudden weariness, and went to seek the calm of her study, where sherry and ratafia biscuits awaited her.

As for Elizabeth, she settled back against the cushions of Lady Gascoine's carriage and breathed deeply. She was pleased her schooldays were over, and yet apprehensive too as to what the future might hold. Her expressive nervous posture was not lost on Bradbury, who was aware of every nuance of the girl's impulsive movements and uneven breathing. She felt an affinity with and affection for Elizabeth and was only too well aware of how difficult her future might be. She thought of Elizabeth's unhappy background and gave a sigh of her own.

Elizabeth was quick to notice it and laughed out loud. 'That was a very heartfelt sigh, Miss Bradbury. Surely you cannot feel sad to be leaving Miss Hanbury for the last time?'

'Why, no, my dear,' Bradbury said truthfully. 'Quite the opposite.' The small dark eyes in her broad pale face looked into Elizabeth's bright blue ones, which sparkled like gems. Bradbury leaned forward and smiled affectionately at the lovely young lady opposite her.

'Well, for my part, now that I've bid farewell to Miss Hanbury, I feel that my life has really begun.'

Looking at the tall slender girl, with her long eyelashes and vivid good looks, Bradbury couldn't doubt that this was the truth. She sighed again and said gently, 'I am sure it has, my dear, but I know that you will remember, because you are a sweet and loving girl, that poor Lady Gascoine has recently lost her close companion. Her own thoughts are melancholy and she must find that a significant chapter of her own life has closed. I beg of you to respect this in the next few months.'

'Of course,' Elizabeth said quickly. 'And how does Miss Gibson, ma'am?'

'She is sad also,' Bradbury said. 'But she tries to comfort and divert her sister whenever she can. Of course, when Lady

Gascoine has recovered somewhat from this sudden bereavement, she will no doubt be looking for another suitable companion, one who is genteel and compatible. Such creatures are hard to find.'

Both of them leaned back, each thinking their own thoughts as they left Bath and looked through the windows at the autumn countryside unrolling before them.

★　★　★

The next day, they arrived in London and after a rapturous welcome from Miss Gibson, all three of them were summoned almost immediately to the south drawing-room for a meeting with Lady Gascoine.

She was dressed in a severe black silk gown and reclined on one end of the red and gold sofas in front of the fire. Her face was paler than usual, but she was by no means discomposed. Her hair was dressed carefully and her lace-trimmed cap was quite exquisite. Elizabeth curtsied and asked prettily how she was.

'Well, I thank you,' Lady Gascoine said. 'In spite of my great loss, I am determined to take up the threads of life again and, of course, I have the support of my sister, Jane.' She smiled mistily. 'My two sons have been so helpful. Frederick cancelled his race meeting on the day after Miss Holmes's death and Robert organized the arrangements for the funeral. Where would I have been without Robert? He has been a rock and support, ever ... ever ... since it happened.' Briefly, she pressed a tiny scrap of lace handkerchief to her lips, but continued almost immediately. 'But no looking back. We must look forward and as soon as possible, I wish to discuss with you all a position for Elizabeth and a plan for her future.'

Elizabeth glanced with some alarm at Miss Gibson, but her guide and mentor was avoiding her gaze. Bradbury was gazing studiously at the fire. Elizabeth felt completely alone. In spite of the warmth of the room, she shuddered with a sudden chill and looked with panic at Lady Gascoine, wondering what she would say next, but it was Jane Gibson who broke the silence.

She smiled reassuringly at Elizabeth and said, 'Lady Gascoine has kindly said that she would like to offer you the post of companion, which has sadly become vacant because of Miss Holmes's sudden death. There is no need to accept or reject her kind offer at the moment. No doubt you would like to consider it carefully before you give her an answer. No, do not try to make a judgement just yet, Lizzie,' she said as she saw Elizabeth about to open her mouth to reply to Lady Gascoine. 'There are many advantages for you in this generous offer, and you may wish to discuss them with me. Meanwhile, let us go and supervise the unpacking and prepare for dinner.'

'Yes,' said Lady Gascoine in a stronger voice. 'We shall be dining quietly en famille this evening and perhaps later . . . ?'

Elizabeth's thoughts were whirling as she followed Miss Gibson and Bradbury upstairs. She was no longer given the dressing-room but had a well-appointed guest bedroom all to herself. One of the maids was already laying out the clothes from her trunk and there was a cheerful fire in the grate.

'Good evening, miss. What was you wantin' me to put out for tonight?'

'Good evening,' Elizabeth said mechanically. 'The aquamarine silk, I think. It never creases and if you hang it while I dress my hair, I am sure it will be perfect. I am so sorry I do not know your name.'

'Susanna, miss. Ooh, miss, you got lovely hair. I could do it for you, I could. I've had some training for a proper lady's maid from Miss Holmes and I knows what to do.'

'Yes,' Elizabeth said distractedly. 'Poor Miss Holmes. She is dead.'

'Mmm . . . It were a pity, her bein' only in the fifties, like,' Susanna said cheerfully. 'But life has to go on, miss, and they say as how Her Ladyship is looking for another refined lady to keep her company now.'

Elizabeth didn't answer but allowed Susanna to assist her in arranging her hair and putting on the aquamarine gown, which Miss Gibson had made for her, for the farewell party of the Hanbury Academy. She'd sought out a super modiste, who had created a dress that was so severe and classical of line that it displayed only the slender shapeliness of the girl's young body, untrammelled by any decorative frills or flounces and was a departure from the more usual white muslin. Added to this, Elizabeth had not a single item of jewellery, nor did she need one. The colour of the dress made her eyes a startling blue, and they glittered and shone like two sapphires.

She sighed deeply as she picked up her reticule and prepared to leave the room, watched with interest by Susanna. She gave her a smile as she heard the gong reverberating through the building and set off to walk down to the drawing-room to join the rest of the family waiting to be summoned for dinner.

There was a lot of familial chat when

Elizabeth walked in — so much so that she was able to forget her initial shyness and enjoy herself, while not forgetting poor Holmes, of course. She glanced frequently at Lady Gascoine, who in spite of her sadness seemed to be on an even keel.

She found herself seated next to Frederick and opposite Robert and as Frederick began telling his brother about yet another wager his friend had made with him, so Elizabeth remained silent. Frederick's eyes sparkled as he leaned towards Robert and said jovially, 'Well, what do you think, Robert? The most capital wager ever. Jack Richards has come about after his last disaster at the September meeting and is so flushed with luck, he has challenged me to have a race with him. I tell you, I am persuaded I can give him a run for his money. Now I have my new curricle, I shall beat him. Fellow doesn't stand a chance. I shall win hands down.'

'I trust you will not be endangering the family estates,' Robert murmured. 'It would be too bad if we were to end up in the Marshalsea as a result of your ventures in the racing stakes.' Robert made a comical face at Elizabeth. 'What do you think?' he asked, smiling at her.

'Well,' she said, smiling in return, 'I think that Sir Frederick is not such a greenhorn as to let himself be challenged to something he can't win, nor such a toady as to not set the prize high enough.'

'Well,' he said. 'At least his answer shows he has thought about all the possibilities, including the one of losing.' Robert exchanged a smile with the waif who suddenly had a voice in their mock debates, and who still, he noticed, had an attractive ounce of blarney in her speech.

'Pooh!' Frederick said loftily. 'I am not such a greenhorn as to go out of my depth. No, it promises to be a famous day out. Male company, fast horses and a decent purse for the winner. Who could ask for more?'

'Who indeed?' Robert said cheerfully. 'And yet curricle racing is not without its dangers, you know.'

'I know, I know,' he said, somewhat pettishly. 'Depend upon it, I shall not do anything foolish.'

His mama added to his annoyance by saying anxiously, 'Frederick, my darling boy, please take care. If anything should happen to you, dearest . . . '

'I know. I know,' he said again. 'I assure you, Mama, lots of fellows go in for curricle racing. Absolutely nothing to it. Easy as falling off a log.'

Robert gave another grin at this, but Lady Gascoine closed her eyes as if in agony at his unfortunate turn of phrase. 'It sounds so dangerous,' she faltered.

'No, Mama, it is little different from riding a horse. I shall take care, have no fear.'

Robert decided at this moment that it was time to change the subject and addressed Elizabeth directly. 'Miss Baines, I understand your schooldays at Miss Hanbury's are now over,' he said softly. 'Am I to take then that we should be raising our glasses this evening in a toast, to liberation?'

Elizabeth looked up into his laughing eyes and found that they were studying her with interest. Returning his look steadily, she realized she had forgotten nothing about him during the last two years. The fine aristocratic features, straight nose and thick auburn hair hadn't changed at all. Neither had the wide, strong shoulders and breadth of chest displayed to advantage by the close-fitting black coat. He was still the good-looking man she remembered.

He was so unchanged, she thought, but she had changed for ever. She was no longer an ignorant ugly duckling. She was a young lady from Miss Hanbury's Academy and could be proud of herself at last.

She gave him a smile and raised her glass,

saying, 'Yes, indeed, sir. I will certainly toast liberation.'

Everyone round the table murmured, 'Liberation', and Robert smiled back at her. He thought of the inarticulate little Irish girl he'd met at Hawton House two years ago, and the change in her fascinated him more than she knew.

Sensing that he was no longer the focus of attention, Frederick now said rather loudly, 'Be careful not to let my cultured brother monopolize you, Miss Baines. He can become boringly tedious if you allow him to run on about his fossils and his classical statues. Not fit subjects for your young ears.'

Everyone, including Robert, smiled at this and now, with the dessert finished, it was time for Lady Gascoine to rise and lead the ladies into the drawing-room. Elizabeth had much to think about and didn't linger. Pleading a headache, she asked to be excused and went straight to her room.

In the dining-room, Frederick set about the port and cigars with some serious intent and dismissed the footman, in order to get his own drinks and converse freely with his brother. 'The Irish girl's turned out to be quite a delicious little armful,' he said and winked suggestively at Robert, who had begun to twist the stem of his glass in long, sensitive fingers, as though to suggest he too was in a relaxed mood.

'But not to be tampered with while she is under Mama's roof,' he said quietly. 'She is a young lady who has Aunt Jane as her patron. You would be excessively cork-brained to contemplate any havey-cavey with Miss Baines, Frederick.'

'Miss Baines, indeed!' Frederick snorted. 'Even Aunt Jane doesn't know her pedigree. The girl's a bag of mystery. On the lookout, I dare say, to do well by herself.' His fair skin was flushed with the drink and there was a light sheen of sweat on his brow. 'Never knew any such consideration stop *you*, bruth, when a tasty morsel was on the menu. At one time we all thought you were like to stay in Milan, chasing all those light skirts at the opera. Let's see, how many of the ladies were you distracting while you were on your Grand Tour?'

Robert smiled lazily. 'All in the past,' he said. 'Ancient history, like my statues. But I have never destroyed innocence, Frederick, I have always gone with experienced and willing partners, who knew exactly what the score would be at the end of the game. I have never seduced any untried virgins. You would do well to take heed of this. Stick to the bits of town muslin that you know. They can look after themselves. Leave Aunt Jane's protégé alone.'

'I was only thinking of a little light dalliance with the chit,' said Frederick sulkily. 'Still, she turned out to be quite a dainty little filly, wouldn't you say, bruth?' He winked again, very provocatively.

'Dally with Elizabeth Baines and you will have Mama to reckon with,' Robert warned him, but Frederick merely laughed again and poured out the rest of the port.

'Fact is,' he said gloomily, 'as you know, Mama has pestered me almost to death on the subject of marriage. To keep her happy, I've had to get engaged to Isabella. Not a looker, but her papa has settled a handsome portion on her. The fact they are still in half mourning for her grandfather at the moment means I've some leeway. I just hope I can please Mama in the way of an offspring and provide an heir . . . Of course there would be no problem with our Miss Baines. Dainty little bit like that. I'd have no difficulty securing the male line if I had *her*.'

Robert had to take Frederick to task once more and Frederick shouted, 'All right, I know,' in a sulky way. Robert thought he had finally got the message, and it was time to join the ladies anyway.

★ ★ ★

As soon as the object of their discussion reached her room, Susanna appeared with water for washing and to brush out Elizabeth's hair.

'I thought you would have been in the drawin' room a while,' Susanna said. 'With Sir Frederick and his brother in attendance, you'd a' been in for a nice evenin'.'

'No,' said Elizabeth quietly. 'I am fatigued with the journey and need to rest. Leave the candle, if you please. I shall put it out when I am ready to sleep.'

She was reluctant to be too friendly with the maid at this stage. In spite of her talk, Susanna was not a lady's maid and had not learned the tact and reserve necessary to do the job successfully. Without wishing to hurt her feelings, Elizabeth wanted to distance herself somewhat. Her instinct told her that it wasn't a good idea to be over-familiar with her maid. After all, if she herself were to end up working for Lady Gascoine, being too close might put her at a disadvantage.

She lay on the high, firm, guest bed and thought over Her Ladyship's offer. It would have distinct advantages, she thought. Firstly, she would not be parted from her beloved Miss Gibson and the loyal Bradbury.

Secondly, she knew Lady Gascoine as a kind and gentle woman, whatever poor, unhappy Holmes might have said. She would be treated fairly, not humiliated, the work would not be menial and she would be mixing with pleasant and civilized people. Then Holmes's bitter words came back to her: 'Nothing belongs to me and I belong to no one. I am the unpaid servant. The ugly unmarried poor relation. The dogsbody and whipping boy for the whole household.'

Elizabeth herself had experienced that sort of persecution with the unspeakable Kate Molloy and her bastard brood. But they were all in the past. She tried not to think of them.

She remembered Holmes saying, 'There is only one person who treats me with any humanity and that is Robert Gascoine and he seems to be half unseeing, more interested in his books and collections . . .'

That seemed true enough, Elizabeth thought. She liked him and wished she could know him better. With his beautiful speaking voice and devastating smile, he seemed so different from Sir Frederick, more mature altogether, almost as if he should be the elder brother. This coolness seemed to persist even when he was with his family. She could never imagine him in a temper or out of control like her father, George Baines. As she leaned to extinguish the candle, she remembered the hateful Captain Preston, and his angry drunken face flashed across her mind's eye making her shudder. Tragic though Holmes's story had been, Elizabeth knew that realistically, comfortable penury at Hawton House would be far preferable to anything in her previous life — or anything she could hope for in the future, for that matter.

3

The next morning she had made a decision and was determined to tell Lady Gascoine, but first she sought out Jane Gibson in the small south drawing-room.

'Elizabeth, good morning,' Miss Gibson greeted her. 'Bradbury is not yet down but she will be joining us for breakfast.' Looking more closely at Elizabeth she said, 'What is it, child? Have you come to your decision already?'

'Why, ma'am, I have and the answer is that I . . . I have decided to accept Lady Gascoine's kind offer. But . . . but I wanted to tell you first.'

Jane Gibson stood up and took both Elizabeth's hands in hers. 'I am so delighted, Lizzie, and my sister will be so much cheered when she knows you are going to be companion to her. I shall tell Bradbury as soon as she is down. Meanwhile, here is my sister now. Great news, Mary. Our little Lizzie has decided to stay with you and will make herself your cheerful young friend and companion.'

'Great news indeed.' Lady Gascoine

beamed. 'If you are agreeable, Jane, in return for her services I shall give Elizabeth her own rooms and all found. In addition I will match the allowance which you made for her when she was at Miss Hanbury's.' She turned to Elizabeth. 'For my part, I shall expect unquestioning loyalty and respect and your company whenever I require it. Meanwhile, we must have breakfast and then I shall take you to my own suite, so that you will be familiar with the house.'

Lady Gascoine's bedroom was even more impressive than Elizabeth could have imagined. The large four-poster bed was upholstered in green Genoa velvet and the graceful bedside tables were inlaid with elegant marquetry. Lady Gascoine's writing desk was dainty and feminine with a silver-bound writing case and ink stand to match. There was a brass bell pull at each side of the white marble fireplace and the cast-iron grate incorporated the Gascoine crest. Everything was the best quality and Elizabeth gazed in awe at the beautiful tapestries on the wall, and the green silk wall covering in Her Ladyship's dressing-room. Leading off from this was a small, cosy sitting-room with a tiny fire grate and a large upholstered chair with many cushions.

Lady Gascoine seemed to understand the

impact that it had all made on Elizabeth and quietly suggested that they should go downstairs. 'Before we go, Elizabeth,' she said, laying a soft white hand on Elizabeth's arm, 'I should like to make you a little gift. Just a trifle, my dear, to mark the start of our friendship, and if you agree, I would like to forgo the custom of calling you 'Baines' and stick to 'Elizabeth'. It is such a pretty name. I own that when Jane decided on sending you to Miss Hanbury's, I was doubtful of the wisdom of it all. As it happens, everything has turned out for the best and you are thoroughly worthy and suitable to be my close companion. Here, this is for you.'

She handed Elizabeth a leather case and Elizabeth opened it carefully. It contained a single row of perfectly matched and graded pearls. 'My papa gave this to me over thirty years ago, as a coming-out present,' Lady Gascoine said. 'Papa believed that young girls look tasteless wearing diamonds and precious stones. He said that a dainty necklace of pearls was all the jewellery a girl needed, until she married, that is. But that won't be for some time yet, will it, my dear?'

'No indeed, ma'am,' Elizabeth said softly. For some reason she discovered her voice had gone quieter, whether it was shyness she knew not. 'But I cannot accept . . . You should not be so generous . . . You cannot make me such a gift . . . '

'Fustian!' Lady Gascoine smiled. 'Turn round, Elizabeth. The catch can be quite tricky but I am used to it and have the knack of it.'

Blushing with pleasure, Elizabeth turned obediently and stood still while Her Ladyship fastened the dainty necklace for her.

'Charming, quite charming, and most suitable for a young and beautiful girl. Papa was quite right. I shall go and write some letters now, Elizabeth, and will see you at luncheon. Perhaps we may have a little outing this afternoon, in celebration of our working agreement. No, really, run along,' she ordered as Elizabeth tried stumblingly to thank her again for the gift of pearls.

Elizabeth went downstairs, pausing in front of a large mirror on the landing and touching the pearls at her throat. Already they appeared to be more lustrous and to have taken on the warmth of her body. It was the first time in all her young life that she had been given such a personal and splendid gift. In her conscious memory, Elizabeth had never had a birthday present. She didn't even know when her birthday was, and no one in the Baines' household had ever enlightened her on the topic. She had felt very excluded at

Miss Hanbury's when the other girls had received the best wishes and congratulations of their companions, and yet she had never been able to celebrate her own.

From the euphoria of the gift, and the simple pleasure of Lady Gascoine in giving her the pearls, she must have gone down a different staircase, or made a wrong turn. She didn't even recognize this part of the house at all. She had turned the corner at the bottom of the staircase and found herself in a long gallery. With Lady Gascoine's need to have a warm house, there was a fire burning in a veined marble fireplace. On either side of it were alcoves specially created to hold specific statues. As Elizabeth began to walk the length of it, she realized this must be Robert Gascoine's statue gallery.

Although Lady Gascoine might have chosen the chairs and settees, of carved and gilded mahogany with the upholstery of crimson silk damask, and the magnificent chandelier, it was Robert who had been responsible for the simplicity of the decorations and the arrangement of the sculptures. Everything seemed designed to emphasize the splendour of these figures. It was full of statues, most of them lifesize, all of them partially or completely unclothed. She walked slowly past them, thinking all the time that she should go back the other way and return to the south drawing-room. One statue in particular caught her eye and she paused and stood before it to have a closer look. It was Diana the Huntress, holding her bow in her left hand, and reaching back with a graceful gesture of her other hand, to pluck another arrow from the quiver on her right shoulder. Elizabeth was entranced. The loveliness of the calm stone face and the curve of the draperies opened her eyes. She was eager for more. She turned round to see the other statues.

'Miss Baines, you seem to be very taken with the goddess of the chase. Does she please you? Does this mean that you can admire such an antique model of brave womanliness?'

It was Robert Gascoine, who had come upon her without her awareness, and Elizabeth turned immediately at the sound of his quiet, distinctive voice.

She looked at him closely before she replied. He was wearing ordinary clothes for a man of his station, yet she could sense the hidden muscle power in his tall but compact body. He seemed to be waiting for her reply without appearing to.

'Well,' she said, hesitantly. 'She seems a warrior, with her bow and arrows, but feminine and graceful also . . . An . . . an

70

ideal of womanly beauty.'

His compelling eyes were bright in the comparative dark of the gallery and she noticed with fascination that they were mainly green today. His shapely lips curved into a smile that his eyes had already begun. 'And does this mean that you can identify yourself with her brave and open warrior spirit?'

In spite of the lightness of his tone, she recognized that his antiques were an absorbing interest and she answered seriously, 'Well, I don't know about that, sir, but I think she is very beautiful.'

'She is the jewel in the crown of my collection,' he said gravely, with the hint of a smile. 'While I was on the Grand Tour, I stayed for some time in Italy. There I met a Signor Bertorelli, who recognized my interest in antiquarian statues. He put several my way including this one. Which had once belonged to Cicero.'

Elizabeth was impressed, not only by the statues but by his knowledge and erudition.

'Should you care to view some of the other statues, Miss Baines?'

'Why, yes, it is an amazing collection, sir. Being newly released from the schoolroom, I have never seen their like.'

At that precise moment, Elizabeth's eye

alighted on a shamelessly naked Perseus slaying the Gorgon.

Noticing her blushes, Robert said sympathetically, 'Many of Mama's friends deplore the lack of any sort of contrivance, which would conceal the nudities of the male statues, but my Aunt Jane considers this to be the most beautiful room in the house.' He paused and then said, 'And of course, it is true to all the Palladian principles of simplicity with restraint.'

Elizabeth, suspecting he was laughing at her, gazed at him severely for a moment. Having little knowledge of Palladian principles, she had nothing to say. Pointing to another carved head, she asked, 'Is that another goddess?' She indicated the head of another Roman woman. With its oval frame and carved and gilded swags and tassels, it seemed the room had been designed just to display this epitome of classical beauty.

'Yes, she was dredged up from one of the Italian ports and sold to me as being a representation of the goddess Juno. Since then I have had some doubts about her identity, but she is still very beautiful, is she not?'

'Yes,' Elizabeth said softly. 'She is certainly that, sir.'

She spoke carefully in her best elocution

voice, hoping that the very faint Irish intonation of her voice, which even Miss Hanbury's sternest efforts had not succeeded in eradicating entirely, wouldn't be too evident. As she looked up at him she saw his bright, lustrous eyes expressing open amusement and bit her lip, thinking she must sound very gauche. As she continued to gaze at him, uncertain as to what to say next and yet unable to look away, she wondered how old he was. She wished suddenly that she could make a witty remark, have a joke with him, tease him a little as she'd been wont to do with her friends at school, but she hadn't the confidence.

Instead, she listened politely while he said, 'If you're interested in art and antiquities, Miss Baines, perhaps you would like to see the pictures in the landscape room?'

'Why, yes, I should like that very much, sir.' She said no more because at that moment one of the maids came to summon her to attend Lady Gascoine in the south drawing-room and she went in haste. Robert was left alone.

He remembered the shy waif of two years ago, who never spoke above a whisper and who looked as though a breath of wind could blow her away. Now she was so changed and he just hoped that Miss Hanbury's Academy had not influenced her to adopt the shallow manners and vapid interests of some of the young ladies of his acquaintance. He'd been surprised and intrigued by her appearance and manner. She was so pretty with her fair complexion and golden curls yet seemed totally unaware of the impact her beauty had on people.

In spite of his apparent detachment, she had aroused his interest. He was obliged to admit to himself that there was definitely a sexual element to this. He wondered fleetingly what she would be like to kiss but stifled the thought as soon as it had begun.

Being personal companion to his mama would not be easy, he thought sombrely. She would be required to always tread the fine line between friendliness and professional correctness. She would be required to mix with other servants as well as gentlefolk; would have to endure unkind criticism and learn to laugh at spiteful remarks and the petty jealousies of other women in the household. He felt an urge to warn her to protect herself in some way from the cruelties that being a lady's companion would hold for her.

He knew from his Aunt Jane that Elizabeth had endured physical cruelty while still a child. It would be a shame to remove this from her childish years only to return to it when she thought she was safe again. Still, for all her fragile appearance, she must be strong and resilient. As far as he knew, she had never had difficulties with bullying or spiteful remarks from the girls at Miss Hanbury's. Perhaps the other girls had recognized the strength in her and never attempted it. He sighed and went back to his self-imposed task of cataloguing his collection in the landscape room.

★   ★   ★

As Elizabeth dressed for dinner that evening, she remembered the first time she had visited Lady Gascoine and how consumed with nervousness she'd been. How gauche and naïve. Unlike tonight, when she was pleasantly excited by the pleasures to come. She was looking forward to dining in the presence of Robert Gascoine, and she dared admit that his conversation and his sense of humour made him attractive.

Miss Gibson had Bradbury to help her to dress and they had Susanna to assist with the preparation of their washing water and the dressing of their hair. Elizabeth had decided to be independent. One of the many skills she'd learned at Miss Hanbury's was adapting the latest hairstyles to her own type of beauty and how to carry herself well in order to show off the fashionable Regency dress to advantage. Many of the girls at Miss Hanbury's had little interest in anything except the opposite sex and the latest fashions. Their conversations were on subtle little beauty hints and the most modish accessories for their various outfits. She knew that some of them changed their gowns several times a day, but this was not Elizabeth's interest. Rather she enjoyed her books, her sketching and her dancing lessons. This did not mean she was indifferent to the interests of her contemporaries, however. She was as interested as the next young miss in how to bite her lips a little, so as to redden them before she made her entrance, or to use a mixture of glycerine and rosewater to whiten her hands.

She was also fully aware that the high-waisted white dress, which was de rigueur for young unmarried girls, suited her to perfection. She put on one that had flounces on the hem, lending it extra weight and ensuring it hung straight and without creases. She had chosen the dress because it emphasized her slender figure and the shapeliness of her arms and shoulders. Once it was on she arranged her hair in the usual fashionable ringlets, which cascaded from the crown of her elegant head to the nape of her slender neck.

She looked in the mirror and was pleased and satisfied with what she saw. She knew that this time she wouldn't disgrace herself or Miss Gibson with her lack of social finesse. Miss Hanbury had instructed her in the art of acceptable table manners. She drew a deep breath and reached for Lady Gascoine's gift, the pearl necklace, and attempted to clasp it round her slender throat. She liked the effect. The luminous beads quickly took on the warmth of her flesh again and reflected perfectly the stunning whiteness of her skin. For a few minutes she fumbled ineffectually with the fastener. No matter how she struggled, the knack of fastening it eluded her. The first dinner gong resounded gently through the house and, sighing with annoyance, she opened the door and went in search of Miss Gibson and Bradbury. She was sure one of them would be able to help her out.

As she stepped on to the dimly lit landing, she was aware of someone coming along the corridor.

It was Robert Gascoine. He was dressed in the usual male evening attire and was looking more relaxed and handsome than he had done that morning.

'Why, Miss Baines,' he said and smiled. 'I hope I didn't startle you. I have just been doing some work on the last entries in my catalogue.'

She looked at him, a confident ex-scholar from Miss Hanbury's Academy just taking the first steps on the rungs of the ladder, which was to lead to a comfortable life with his mother Lady Gascoine. The smile she gave him and the polite request to aid her with the string of pearls was a very correct one, so why did he think it so provocative?

He supposed that it must be because she was so young. He hoped that no one took advantage of her innocence, and gave a self-deprecating smile as he realized that must mean him too.

'I can't fasten it, sir,' she said rather breathlessly.

'Turn round for me then,' he said gravely.

She felt a certain quickening of her heartbeat as she handed the pearls to him and stood obediently with her back to him. As she felt the gentle fingers fastening the string of pearls, she was aware of the sensation on her skin and the way his light touch encouraged feelings she never knew she had.

As for Robert, he had the strange feeling when he saw the bent head that he should raise it and make the beautiful lips his own.

He was shocked at this thought, which was no better than Frederick's and he quickly dropped his hands from her neck.

Elizabeth, who had enjoyed the feeling of his hands touching the back of her neck and the strange sensations these had given her, stuttered, 'Th . . . thank you, sir,' before she fled downstairs to the dining-room.

Robert stayed where he was for a few moments. He had to acknowledge that she was very alluring with her pretty curls and blue eyes. The skin at the nape of her neck was white and of a texture most fashionable ladies would die for. The feel of her soft curls beneath his fingers was absolutely beguiling. She seemed quite a poised and confident young lady after two years at Miss Hanbury's and yet she had the quality of artless innocence, which he found totally seductive.

4

That night at dinner, Lady Gascoine mentioned that they would be going to the family estate in Norfolk for Christmas.

'We shall all be together as a family at the most holy time of the year, Elizabeth, and you will like the country atmosphere at Waringham,' she said, smiling. 'Christmas celebrations seem so timeless amid the farming folk, and the ritual of church on Christmas morning followed by a luncheon of roast Norfolk turkey is something I remember from being a tiny child.'

'When Sir William was alive it was a family tradition to all go to Norfolk for Christmas,' Miss Gibson said. 'Bradbury and I would be delighted to revive that particular celebration.'

Looking round at the kindly faces, Elizabeth knew that Baines could never catch her now. She felt pleased and grateful that she had found such a safe haven from her stormy existence and offered up a silent prayer of thanks at her good fortune.

Something of this must have shown in her face because Miss Gibson said kindly, 'It will be such a diversion for dear Lady Gascoine, Elizabeth, and there will be the added pleasure of being in the company of such charming young people. We shall be seeing something of Frederick's intended, Miss Isabella Mason, and her sisters.'

Elizabeth said nothing. It was not at all appropriate for her to express her heartfelt gratitude to feel so safe in what Holmes had described as 'comfortable penury' and it wasn't in her authority to decide on the movements of the Gascoine family. She glanced up and saw Robert Gascoine observing her closely, as though trying to penetrate her mind.

Noticing his look she raised her chin and said, 'And how is your task of cataloguing progressing, sir?'

'Well, I thank you,' he said and smiled at her as though he had already guessed what she was thinking.

'Pooh!' Sir Frederick Gascoine exclaimed rudely. 'What does it signify, Robert, all this fiddle-faddle with your dusty old collection? Who, apart from a few ancient old fogeys, can possibly care about such stuff?'

'Well,' Robert said, smiling, 'Miss Baines for one has expressed an interest in viewing the landscape room and no one could think her an ancient old fogey.'

'She's a polite and considerate young lady,' Frederick said, 'and if to be Mama's new companion, she must learn to protect herself from such tedious experiences. Am I not right, Mama?'

Lady Gascoine smiled fondly at him. 'Why as to that, Frederick, Miss Baines is her own person and the way she wishes to spend her own leisure time is entirely her own choice.'

Frederick frowned at this but Jane Gibson said quietly, 'The pictures in the landscape room are indeed interesting, Elizabeth. I'm sure you will enjoy them.'

Frederick immediately changed the subject and began to speak rather loudly and rapidly about a mill he had enjoyed that morning in Richmond. 'They went twenty rounds,' he said. 'Gentleman Rogers and The Wimbledon Wonder. The Wonder won, of course. I made a modest sum from backing him. You would have enjoyed it, Robert.'

'I feel there is little pleasure to be gained from watching two grown men beating each other senseless and putting money on the result,' Robert said. 'As soon as the claret starts to flow, I feel it's time for me to leave the scene.'

'Pooh!' said Frederick again. 'Like I said, you're just too mean to tip the brads where a gentlemanly wager's concerned but I tell you this, bruth, after Christmas we're taking our curricles down to Brighton and I warrant we'll see some sport there. There might be an occasion when even you would be tempted to part with your blunt.'

'Oh, my dear,' Lady Gascoine said anxiously. 'Please be careful, Frederick. One foolhardy act could have such devastating consequences.'

Jane Gibson and Bradbury both looked at him and Frederick, glorying in the consternation he had caused in his mother's breast, went on to describe the sort of sport that he and the rest of the splendid chaps would enjoy.

'Now that he's come about and has the wherewithal, Jack Richards is thinking of taking a house for a few days. He'll organize a few events with The Wonder and no doubt we shall have a race with the curricles, of course. There will be cards for those who have no stomach for curricle racing.'

It was obvious he was looking forward to the trip, and equally obvious that his brother was not. His mama continued to gaze at him fondly.

Under cover of the conversation, Elizabeth turned to her silent neighbour.

'And so you have no inclination yourself to take your curricle down to Brighton, sir? It is said to be very splendid indeed, now that the Regent has developed his Royal Apartments.'

'Well, yes,' Robert replied. 'I have been to Brighton, but never as a personal guest of His Royal Highness. A friend of mine from my Oxford days has had that privilege, and was most impressed by the Pavilion. He described to me the Prince's taste for *chinoiserie*. He wrote too of the astonishing southern wing, which has a Chinese passage of painted glass decorated with exotic flowers and insects, fruit and birds. My friend says that when it was illuminated the experience was just as though one had passed through a giant Chinese lantern.'

He spoke in a low voice so as not to intrude on his brother's conversation, and Elizabeth followed his lead and spoke softly. 'I have never visited Brighton,' she said wistfully, 'but I own that I thought Bath was quite grand enough for a humble schoolgirl.'

'But you are no longer a schoolgirl,' he said. 'And you should never consider yourself as humble. In fact, you are quite the smart young lady. Perhaps next year Mama might care to visit Brighton herself and you could accompany her.'

They were interrupted by Frederick, who said rudely, 'What you two whispering about?

You act like the dashed conspirators in the Gunpowder Plot.'

Lady Gascoine took this as a hint that it was time for the ladies to withdraw and they left the brothers together.

In the drawing-room, while Bradbury sat drinking tea with Lady Gascoine, Jane Gibson told Elizabeth about the family seat in Norfolk.

'It is truly magnificent, Elizabeth. My brother-in-law, Sir William Gascoine, was as keen a collector as dear Robert, and the pictures and the tapestries must be seen to be believed. The soil is like black gold and all the farms are thriving. If ever there was needed a model of excellence in agricultural management, the Waringham Estate is it. The hard work put in by Sir William in his lifetime provided funds and resources to fund the great house, but also ensures that the fabric of social life remains intact.'

'Are not the tenants put in hardship by the recent war at all?' asked Elizabeth diffidently.

'No, my dear. There are more than a hundred cottage dwellings owned by the estate, all of which are either lived in by families who work on the estate or in the locality. His patronage has kept the village inn alive and even provides players for the cricket team. There is a Sunday school for the children and before he died, he had set up plans for a day school with a teacher. This is no mean achievement in the present situation where rural poverty is so widespread.'

Elizabeth listened carefully. She knew nothing of the problems of the landowners, yet she felt that Miss Gibson was particularly admiring of the late Sir William Gascoine. She wondered if Miss Gibson had ever been in love with him. Her love would have been unrequited, of course, for Sir William had married Lady Gascoine — the sort of situation which had occurred many times in the romantic stories from the subscription library that Elizabeth and the other girls at Miss Hanbury's had delighted in reading.

'It sounds really splendid, Miss Gibson. What . . . what happened to the young lady who was to be the teacher?'

'Nothing,' Miss Gibson said shortly. 'That part of Sir William's vision had not been developed at all. Sir Frederick has not, so far, expressed much interest in his tenants.'

She stopped short as if aware she had said too much and then changed the subject. 'But enough of this, Elizabeth. You don't need to fill your head with such things. Suffice it to say that you will be enchanted by Christmas Norfolk. The house is a long way from the Baines' and the servants desire only to please.'

'I'm sure that I'll be enchanted, ma'am,' Elizabeth said. 'And how will the gentlemen pass the time?'

'There are many social opportunities with Lady Gascoine's neighbours and friends of Miss Isabella Mason. The gentlemen enjoy cards and billiards, organize shooting parties and in the summer trout fishing, of course. There are so many social engagements and opportunities for young men to meet refined young ladies that they never cavil at attending their mama to Waringham.'

Bradbury handed Jane Gibson her tea and Lady Gascoine said wistfully, 'I miss Holmes. She used to sing so well and entertained us quite royally after dinner. What about you, Elizabeth? May we expect a little tune from you now that you have graduated from Miss Hanbury's establishment?'

She smiled in such a kindly manner that in spite of her initial shyness, Elizabeth longed to oblige her. She looked questioningly at Miss Gibson, who nodded and smiled reassuringly at her.

'Yes, Elizabeth, you have a pretty voice and a light touch on the pianoforte. Give us a song, my dear.'

Elizabeth walked obediently to the piano.

Her music books were upstairs and so she played an old Irish song, which she could play by ear. She sang in a high, clear voice, her youthful feeling fitting well with the sentiments of the song, and the women were charmed by it.

'That was a change from the usual drawing-room offering,' Lady Gascoine said generously. 'Now, my dear, give us another one like that — no matter you haven't your music in front of you.'

Quite forgetting Lady Gascoine's continuing sadness about the death of Holmes, Elizabeth chose a tragic air and sang it with such feeling that she finished the song with her young bosom heaving and her eyes bright with unshed tears. There was a pause as the last chords died away and then the door opened and Sir Frederick and his brother entered the room.

'Upon my soul, Elizabeth, that was a very affecting piece. Well done, my dear.'

Elizabeth wasn't sure whether Sir Frederick was being sincere but there was no doubting the pleasure her singing had given to Lady Gascoine, or the open admiration in the eyes of Robert Gascoine.

She rose from the piano stool and went to sit on a small brocade sofa nearer to the fireplace. Frederick threw himself across a very comfortable armchair and ordered the footman to bring him more claret. Robert, though, refused the claret and seated himself on a low chair immediately opposite to her.

'That was a very moving ballad that you sang, Miss Baines,' he said. 'May we hope that you will entertain us on other evenings. In Norfolk, perhaps?'

'Perhaps, sir,' she said shyly, 'but I have had only a few piano lessons, and have a somewhat limited repertoire of songs.'

'I think I will be the best judge of that,' he said. 'From my own selfish point of view, I look forward to hearing more of your voice, and will endeavour to entertain you in return, with a view of my collection. If you are able to take an hour off your duties sometime,' he said, 'you may perhaps enjoy a tour of the landscape room.'

'I should like that very much,' Elizabeth said. 'But how do you spend your time when you go to Norfolk, and you are absent from your treasures?'

He smiled as he answered, knowing her question had been somewhat tongue in cheek. 'Well,' he said, 'Papa was no less a collector than myself. If you enjoy my poor artefacts, you will take great pleasure in the treasures of Waringham.'

Elizabeth was sure she would, and she felt a

tingle of anticipation at the idea of Robert Gascoine showing her his collection of 'poor artefacts'. She looked at him while he was speaking. His hands were long and capable, she couldn't imagine such hands letting her down in any way. His eyes shone mostly brown in the mixture of fire and candlelight and he looked delighted at the idea of showing her his pictures.

★ ★ ★

There was no time for looking at Robert's collection over the next few days. As so often in early December, there followed a spell of exceptionally fine weather and Lady Gascoine usually insisted they might take a turn round Hyde Park in the open carriage.

'See and be seen, my dear,' she said. 'We seem to be having a most gentle autumn and there are so many friends and acquaintances abroad, enjoying this unseasonable weather.'

Then there were invitations to pretty new companions and to some who weren't so pretty. There were condolences over the death of Holmes and there were many invitations issued for dinner or card evenings. Elizabeth was conscious of the curiosity she aroused among Lady Gascoine's many friends. Although Frederick was frequently away from home, Robert was usually on hand to entertain the company and act as host at the various soirées organized by his mama. In a few weeks Elizabeth had grown to like him for his unfailing courtesy and consideration to his mother and her friends, but she wished sometimes that she could penetrate his air of cool politeness.

This persisted even when Lady Gascoine's friends came in to play cards or have an informal dance. If Frederick was present, things were lively and enjoyable. Frederick knew all the latest dances and Elizabeth was happy to learn. Even when there was a group of pretty young girls, Robert could not be persuaded to dance and Elizabeth wondered why.

As promised, when the weather turned to blustery rain again, Robert took her on a tour of the landscape pictures. Elizabeth at first had only an impression of the stately room with its two doors and central fireplace. This was made of white marble with a black chimney back on which was moulded Pegasus, the mythical winged horse. The massive fire irons were brass griffins' heads and Elizabeth spent so long gazing in awe at these that she was almost unaware that he was still standing beside her.

Robert laughed softly, and murmured,

'What is it that fascinates you so about the fire, Miss Baines? Can it be that you prefer the ironmonger's craft to my poor art collection, or do you see pictures in the fire which are superior to those around us?'

Elizabeth at first hung her head, feeling a little rebuked, but when she glanced at him she noticed he was smiling with such kindness that she smiled back.

'Not at all, sir,' she said with some spirit, 'but it lacks only three weeks to Christmas and a cosy fire is always a draw on a bluff December's day.'

As he led her round the gallery, she noticed that all the pictures were hung one above the other as was the fashion in the big houses. All were surrounded by gilded frames, which showed to advantage against the deep rose-coloured wallpaper.

He paused before a picture placed at the side of one of the doors. 'This one,' he told her gravely, 'is the first picture I ever bought so it has some sentimental attachment for me. It is as you see a representation of our Lord calling the fishermen to be his disciples, and is painted by Grimaldi.'

Elizabeth looked curiously at the painting. In the foreground were the fishermen tending their nets. They were dressed in the costumes of biblical times and the figure of Christ was half turned towards them. He was wearing traditional white flowing robes. His hands gestured that he wished them to leave their boats and join him. The poses of the men's bodies showed them to be both curious and afraid of the challenge which lay before them. Their dark eyes narrowed against the sun and their hands stilled at their tasks as they looked at Jesus in wonder. But it was the greater view of the background that she noticed more closely. To the side of the picture was a particularly detailed depiction of a goat herd with his flock, set in the sort of scrubby landscape typical of the Holy Land. Elizabeth was fascinated not only by the obvious skill of the painter, who had brought this scene to life, but at the imagination the artist had shown in visualizing the lives of those who had lived long ago.

He waited patiently for her to speak. 'It is painted by an Italian artist, and did you buy it in Italy, sir?'

'Yes, I did, and for a very good price.'

'One may see the whole story of Jesus calling his disciples,' Elizabeth said. 'It is very striking and I like it. I know that Miss Pemberton has always admired this narrative style of painting . . . ' Her words petered off because she was not sure how they would be received.

He seemed pleased and watched her with bright eyes. He moved on to show her another picture on the opposite side of the door. 'This is without doubt one of my favourites,' he told her. 'It is a river scene by Poussin. One of his favourite subjects for a landscape painting. I fell in love with it as soon as I saw it, and could never part with it.'

Elizabeth was intrigued by the words 'I fell in love with it'. She wondered what he would be like if he fell in love with a real flesh-and-blood woman like herself, for instance, rather than a painted canvas. She looked with interest at the painting which had made him fall in love. There was a castle built on a high rock with a beautifully painted sky beyond it and, in the foreground, two figures reclining on a bank. She thought fleetingly of Miss Holmes that evening years ago when she had sung: 'As the rock remains unmoved against the winds and storm, so this spirit is still strong in its faith and its love and she will never be unfaithful to her lover.'

'I think it would be my favourite, too,' she said. 'The art teacher, Miss Pemberton, always hoped we could achieve that with our watercolours, the sort of opalescent blue and clouds that . . . that the artist has created in this picture.'

This was a long speech for Elizabeth and

she realized that she was gradually losing her crippling shyness with Robert Gascoine. She glanced at him to see what effect her spontaneous opinion of the picture had on him. He was looking approvingly at her.

'I'm sure that Miss Pemberton would be most interested to see your Poussin,' she went on daringly.

'Alas, I cannot imagine that it would ever be possible,' he said with mock regret and Elizabeth smiled. She was even learning to recognize when he was being humorous.

Then they heard Lady Gascoine's maid calling Elizabeth and the smile faded from his eyes. 'It seems my mama has need of you,' he said and Elizabeth was disappointed because he expressed no great desire for her to stay longer, or a wish to tell her more about his pictures.

As the days passed she became increasingly impatient with him. He seemed so restrained and quiet and was apparently content to be in Frederick's shadow all the time. Yet she knew that such was his strength, it was Robert the family would turn to in a crisis.

The last day before their departure for Norfolk was wet and miserable. All the household servants seemed to be involved in preparations for the Christmas holiday and Lady Gascoine sent Elizabeth with the maid

Susanna to change her books at the subscription library.

'Bring something romantic but with adventure, Elizabeth. There are bound to be a few tedious interludes in the country and I shall need some diversion when the weather is inclement.'

When they returned later in the afternoon, Elizabeth put all the books on one of the small tables while Susanna took their outdoor clothes upstairs. Elizabeth picked up two volumes and turned to go to the south drawing-room, to seek out Lady Gascoine.

'There is no need to carry those. Pray allow me to do that for you.'

She looked round in surprise and saw Sir Frederick Gascoine standing behind her. He had reached out a masterful hand and taken the books from her before she had time to prevent it. 'No, really . . . I thank you, sir. But . . . I have to take the books to Lady Gascoine . . . I can manage quite well, thank you, sir.'

'I insist,' he said suavely. His brown eyes were provocative and she saw the open amusement in his face as he read the book titles out loud. 'Upon my soul,' he said. 'Here is an intriguing tale for a refined female. *The Perils of Miss Maxwell*, dear me! A story of romance and danger, but with a happy ending. What drove you to choose that one for dear Mama? What can a young lady who has just left school possibly know of romance and danger? Perhaps it is merely that you would like to know. Is that it?'

Elizabeth stood looking at him helplessly. She could smell the spirits on his breath and knew from the expression on his face that he was trying to flirt with her but she was at a loss as to how to act.

'Please, sir, I beg you to give me the books so . . . so I can take them to Her Ladyship . . . '

He ignored her plea and said, 'I have no doubt that a lady as pretty as yourself must have some experience of romance or danger, or both.' He took a step nearer and she felt anger start in her heart at the old familiar sensation of being trapped by a bully.

'Come, Frederick, stop teasing Miss Baines. Cannot you see that she will be in Mama's bad books all day if she doesn't discharge her errand efficiently?'

Robert was looking down at his brother from the top of the marble staircase. He spoke lightly and with a pleasant smile, but Frederick knew that he would have to be obeyed. Robert took in the little scene in front of him. The hint of tears in Miss Baines' eyes was not lost on him and he approached his brother steadily and with determination, holding out his hand.

'When one is brought up with a brother, Miss Baines, teasing becomes second nature. You must forgive him. He means no harm but I know you had no such problems at Miss Hanbury's, among such refined girlish company.'

Elizabeth thought of the three Baines boys and shuddered. Frederick released the books and Robert gave them back to her. She felt too upset to thank him properly. She took them gratefully and sped away, hoping that Lady Gascoine wouldn't notice her agitation.

Preparing for dinner that evening, Elizabeth thought again of how strong Robert could be in contrast to his selfish brother, who seemed wayward and weak. As he had given her Lady Gascoine's books, for a moment his cool hands had touched her own and she had to admit the sensation was very pleasurable.

At dinner the talk was all about the social evenings that they were to enjoy in Norfolk. Lady Gascoine seemed to have thrown off entirely her depression at the death of her long-term companion and was effusive in her praise of Elizabeth.

'She is so refined and tactful,' she said warmly to Jane Gibson. 'Elizabeth has exceeded all my deepest hopes of a genteel

98

companion and all your opinions of her qualities are entirely vindicated, my dear Jane. She will be such a helpmeet and support this Christmas when we will have the pleasure of seeing Miss Mason and her family.'

Elizabeth blushed and looked at Sir Frederick. He was staring angrily at her and didn't seem at all like a happy prospective bridegroom. His face as usual was flushed with wine and he seemed impatient of his mama's Norfolk plans.

'The family is only just out of mourning for Isabella's grandpapa. They will not be planning a wedding before May,' he said. He took another gulp and glared at Lady Gascoine, who took no notice, but continued to talk of the future.

'May is such a lovely month for a wedding,' she went on, ignoring his scowl. 'And Isabella has two pretty sisters to attend her as bridesmaids. There is so little between them I shouldn't wonder if her mama hasn't dressed them in identical gowns. But suffice it to say, Frederick, I look forward to a warm coze with dear Mrs Mason when we're both in Norfolk. You will like her, Elizabeth. She is so unaffected and totally without side whatsoever. And Miss Mason, Frederick's bride-to-be, is a very charming young woman. I'm afraid it's taken a long time with Frederick's shilly-shallying about the date and then the mourning for the grandpapa, but all is well now.'

Elizabeth noted at this point in the conversation that Jane Gibson and Robert Gascoine exchanged the merest flicker of a glance. It was so subtle as to be almost unnoticed but Elizabeth spotted it all the same. After all, her very survival in the Baines' household had depended on her skill at reading faces and guessing if something evil was about to befall her. She had no idea what the meaning of the exchanged look was and at that moment the dessert was served and the meal came quickly to an end. She attended Lady Gascoine in the drawing-room and as soon as she could escaped to her own room.

Next day was the sixteenth day of December and they made an early start. Luggage, jewellery, writing cases, refreshments and maidservants were all packed speedily and efficiently into the various Gascoine vehicles. No one had seen Sir Frederick Gascoine who seemed to have set off alone in his curricle. Robert and his valet were travelling together in his post-chaise with four horses for greater speed and the four ladies were all travelling in the imposing Gascoine carriage.

The journey to Norfolk on the coach road was uneventful. The inns were comfortable and although they were pleased when they finally arrived at their destination, they were not exhausted. Lady Gascoine quickly organized the servants to make her guests comfortable, then she went through the visiting cards on the silver tray. Robert Gascoine had already arrived, but there was still no sign of Sir Frederick.

'The tiresome boy will no doubt have stopped for some sporting event,' his mama said fondly. 'But he'll be here well before the twentieth when dear Isabella visits us. Oh look, Jane, we're invited to a ball at the Masons' on Thursday. That should be quite a splendid occasion, my dear,' she explained to Elizabeth. 'We must look out our best gowns for such an occasion. They are very wealthy and although Mr Mason's grandfather made his money in manufacturing the family is all that is refined and Isabella is so genteel and well educated.'

The next day Sir Frederick Gascoine's curricle swept up to the front door of Waringham Hall. In the most black temper, he threw the reins of his perfectly matched bays to the tiny under-groom, who leapt down from the box to catch them. Then, as the animals were led round to the stables, he entered the hall and, in the same ungracious manner, threw his whip to the footman, and shrugged himself impatiently out of his many caped greatcoat. There were now several flunkeys in the hall divesting Sir Frederick of his boots and gloves and, looking over the beautifully carved banister rail, Elizabeth watched silently as he stalked into the study, shouting for wine and refreshments to be brought to him forthwith. For a prospective bridegroom about to meet his beloved, he seemed in a most ill humour.

The dining-room at Waringham was so immense that the walls seemed to be always in shadow. This gave Elizabeth every opportunity to observe Miss Isabella Mason as she entered the dining-room on the arm of Robert Gascoine. Mr Mason partnered Lady Gascoine and Frederick led in Mrs Mason, a stout little body in her late forties.

Genteel she might be but Isabella Mason was no beauty. She was twenty years old, small like her mama and rather dumpy. She had a serious, almost anxious expression. As she turned her head adoringly towards Sir Frederick, her round face resembled a plate of cheese or a full moon, the eyes pale blue like moonlight. She was exquisitely dressed with her hair in rather tight, mousy curls, which added to the impression of her broad, homely face. She was clearly very deeply in love with Sir Frederick and hardly able to take her eyes off him.

For his part he addressed few remarks to her and positively scowled when she spoke to him. He seemed to find her sisters Lydia and Caroline more to his liking but the young damsels, aged sixteen and fifteen respectively, were in awe of the situation and though tolerably pretty had little conversation or poise.

Elizabeth, seated opposite Mr Mason, warmed to him immediately. His conversation was sensible and his manner courteous without any pomposity; he was entirely unpatronizing. She had been introduced to the visitors as 'Lady Gascoine's young companion,' but this did not deter any of the Mason family from treating her as a fellow human being and an equal. Mr Mason in particular seemed to enjoy her company and she was soon at ease with him as he told her tales of bygone Norfolk.

'I've lived here all my life, man and boy, you see, Miss Baines, and this area in the past was known to be a very close community, almost cut off from the world. Perhaps that's why our grandfathers and fathers were so enamoured of their tales and legends and now that I myself am an old codger — over fifty, you know — it will fall to my lot to tell the chimney corner tales. Did you know, for instance, that the origin of 'nosey parker' was a sixteenth-century cleric from Norfolk? He became Archbishop Matthew Parker of Canterbury in the reign of Elizabeth I. He delved so deeply into the affairs of his fellow clergy to influence ecclesiastical morals that he became known as 'Nosey Parker'. His continuously inquisitive nature earned him that well-deserved title.'

'And what of the famous Norfolk females?' Elizabeth asked, smiling.

'Two come to mind immediately,' he said. 'Anne, daughter of Charles IV, the Holy Roman Emperor, was married to King Richard II and when they visited Norwich in 1383 they were received with great pomp and honour and Queen Anne made a great and lasting impact on Norfolk life. It was she who introduced a new concept in riding to the ladies. She introduced a new style of riding with the side saddle. Before that, women used to ride astride, like men.'

'And the other, sir?'

'Oh, undoubtedly, there is the legend of poor Anne Boleyn whose ghost is said to haunt Blickling Hall where she spent some of her childhood. Every year on the anniversary of her death, on 19 May, she is said to travel up the long avenue to Blickling in a phantom carriage drawn by a headless coachman. So you see, we old codgers have our fund of chimney corner tales, Miss Baines.'

He smiled and Elizabeth smiled back at him, enjoying his lively conversation. As the various meat dishes were brought in and the talk became more general, he said, 'And what of yourself, Miss Baines? I understand you are from Ireland, but I'm persuaded that Baines, is not a particularly Irish name. When I was young, I mind there was a family of that name in Copthorne village, near Ridgeway. At least I think it was Copthorne. Are you familiar with Norfolk at all?'

'Why, no, sir. This is my first visit. I understand from Miss Gibson that there is good agricultural land in these parts.'

'That is certainly true and Frederick's papa, Sir William Gascoine, was a very successful landowner. It's early days yet, but I trust that Sir Frederick will prove as dedicated as his father and grandfather.'

This was the second time that Elizabeth had heard of Sir William's love of the land and his care of the tenants. She said softly, 'I am sure that will prove to be the case, sir, especially if he has your daughter's love and support.'

Edward Mason positively beamed at her

tactful reply. 'Tradition is so important in the country, Miss Baines, but enough of this old man's prating. Shall we see you on Thursday? Emma — Mrs Mason, that is — seems to have invited half of Norfolk. As a mere man, I just hope that it will not be too sad a crush but as always, I shall be outvoted by the females of the family.'

The talk now turned to plans for the dinner dance at the Masons' manor house and Emma Mason said mistily, 'Take no heed of Edward, Lady Gascoine. There will be plenty of room at the manor and we need to extend the hospitality to as many of the county as possible. Now that we are out of mourning for my dear papa, we will be able to make a formal announcement of Isabella and Frederick's betrothal. After the New Year's festivities, we shall be pulling out all the stops for the wedding.'

Sir Frederick gave an even larger scowl at this and a meaningful glare at Lady Gascoine, who now indicated that it was time for the ladies to withdraw.

Once in the drawing-room, Elizabeth remained slightly on the fringes of the female company, aware of her lowly status as paid companion, although her dress and deport-ment were such she could pass for an equal. In no time, though, the younger girls had joined her in the window recess, sitting on small mahogany chairs and sipping lemonade rather than tea. They forgot their earlier shyness and were chatting as though they had known her for ever.

Elizabeth thought with regret that she had never had a sister and she found the warm and open manners of Lydia and Caroline very attractive. They were full of excited talk about Isabella's wedding, Mama's plans for the cake, the design of the bride's dress, their own role in the important day and, of course, the handsome bridegroom, so like the prince from a fairytale. For the first time in her young life, Elizabeth discovered in herself a talent as confidante.

'Isabella met Frederick two years ago at her come out,' Lydia confided. 'She's told me it was love at first sight.'

'Just like a romance,' Caroline chimed in. 'I hope I meet someone like Frederick when I have my coming out.'

'And what of the wedding plans?' Elizabeth prompted them. 'Have you planned your outfits for the important day?'

'Mama thinks we may have matching gowns,' Lydia said. 'But I am fourteen months older than Caroline and taller,' she said proudly.

'And my hair is fairer and very curly. We

107

feel we should both have our own style.'

'We are both going to see if Mama would agree to different gowns for us.'

They were interrupted at that moment by Jane Gibson. 'Your sister has agreed to play for us,' she said to the girls. 'I know she is reckoned to be a very fine pianist, and we have managed to persuade her.'

The women regrouped a little as Isabella Mason took her place at the pianoforte. She played extremely well with absolute accuracy, if a trifle lacking in light and shade. No expense had been spared to provide the best teacher for her and the piece she chose was rather ambitious for an amateur.

The gentlemen entered as Isabella was playing the second movement and though every note was perfect, Robert Gascoine felt that somehow it was lacking in any musical expression or feeling. He thought there was no comparison between this rather stilted rendering and Elizabeth's singing, which had been so poignant and moving. Amid the polite clapping and murmurs of admiration, his eyes rested on Elizabeth and she seemed happier and more relaxed than he had ever seen her before, surrounded as she was by Miss Mason's sisters. Some young people nearer to her own age would be good for her, he thought. He moved towards her as though compelled by some force beyond his control. As the younger girls shifted their chairs and made room for him, he merely nodded to them in a kindly greeting while his eyes sought Elizabeth's.

'That was wonderful, my dear,' said Lady Gascoine. 'What a fortunate young fellow my dear Frederick is to have such a talented bride. I think we are in the mood for more and I know that Elizabeth plays some Irish airs very prettily. My sister Jane has taken the liberty of placing your music for you my dear,' she said to the embarrassed Elizabeth, who looked up in some surprise at being called upon so unexpectedly.

It never occurred to Elizabeth to demur or protest just so that she could be persuaded. That kind of vanity was absolutely alien to her nature. She merely walked obediently towards the piano and sat in front of it. As she sat down she was pleased and at the same time embarrassed to see Robert Gascoine come to turn the pages for her. For some reason the first piece, 'The Harp That Once Through Tara's Halls', seemed to affect her most profoundly. For some reason, her heart was so full tonight, that she sang with a passion previously unleashed.

She felt the last lines: 'As when some heart indignant breaks, to show that still she lives.'

Her eyes filled with tears and she felt her own heart breaking, and yet she knew not why. Suddenly, all the pent-up anguish and longing, left over from her miserable and abused childhood with the Baines family, threatened to overwhelm her. In spite of the kindness and generosity of the two women, she was beset by a tremendous sense of emptiness and loss. She had no mama to love and care for her, and she still remembered with horror the hateful Captain Preston.

As the song closed there was a moment's silence, and Elizabeth remained for a few seconds with her head bent. She felt she would die of embarrassment as all eyes in the room were on her. Then she stood up and curtsied to the applause. Robert was at her side now and he led her back to her seat. He gazed at her in wonder. How was it possible for such an obviously innocent young thing to feel and express so much passion and despair? Through her music, she had openly shown her unhappiness and heartbreak to the assembled company and he found it awesome.

The tea tray was brought round and he handed Elizabeth a cup of tea and went to sit near her.

He took a drink of his own and said, 'You sang that with some feeling, Miss Baines. Is it a song you learned in Ireland?'

She didn't reply but just nodded.

'Are your parents still living in Ireland?'

Her voice was practically a whisper. 'My father is, sir, but my mother is dead.'

He could see she did not wish to discuss her former life and remembered then some hint that his Aunt Jane had given him about the girl being ill treated by her father and stepmother. He didn't press her and saw that she looked grateful for this. Very pleasantly he changed the subject. 'My mama acquired a special painting for my birthday at the beginning of the month,' he said. 'Now I have officially received it, I shall invite you to a viewing ceremony in the portrait gallery, if I may.'

Elizabeth was only able to manage 'Thank you, sir,' in a low voice before his brother Frederick approached and asked him for a game of billiards.

'This dashed petticoat brigade and their prattle about bride clothes ain't what a fellow wants to listen to after a good bottle of port,' Frederick said. 'Mr Mason and I are all for a cigar in the billiard room. If you sit charming females, you'll get like them. Deuced effeminate game, gabbing to women.'

Robert smiled, and said that it was just because Elizabeth was so beautiful that

111

Frederick was jealous. He bowed respectfully and said, 'Well, you see how it is with older brothers, Miss Baines. There's no rest for the weary.'

Elizabeth smiled at him as he excused himself and followed his brother from the room. She was becoming a trifle weary herself as the Mason girls tirelessly discussed their outfits for the ball and the guest list that their mama had prepared.

'Mama has planned to have a lot of country dances on the programme so that Caroline and I may get a look in with the dancing,' Lydia said.

'And Mama has said that Isabella may do the waltz,' Caroline chimed in enviously. Both girls were eager to tell Elizabeth that they visited the home of a friend on Monday afternoons because the friend's mama engaged a dancing teacher once a week and they shared the lessons.

Emma Mason's face beamed with pleasure as she listened to the excited chatter and even Jane Gibson and Bradbury seemed interested in the girls' plans. Only Isabella was quiet and distant, her lips drooping disconsolately and a faraway expression in her pale eyes.

Elizabeth wondered why she should be so sad. She had a wealthy family, she was young, and she was soon to be married to one of the most handsome men in London. Elizabeth thought of the contrast between Isabella's happy home life with such good and happy parents, and her own upbringing with the unspeakable Baines and Kate Molloy's cruel brood. She tried to look more cheerful for the sake of Lady Gascoine, who had made such an effort for her guests. Even the few words she had exchanged with Robert Gascoine seemed of no significance now. Nevertheless, she was pleased and relieved when the company had gone and she could escape to her bed chamber.

As she settled down in bed, Elizabeth remembered that Mr Mason had mentioned a Baines family at Copthorne, near Ridgeway. Then, as she began to drift into sleep, there came unbidden to her mind, someone — her mother, father, someone — whispering, 'Everyone knows as goose dinners at Ridgeway Fair is just rabbit dipped in goose fat, my pretty.'

She sat up with a start. Where had the thought come from? Who was the 'someone' who had spoken those words to her? When?

She remembered the voice now. It was a woman's voice. Vainly, she clasped her temples to try and remember more. Nothing came and, quite exhausted, she was obliged to lie down and sleep.

5

The evening of the Masons' ball was clear
and crisp. There was a hint of frost in the air
as they arrived at the manor and were held up
in the queue of carriages on the drive.
Although she knew she was looking her best
in a pale blue evening dress and regulation
white gloves, Elizabeth experienced a sudden
attack of stagefright at the thought of all
those people.

Jane Gibson seemed to sense her panic,
and said, 'Elizabeth, dear, you look absolutely
charming.'

'Yes, charming,' Lady Gascoine said, 'and
the pearls suit you to perfection. I just hope
you don't meet some wonderful man this
evening who will sweep you off your feet away
from me.'

They all laughed and Bradbury squeezed
her hand sympathetically. 'Elizabeth's far too
sensible for that ma'am,' she said. 'She's not
the sort of girl who could be swept or
whisked away by any Prince Charming. Her
pretty feet are firmly on the ground.'

Under the pretext of smoothing her dress
so that it had no creases, Elizabeth thought

about what Bradbury had said. She had read about falling in love in some of the books from the circulatory library, and now, suddenly, she thought of Robert. How he looked at her with the demon of amusement lurking in his eyes. His way of showing her the paintings and the tremendous knowledge that he had. And finally, his consideration for her feelings. She would have to travel a long way to find such a man. But she knew it was no use even to think of him in that way, and resolutely put him out of her mind. She must concentrate on her duties towards Lady Gascoine.

And then they were all at the door and starting their long, slow walk up the grand staircase, announced by a liveried Master of Ceremonies as 'Dowager, Lady Mary Gascoine, Miss Jane Gibson, Miss Beatrice Bradbury, and Miss Elizabeth Baines'. For the first time in her life, Elizabeth was making an entrance at an exclusive party.

As if in a dream, she walked to the top of the room, where most of the elderly ladies were sitting, and sat down modestly, slightly behind Lady Gascoine, so as not to intrude on the other ladies' conversation. She looked round her at the Masons' glittering ballroom, the beautifully dressed men and women greeting each other, the huge chandeliers causing the jewels of the women to flash and sparkle, as they nodded and smiled at Lady Gascoine and her companions.

Miss Isabella Mason said a few pretty words as she curtsied to her future mother-in-law, then the younger girls, dressed in white with blue ribbon sashes, and last of all Mr and Mrs Mason. They were all that was polite and charming as they welcomed their guests and moved forward to meet the next group. As Mr Mason had predicted, it was a sad crush and the dancing hadn't even started yet. Many of the guests were already in the refreshment room or playing whist, but there was no shortage of handsome young men and pretty young women, many of whom knew each other, while others as yet unacquainted were eyeing each other discreetly and hoping for a dance.

Elizabeth kept her eyes lowered modestly and seemed entirely lacking interest in any of the young blades who looked at her so curiously. She heard Sir Frederick and Robert Gascoine announced and they entered the ballroom together. Now that the guest of honour had arrived, the first country dance was given out by the Master of Ceremonies and the young ladies present were soon filling in their dance cards. Sir Frederick and Miss Isabella Mason were in the first set to be formed and she saw Robert Gascoine sitting chatting to an elderly gentleman at the far end of the room. She looked down at her hands. She knew she was not likely to dance and told herself she must accept it. Lady Gascoine did not pay someone to be a companion and then do the job herself. Still, she couldn't help feeling disappointed. She composed her features into one of pleasant acceptance. Meanwhile Lady Gascoine started fidgeting about her fan and looked round ineffectively to try and see where she could have dropped it. Elizabeth offered to go to the ladies' cloakroom and fetch it for her.

'Depend upon it, Elizabeth, that is where it will be,' Lady Gascoine said and bestowed a gracious smile on Elizabeth as she sped off to the cloakroom, glad to have something to do.

Returning with the fan, Elizabeth was held up in a crush of people in the entrance to the ballroom and was spotted by Mr Mason, who said, 'Miss Baines, is there room on your card for an old codger, in the quadrille, perhaps?'

He was smiling at her and she felt flustered. She blushed and her eyes darted this way and that, trying to find some way out of a situation that she found so embarrassing. 'I . . . I . . . didn't think to . . . join the dancing this evening,' she stuttered. Elizabeth

117

had little worldly wisdom but her instinct told her that she liked Mr Mason and there was no harm in him. Yet she was unsure as to what Mrs Mason and the other ladies would think of her standing up with him in public.

The question was answered by Mrs Mason herself, who suddenly appeared at her husband's elbow and said smilingly, 'Do dance, Elizabeth. It would make his old heart glad to stand up with such a beautiful young lady.'

'Very well. I ... I ... thank you, sir. I should be pleased to dance.'

'I am only claimed for two dances, my dear, so I shall come for you in good time for the quadrille.'

Elizabeth blushed again and, curtsying to Mrs Mason, hurried back to Lady Gascoine with her fan. Her Ladyship seemed content with the idea of her young companion enjoying the dancing, smiling at her and merely saying that she wanted her to have a good time, but she wished Elizabeth to attend her when they went in to supper.

On the dance floor, Edward Mason was all that was affable. His instinct, so acute when dealing with tenants and people from all walks of life, told him that there was something special about this delicate young girl.

As they joined and parted and joined again in the dance, he managed to say to her, 'You are quite a remarkable young lady, Miss Baines, to be chosen as a companion to such a one as Lady Gascoine. You are not only beautiful, you seem to be clever, which my dear Isabella, alas, is not.'

Elizabeth remained demure and didn't respond to his praise but when they were facing each other in the next figure, he said, 'You seem to display a maturity beyond your years, Miss Baines. Lady Gascoine is indeed fortunate to have you as her companion. I am sure that Her Ladyship would not mind if you were to allow yourself to enjoy the dance. Even with an old fogey such as myself.'

She smiled at this and when the dance temporarily parted them again, she had time to look round and observe who else was dancing. Sir Frederick Gascoine was partnering Lydia Mason and while they danced the young lady was gazing at him just as adoringly as her elder sister. Robert Gascoine, she noticed, was dancing with Caroline. Edward Mason, noticing her glance in Robert's direction, and her smile, came to a sudden decision. This young lady was as deserving of happiness as were his own dear daughters, he thought. Why should she be confined to a life of genteel servitude when she was obviously superior in both intellect and accomplishment? The name Baines still rang a bell in his distant memory. By the time the dance had ended, he had decided to make some enquiries.

He delivered Elizabeth back safely to the other ladies and stayed to talk for a while during the next few dances and then it was time for supper. Edward Mason found them a table to themselves, and Elizabeth was able to attend to Lady Gascoine's comfort personally. Robert joined them and after supper Edward Mason announced to the assembled company that he and his wife were delighted to be able to announce the betrothal of his eldest daughter to Sir Frederick Gascoine. Champagne glasses were raised to the health and happiness of the engaged couple and there was polite applause when Sir Frederick and Isabella were the first to take to the floor in the next dance, which was a romantic waltz.

She watched the dancers, gliding past in each other's arms, and saw Robert dancing with one of the girls from the dancing class in the village. Then her thoughts drifted to Signor Guiseppe, his patent leather shoes twinkling like his black Italian eyes, as he coached the gauche schoolgirls so patiently and humorously in the dance steps. She remembered that she had been chosen to demonstrate to the others and sat up a little straighter. She wished that she were dancing the waltz with Robert Gascoine and that for a few moments she could show off her waltzing in front of the assembled company. Her eyes sought him out. He looked tall and masterful as he led the small girl across the floor, turning her with style and panache to make it look as though his partner were better than she was. Elizabeth had never questioned the unfairness of the hand that life had dealt her when she was a child in thrall to the Baines family. Now, watching the beautiful ladies and gentlemen moving in time to the graceful music, she screamed inwardly at the injustice of it all. Just by an accident of birth, just by the unfairness of life, she was condemned to what poor Holmes had rightly described as 'comfortable penury'.

She was immediately ashamed of her ignoble thoughts and tried to think instead of all the kindness and generosity that she'd received at Hawton House. She had nourishing, plentiful food instead of the crusts and scraps she'd been thrown when she lived at home. She glanced down at her elegant dress and thought of the filthy rags and bare feet she'd endured before she met Miss Gibson. Now her bed linen was immaculate and of the finest quality. She gave a sigh. She had no right to be dissatisfied. Her life was easy and she was with well-meaning, genteel people, moving in polite society. She should be grateful for the change in her fortunes.

But her wish to dance was granted less than an hour later because there was another waltz. This time, it was her hand that Sir Frederick was bending over, it was she whom he was now begging for the honour of the dance.

'Do you waltz, Miss Baines?' His tone was faintly sarcastic as he called her 'Miss Baines' but she didn't care. She was just longing to dance. As in a dream she looked towards Lady Gascoine and, seeing her consent, she allowed Frederick to lead her on to the floor.

She would remember Holmes's words for ever after this night: 'There is an old Spanish proverb which says: 'Have what you want. Have it and pay for it.' '

As she moved into the dance, it was just as though she were dancing again with Signor Guiseppe. Frederick's clasp was light, his body firm as he waltzed her to the end of the room. She could feel his surprised reaction at her confidence in the steps, knew that he was aware of her slim waist under his hand. It was a wonderful experience to be moving in such harmony with a skilled dancer like Sir

Frederick Gascoine. She knew that she didn't much like him as a man, didn't feel she could trust him, but here on the dance floor, in full view of his friends and fiancée, Elizabeth felt confident. She could give herself up to the pleasure of the dance and never, by word or deed, did he do anything improper.

It was afterwards that things began to go wrong. She was escorted very correctly back to Lady Gascoine and Miss Gibson. He bowed and thanked her most politely and moved away to join a group of friends. Minutes later Elizabeth had to visit the cloakroom again, this time because the room was so hot that a window had been opened and Lady Gascoine was in a draught.

Lady Gascoine wanted her shawl. 'I have only just noticed what a draught is coming from that window. Elizabeth, be an angel and fetch my shawl, my dear. It would make me so much more comfortable.'

Elizabeth went obediently to get it. It was nearly midnight and most of the servants were clearing tables and having their own supper. Many of the maids were attending ladies who were seeking their host and hostess before departing for their carriages. The cloakroom was deserted but she quickly found Her Ladyship's shawl and set off back to the ballroom. The corridor was dimly lit and she was startled when a figure suddenly leapt out of the shadows and held her in a suffocating grasp.

'Don't scream,' he said. 'I won't hurt you. Just one little kiss from your sweet lips, dear Miss Baines. I so enjoyed our waltz. No. Don't pull away. I won't hurt you. Just one little kiss is all I ask.'

She panted with the effort of trying to tear herself free of him but, looking up into his drunken face, she knew it was useless. 'Please, sir, please let me go,' she begged, but he merely laughed softly and she was reminded of the hateful Captain Preston. Fear crept up the back of her neck like an icy hand, and she tried to scream for help but it was no good. There was no one around.

Suddenly, there came unbidden to her mind some choice and filthy language she had heard from the slut Kate Molloy and she indignantly let rip at him with the same sort of verbal abuse.

At first his eyes widened in shocked surprise and then he laughed and tightened his grip.

'That's enough, Frederick. Release Miss Baines at once. She is not a suitable subject for your silly larks.'

It was Robert Gascoine, speaking in a quiet voice but with authority. Whether he had heard her unladylike talk she didn't know, but his own words had an immediate effect. Frederick ground his teeth and released her immediately, insisting that it was only a bit of fun.

'You'll have to forgive my brother yet again, Miss Baines. What he finds fun isn't so for everyone. When drink's in, wit's out, you know.'

He wondered at first if she'd even heard him. She was gazing unseeingly in front of her, seemingly miles away, as though something had gripped her imagination and she was unable to rouse herself from her inner vision.

At last she spoke in a low voice. 'I do beg your pardon, sir. I should not have spoken to Sir Frederick so. It was just . . . just that . . . '

She was unable to complete the sentence, unable to tell him of the unbelievable torture inflicted on her by James Preston. Two large tears rolled down her cheeks unheeded and she pressed her shapely lips together hard, to try and stop them trembling, bowing her head in despair at the way she had spoken in that hoydenish fashion. She could never explain. She could never tell him about her miserable life in Ireland. Never.

In two quick strides, Robert had reached her and had her in his arms, her tearful face pressed against his chest. He held her trembling girlish body as he would hold a child, to soothe away its tears and comfort its hurt.

Elizabeth recognized the humanity and kindness in this gesture in contrast to Frederick's drunken amorousness and Captain Preston's cruelty. She sniffed loudly into his immaculate evening coat and leaned against him, accepting the safe haven of his arms. All she was conscious of was the warmth and reassurance of his powerful body next to hers, the gentleness of his large hand as he stroked her soft curls without speaking. They remained like that for some moments until gradually her trembling ceased and she made an effort to compose herself.

In that short space of time, Robert was overwhelmed by a feeling of tender protectiveness towards his mama's young companion. He was aware that her early life had been a troubled one, and he had certainly been aware of the unladylike obscenities which had issued from those beautiful young lips. He had no idea what difficulties she'd had in Ireland or where she'd learned such loose talk. All he knew was that he admired the brave independence of spirit, which had made her invent herself from the gauche awkward child that she had been to this lovely young woman. Where had she come from? And what had her unhappy past been? Involuntarily, his arms tightened round her and for a long moment he held her close. Then he gently released her. It was all too seductively easy just to enjoy the sensation of her soft warmth and alluring scent and feel once more the silken curls against his fingers, as when he had fastened her pearls.

He stepped back and Elizabeth gazed up at him sombrely. She caught a look in his eyes and it was anything but cool. He was offering only comfort, she knew that, she wasn't a fool. But oh, how wonderful it felt to be in those strong reassuring arms. She had felt so safe and calm. Her whole body had melted when he held her to him and pressed her against him in that intimate way. She must get a hold on her senses and speak calmly.

'I beg your pardon for giving way like that,' she said. 'I'm sure that Sir Frederick meant no real offence. I . . . was . . . just taken by surprise, that is all. I'd like to rejoin Lady Gascoine, if you please, before anyone notices my absence.'

He continued to look at her as she stood in front of him, apparently calm now. Ready to go to his mama and yet seemingly didn't have the will to part from him. If she doesn't go soon, he thought, I shall be holding her in my arms again. She looks so sweetly sad. No girl of her age should look like that. Damn Frederick! Why does he have to interfere so carelessly with an innocent girl who means no harm?

He said nothing of this, but taking care to see that she was composed and tidy, he left Elizabeth to hurry back to the ballroom.

The last coaches didn't leave the manor house until two in the morning and the older ladies were quiet on the way back to Waringham, but all three declared it had been a successful evening, in spite of the sad crush. They seemed not to notice that Elizabeth was quiet, no doubt they just thought that she was exhausted by the long evening.

'Did you enjoy the dancing, Elizabeth?' Jane Gibson asked.

'Why, yes, ma'am,' she answered and then, remembering the scene with Frederick Gascoine, was not inclined to continue.

'Signor Guiseppe must have taught you very well,' Bradbury said quietly. 'You waltzed divinely, Elizabeth.'

In the dim light of the carriage, Elizabeth blushed and Lady Gascoine said quickly, 'But my Frederick is such a superb dancer, is he not, Elizabeth? There's no wonder that dear Isabella is so in love with him.'

In the silence that followed, Elizabeth

wondered inwardly what it was that Isabella did find to love in him. True, he was handsome, the best-looking young man that Elizabeth had ever seen, and she was prepared to believe Jane's opinion that he was the most handsome man in London. This was not all. He was tall, elegant, beautifully dressed, a notable whip, an athletic boxer, and an out-and-out Corinthian. He came from an illustrious and noble family. His parents and Isabella's had encouraged the match for dynastic reasons. Any number of women must be in love with him. And yet he was a gambler, drank to excess, and was an obvious philanderer, one who seized any opportunity to prey on helpless females such as herself. She shivered. Life with a confirmed whoremonger such as Frederick Gascoine would be difficult indeed. Unless, that is, he became a reformed character as soon as he was respectably married to dear Isabella. In some of the books she had read, the drunken bachelor rake had miraculously turned into a respectable model husband when he married a good and loving wife. But in the novels, the wife was usually strikingly beautiful and strong-minded. She thought of the timid, dumpy Miss Mason. It would be hard to imagine the dashing Sir Frederick giving all for love of such as she. If Robert were engaged to Isabella, the problem would be non-existent. And yet, if Frederick could be a kind and attentive husband, Elizabeth knew that Isabella would be deliriously happy and there would be no problem.

It was none of her business except that she must make a bid to avoid being alone with Frederick. Of all the resolutions she was thinking of, this one remained with her as she fell asleep.

6

Elizabeth saw little of Frederick Gascoine in the days before Christmas. Having a few spare moments one afternoon, she decided she would look round Sir William's collection. She knew which room it was in and was intrigued. The door was not locked, but it was heavy. When she opened it the room seemed too neat and tidy, and rather bland.

She went to a nearby case and looked in. It was the loveliest of little pieces of material from the summit of a mountain in India. She surveyed them gravely. They were absolutely perfect and each one looked like a little coil of rope.

Suddenly, she became aware of the door opening. When she looked up she suddenly felt guilty and stared at the floor instead, with a deep red blush covering her face and neck. It was Robert Gascoine.

'Miss Baines. I hope I don't intrude. So you have finally come to see Papa's collection?'

She wanted to explain about the language used when Frederick pinioned her arm and

131

would not let her go. It was only because of Preston having her in his power. Her voice trailed away and she was silent.

'Shall we just say that it was in the heat of the moment and his stupid larks were a complete surprise? That would explain your shock,' he said.

As though she hadn't spoken, he carried on talking, taking her round the gallery, showing her the artefacts and explaining where they had come from, until gradually she lost her feelings of acute embarrassment.

She stood next to him, unaware that she was so straight and tall now that she had reached eighteen. He was very conscious of her and thought of facts which would be of interest to her, meanwhile watching her face to see which fossils she liked.

He thought she liked the strata of the Alps. It was a much convoluted one due to the convulsions on a stupendous scale, due to the volcanic action, he told her. The offering from this part was a small piece of material alive with the tiny shells from the bottom of the sea. She liked these, and the open and expressive face told him so.

Soon it was time to go and see if Lady Gascoine was ready to go to tea with another friend of Isabella Mason's. They were all looking forward to Christmas and Elizabeth

132

felt a quiet happiness about her position in life.

It seemed that Frederick Gascoine was not. Although she saw little of him in the days immediately before the festival, she noticed that at dinner he was either morose or truculent until even his fond mama began to lose patience with him. It was obvious that he didn't win as many wagers as he would like her to believe and his intended father-in-law was proving to be a disappointment to him.

'He seems such a killjoy,' he said. 'I know that when she marries me, Isabella's fortune will pass into my hands and yet he is so miserably mean, he won't consider advancing anything of the loot on my account.'

There was an uncomfortable silence and even Lady Gascoine seemed to find this sort of talk unsuitable. She and his aunt made no response and Elizabeth looked down at her plate, reluctant to hear any of Frederick's confidences about his finances. Only Robert expressed polite interest and asked what had happened.

'Why, I put to the old miser that as Isabella and I were to be wed in less than five months, it wouldn't be behind the door for him to consider a few thou' in advance. I pointed out the expenditure I'd be incurring in refurbishing Hawton House and enlarging the dower house at Waringham for dear Mama, not to mention the expenses of my own wedding clothes and the celebrations for our friends in town and celebrations in Norfolk.'

'And what was Mr Mason's reaction, Frederick?'

'Papa's will, sealed and delivered and that was his final word. He hinted that as Papa had died such a wealthy man, there should be no need for his heir to look for an advance of any kind.'

'I am sure that Mr Mason feels he is doing right by Isabella and acting in her best interests,' Robert said guardedly. 'It would be foolish indeed of him if he were to break into Isabella's portion without assurances of seeing her settled in wedlock. Has a date been settled for the signing of the marriage settlement?'

'Middle of February,' Frederick muttered resentfully, 'but I shan't feel secure in my mind until that fortune is in my hands.'

Robert said mildly that Hawton House was large enough as it stood and Frederick's mama exclaimed that she would manage famously in the dower house, with no more extra expenditure than some new drawing-room curtains. Robert added that Frederick's wedding clothes need not be ordered yet.

'There's plenty of time to get your tailor to

supply you,' he said kindly. 'And you needn't pay him until the year's end, you know. As for myself, I know you will want Hawton House for yourself and your bride. When Mama moves to the dower house, I shall buy myself a modest townhouse and set up my own establishment.'

Frederick dismissed his brother's plans contemptuously. 'Pooh!' he exclaimed as usual. 'That's typical of you, Robert. A modest townhouse is the summit of your aspirations and that's all your stupid collections of pictures and fossils warrant. Not everyone has such trifling ambitions. I'm seeking to extend my estate and take my bride to a far grander home. I shan't feel comfortable in my mind until Isabella's fortune is in my hands.'

And what of Isabella's happiness? Elizabeth thought. Wouldn't that be in Frederick's hands too? She felt a pang of sympathy for Isabella Mason, about to be wed to such a dissolute and selfish man. She wondered why he never spoke of Isabella — only her fortune which would one day be his. Once more, she wondered at the blindness of love. Would Isabella gradually have her eyes opened to Frederick's true character when they were wed and it was too late?

Christmas was now nearly upon them and

Lady Gascoine's plans to entertain her sister and the Mason family were well under way. She gave Elizabeth a few hours off in order that she might do some shopping in Norwich and Bradbury was also keen to go. At the last minute, Robert offered to accompany them in his carriage, saying that he wished to visit a dealer who had a small sculpture he was interested in. They arranged to meet at the King's Arms for luncheon when they had completed their purchases. There was a light flurry of snow before they set off but it didn't seem to be settling and the three of them were in good humour as they parted to go their separate ways. Elizabeth and Bradbury had plenty of time to shop before luncheon and set about it with some intent.

Elizabeth was unsure about Christmas gifts. Bradbury advised that a small token for Lady Gascoine and Miss Gibson would suffice and that the two gentlemen would neither expect nor appreciate any Christmas tokens.

'In any case,' she said, 'what possible gift could either of us afford that would please a wealthy gentleman? Leather riding gloves? A silver brandy flask? Either of those would take a whole year's allowance and, in any case, both gentlemen have an abundance of such articles. Anything less than these trifles would be insulting. For the ladies, though, a lace handkerchief is possible, or a box of sweetmeats, perhaps.'

Elizabeth was thoughtful. She understood the impossibility of buying gifts for Robert and his brother but was determined to get something for Bradbury as well as the two other ladies. In the end, after much inward debate, she obtained a top-of-the-range, sable-hair watercolour brush for Miss Gibson and a small, exquisitely worked sachet of Norfolk lavender for Her Ladyship's dressing-table drawer. The choice for Bradbury was much harder, but she knew that lady was a skilled seamstress who made many of her own clothes. After much hesitation, she went back to the drapers on her own and purchased a length of fine Bruges lace, enough to edge a petticoat. It was all of two inches and bound to please a lady as skilled with a needle as Bradbury.

As they waited for the coach to take them to the King's Arms, Elizabeth clutched her precious purchases and hugged herself with the thought that even after a morning's shopping, she still had luncheon with Robert Gascoine to look forward to. He'd booked a private parlour for them, and the two ladies were soon settled in front of a cosy fire, surrounded by their parcels, bonnets and cloaks removed and enjoying a glass of Madeira, as they waited for their host. They were to be entirely private and serve themselves when the luncheon was brought in, and both of them were in a relaxed mood.

He strode into the room a trifle late, bringing a waft of the cold December air with him and carrying a small package done up in brown paper. His face was glowing and alive with the cold and his unusual brown and green eyes were sparkling with pleasure. If Sir Frederick Gascoine had once been the most handsome man she'd ever seen, she was obliged to revise her opinion. There was nothing of Frederick's petulance or bad temper in Robert's fine-featured face. He was openly pleased to see them and delighted with his little marble statue of a tiny cherubic baby by Bernini, its face angelic and chubby, its little arms and legs plump and curved.

'I got it for a song,' he declared and for the first time Elizabeth dared to tease him a little. She looked at him mischievously from under her long lashes.

'Oh, you sang, did you, sir? And was the dealer kind enough to let you have it on condition that you went and sang elsewhere?'

He laughed at this and even Bradbury smiled. 'No, you baggage,' he said. 'I merely offered the right price at the right time.'

'And were there other gentlemen desiring to buy the sculpture?'

'There were some, but most of them were not as single-minded as I am myself. Most of them have other things to occupy them. But tell me, what do ladies buy when they have no other occupations?'

'That is Miss Bradbury's and my secret,' Elizabeth laughed. 'But I do assure you, sir, that they are not the result of us having no useful occupation. Miss Bradbury and I are always occupied. We sew and sketch and keep Lady Gascoine and Miss Gibson company. We read, change our library books, go for walks . . . '

All the while, she was laughing and Robert was quite enchanted by the animated girl in front of him. His eyes held hers for a long moment before Bradbury broke the spell by pointedly removing the cover from a roasted chine of mutton, surrounded by beans and bacon.

Robert served it out gravely and poured three glasses of fine claret. The three of them were in such good mood, no one wanted the luncheon to end.

'You must acknowledge, my dear Miss Baines,' Robert said with mock formality, 'that the Bernini is a prize I never hoped to possess.'

'It certainly looks beautiful,' she said.

'Yes and so lifelike that the eyes seem to be looking at one with absolute trust and innocent delight.'

'No. Do they? Then I must look at the eyes very carefully, sir.'

'Yes. If only *you* would bestow such a look upon me. I wish you would.'

In spite of the lightness of his tone, Elizabeth's heart suddenly seemed to jump into her throat and then began to thump so violently that she felt breathless and uncomfortably hot.

It was difficult to speak but she stammered, 'Sir, I think . . . I think that . . . you cannot mean that . . . You are just . . . just flirting.'

'No. Believe me. I have never tried to flirt with you,' he protested, but she could hear the laughter in his voice.

Bradbury maintained a tactful silence at this and Elizabeth wondered how she felt at the idea of acting as duenna. She felt compelled to glance at him from under her lashes. Immediately, she realized it was not a very prudent thing to do. She saw the smile in his eyes and he was looking at her, while pretending not to, in a way that made her heart beat more violently than ever. Neither of them spoke and Bradbury matter-of-factly served out the apple dumplings and English custard, as though completely unaware that Elizabeth's heart was turning somersaults and that she was now afraid to look at him.

The meal ended all too soon and they gathered their packages together and dressed ready to depart. While Robert settled the tally, Bradbury and Elizabeth adjusted their bonnets and fastened their winter cloaks against the cold. Elizabeth was acutely conscious of Robert by her side as he pressed her hand briefly and mentioned the statue again.

'You must come to the statue gallery tomorrow, Miss Baines, and see my new treasure,' he said to her. 'And Miss Bradbury too, if you should wish it, ma'am. This is smaller than any in my collection and yet I think it is absolutely exquisite.'

★　★　★

The next day was Christmas Eve and it was curiosity that drove her to the statue gallery. This was a room she had not been in. It opened off the room with the stones and fossils. She noticed the new acquisition straight away. Showing it off in the King's Arms did not do it justice. In the statue room it seemed almost to live and breathe. The lovely little arms were raised as though the

141

baby wanted to be picked up and Elizabeth thought the face must be that of an angel. The eyes were just as appealing as Robert said and, as she stood in silent contemplation of the little marble figure, she was suddenly aware that he was standing beside her.

'You've found my Bernini,' he said. 'Is it not as tender and lifelike as I said?'

'It certainly is, sir.' Then she smiled at him. 'Well worth the song, I think.'

'Yes, indeed. It is difficult to evaluate a sculpture by Bernini. They can usually only be judged in the setting for which they were made. It came from one of the ruined Baroque churches in Rome and at first I thought it might be a piece attributed to a sculptor of Bernini's following. Now I am convinced it is by the master himself.'

'I hope you didn't mind my curiosity, sir. Lady Gascoine is lying down. And I had a few minutes to spare so I . . . I . . . '

'Not at all,' he said. 'I am delighted that you are able to take pleasure in my few artefacts. Tomorrow is Christmas Day and you will have very few minutes to spare. The Gascoine family has a long tradition of going for a ride on Christmas Day after luncheon. I expect my mother has mentioned it to you. Shall you be joining us, Miss Baines?'

'Well . . . I . . . am but an indifferent

horsewoman,' Elizabeth stammered. 'I went riding at Miss Hanbury's, of course. I have never . . . never been any good at it. I should probably disgrace the Gascoine family by my . . . my inept riding skills.'

She was remembering the humiliation of her very first time on horseback, at the Hanbury Academy, when she was so frightened of mounting the gentle hack assigned to her that she nearly fainted.

Once more he was looking at her with amusement. 'I fear you're too modest, but I can mount you on the gentlest little cob, if you should care to join us.'

And there was no escape. Even Lady Gascoine and Bradbury joined the riders after lunch as they assembled in front of Waringham Hall, with the Mason family and a couple of grooms. Elizabeth blessed Miss Gibson, who kitted her out so splendidly for her riding lessons at the academy. Her elegant habit was still a perfect fit and with the help of the groom she was able to mount gracefully and sit beautifully on her horse. She adjusted her skirts, pulling on her gloves and holding her small ladylike riding crop. Her mount was called Lucinda and once on her back, Elizabeth displayed a confidence she didn't feel. But then, she thought, appearance was all. The first six riding lessons she'd had at Miss Hanbury's had been devoted exclusively to mounting and sitting with graceful ease, first on a wooden mount and then, when she and the other novices were deemed ready, they were allowed to progress to a living, breathing beast. In spite of her fear, she had never disgraced herself by falling off and after the first few minutes she felt firmly in control of the gentle Lucinda.

The Mason girls came across to speak to her and Lady Gascoine outlined briefly the route they would take. 'We shall go through Waringham village to the Fitchwell high road which leads to the clifftop bridleway past the lighthouse and St Edmund's arch, as far as Fitchwell and then turn back down along the old road to Waringham.'

The party set off at a steady pace and Elizabeth was careful to keep near to Sir Frederick's groom, Kelly, who was mounted on a huge chestnut gelding. The horse was to have a bit of a canter along the cliffs but for now was moving as sedately as any of the ladies' mounts. Kelly was tall and broad, handling the horse easily, and Elizabeth gradually began to relax into the rise and fall of Lucinda's rhythm as she kept abreast of him.

The watery sun was now beginning to thaw the hoar frost which touched every leaf and grass blade along the way, making everything sparkle like fairyland. Elizabeth began to feel exhilarated. She looked about her at the view of the pounding grey sea, so far below them, and her eyes sought out the figure of Robert Gascoine, mounted on a magnificent grey and deep in conversation with Miss Isabella Mason. Several people came up to her, the youngest girl, and then Mr Mason, who seemed determined to speak of Ireland.

Kelly moved forward to canter along the grassy cliff with Sir Frederick. Elizabeth continued to admire the magnificent view and breathe in the cold air as she chatted quietly to Edward Mason. She felt suddenly at peace, as consciously happy as she had ever done in the whole of her life.

Everything went well until they turned back to go along the old road. Then, Frederick galloped towards her, still giving his horse the opportunity to stretch its legs and have its head for a brief time. As he slowed down behind her, for some reason Lucinda took fright at his sudden approach and began to throw back her head and then duck it down again as she danced sideways. Elizabeth shortened the rein as she had been taught by the riding master, but Lucinda was decidedly unsettled and continued to side-step and buck, as Elizabeth tried in vain to control the normally serene little mare. The situation was hardly helped by Frederick, now coming alongside and slapping Lucinda on the rump, telling Elizabeth roughly to 'get a grip on the damned animal'.

This was the last straw. Lucinda gave one last almighty heave and Elizabeth was unseated. She sailed over the horse's head and landed in a heap on the wet, frosty road. Isabella, who was close behind them, gave a sharp scream of alarm and Robert galloped up immediately and flung himself down from his horse to crouch beside her. Frederick's reaction was slower. He climbed down from his horse and motioned to Kelly to take the still-bucking mare under control.

The others gradually grouped themselves round as Robert carefully supported Elizabeth's head and looked anxiously into her white face. He took her gloved hands and began to chafe her wrists.

'Thank God at least there's a pulse,' he said.

Edward Mason crouched on the other side of her. Her smart riding hat had fallen off and rolled a little way away. He picked it up carefully and said, 'Her eyes are fluttering, old chap. The road is very cold and hard. Perhaps she would be more comfortable if we could help her to sit up.'

He reached inside his greatcoat and produced a little phial of brandy. It seemed like an eternity, but at last the blue eyes opened and she began to splutter and choke on the brandy that was being forced between her white lips. Her face was deathly pale but her eyes sought those of Robert Gascoine's as she attempted to sit up.

'Steady, Elizabeth,' he said. 'Easy does it, my dear.' He slid an arm under her shoulders and Edward Mason attempted to replace her hat.

Elizabeth winced and let out an involuntary groan of pain as his gentle fingers caught the lump on the back of her head. 'What is it? Where does it hurt you?'

Robert's eyes expressed such anxiety and alarm that Elizabeth attempted to reassure him. 'I told you I was an indifferent horsewoman,' she said, attempting a smile, 'and now I have a headache to prove it.'

With the utmost care and gentleness, he removed the hat once more and carefully felt the back of her head, searching for injury. There was no cut or wound, only a massive egg-shaped lump. 'Do you have any pain anywhere else?'

'No, I . . . I . . . don't think so.' With Edward and Robert's help, she managed to stand upright, albeit on legs that were trembling uncontrollably, and she had to lean against Robert for support.

Kelly appeared at that moment, leading the now docile mare and said, 'Begging pardon, sir. Shall I help Miss Baines to remount?'

'No,' said Robert shortly. 'Miss Baines will ride with me. Lead the mare back home.'

The whole party now expressed relief and pleasure that Elizabeth was not seriously hurt and regrouped for the rest of the journey home as Edward Mason and Kelly lifted her up in front of Robert on his large grey horse. Still shaken and dizzy, Elizabeth found herself once more in his sure and comfortable grasp. From the safety of those strong, protective arms, it seemed such a long way to the wet, hard ground and she shuddered. He felt the tremor and tightened his hold somewhat, drawing her even closer to him. She tried to sit a little straighter to avoid too intimate a contact but it made the pain in her head throb unbearably. She couldn't help leaning against him and pressing herself against the warmth and comfort of his body. Thankfully, she rested her aching head on his strong chest and, what with the brandy and her slight concussion, she was forced to relax and enjoy the moment.

Bradbury had ridden on ahead to organize the maids to prepare a bath for her and

Robert Gascoine leaned closer to say, 'We shall soon be home, my love, and then you can be cared for properly. I shall ask Dr Godfrey to call in the morning.'

As he spoke, his lips brushed against her hair and Elizabeth almost wept at the tender concern in his voice. She knew he was only being kind to his mama's insignificant young companion but for the first time in her life Elizabeth began to have an inkling of what it must be like to be loved. Once again, she had the elusive feeling of her mother's presence, and wondered what it would be like to be loved unconditionally, as her mama would love her. She wondered what it would be like to have a man's love. Not the quiet motherly love of Miss Gibson and Bradbury, or the hateful attentions of Captain Preston, but the close intimacy which could exist between a man and a woman who loved each other. A gentleman like Robert Gascoine, who could show her the kind of romantic love that so constantly preoccupied the young girls at Miss Hanbury's. It would be such a privilege to feel the passion and affection that Robert could give a woman. To feel his touch, not merely the cool contact of his caring hands, but the hot caress of a lover. She longed for the firm pressure of his lips against her own as she swayed backwards, even nearer to him, and she knew that she would return such a kiss with unbridled passion.

The object of her thoughts remained outwardly calm as they made their gentle progress back to Waringham Hall, but inwardly he was only gradually losing the sensation of horror that he felt when he'd seen that slight crumpled body in the middle of the road. His heart had pounded and his mouth had been dry as he'd bent over her, fearing the worst. Now he was somewhat calmer, he remembered other details of the accident. The delicious softness of her hair as he'd felt for the injury to her head, the trust in her blue gaze as her eyes had opened and sought his own. He had to confess to himself how much this meant to him, how pleasurable he found having the yielding young body so near to him, how much he wanted to rest his lips on the soft fragrant hair so close to his cheek.

Stop! Stop this at once, he thought wildly. It was not a suitable thought for a man in his position. She trusts you and you've no business to think of her in such a way. You would be a libertine and a scoundrel to even imagine taking advantage of her!

They turned into the drive at Waringham Hall and as soon as the front door was opened, he lifted Elizabeth down and carried her up to her bedroom. Miss Gibson and Bradbury were soon in attendance and he noticed that even his mama was inclined to fuss round the bedside, ordering the maid to put her in her nightgown and bring up a hot brick and an extra blanket. Inwardly, he was relieved to relinquish his beautiful burden and go to his own bedchamber for a warm bath after that ride. But he couldn't rid himself of the feel of her slender waist as he'd held her in front of him. He stretched himself more voluptuously in the warm water and gradually began to relax.

What would it be like to have those shapely young lips next to his, to feel her softness against his naked body? The thought of that golden hair, loose and brushing against his skin, made him wild with longing for her. But this was madness! He must take great care not to be alone with Elizabeth Baines for both their sakes.

7

By the time Boxing Day arrived, Elizabeth was feeling stiff and sore and distinctly sorry for herself. She was bored with doing nothing and yet if she tried to read her head began to ache again. The doctor visited first thing in the morning and declared that there were no bones broken and that the young lady could partake of light food in moderation, should stand or lie down, but not sit for long, and take his special preparation of laudanum with hot milk before retiring.

'You are strong and healthy, my dear young lady. Rest and a light diet will soon effect a cure, without any help from a doddery old medical man like me. Good day, ma'am.' He bowed politely to Lady Gascoine and departed smiling.

On Boxing Day night, the house party and the Mason family were due to have an early dinner and attend a soirée at one of Mrs Mason's oldest and dearest friends. Mr and Mrs Atherton had a fine home on the outskirts of King's Lynn and had known the Masons all their lives. They had one son, David and it would have been their dearest wish if David, and Isabella had fallen in love and united the two families in marriage.

'It was not to be,' Mrs Atherton said to her friend ruefully. 'We can't order these things, my dear Emma, and I'm sure I wish dear Isabella happy with Sir Frederick. There will be time for David to find the right one, especially if Isabella is able to introduce him to other young ladies. Now, tell me, Emma, who is this chit that Her Ladyship is employing as a companion?'

There was to be a champagne supper and the evening would include dancing and carol singers. The cream of Norfolk society was expected to attend the soirée and Lady Gascoine declared herself very well pleased that they had been invited. When Mrs Mason had explained to her friend that 'the chit' was a protégé of Lady Gascoine's wealthy sister, the invitation had been extended to include the young companion as well. Elizabeth knew nothing of this as she lay in her room, nursing an aching head and bruised legs. Feeling as she did, a soirée was the last thing on her mind.

Lady Gascoine came to visit the sickroom after luncheon. 'If you are not well enough for an evening at the Athertons' my dear, don't fuss yourself,' she said. 'I can easily arrange for one of the maids to keep you company and order some refreshments in your room. There will be plenty of young women to attend me at the soirée and numerous old acquaintances to keep me entertained. Now I must go and let Maria put my curl papers in. I shall lie down until it's time for dinner.'

But Elizabeth, with the impatience of youth, was already chafing to get into normal company again. 'I'm taking the draught that Doctor Godfrey left me, ma'am,' she said bravely, 'and if I stay in my room beforehand and have a light meal, I may feel well enough to attend you this evening.'

Lady Gascoine smiled at this and said, 'Well, we'll see,' before disappearing off to her own room.

Left alone, Elizabeth lay down on the bed, resting her throbbing head in one hand. Her thoughts turned to Robert Gascoine and the feeling of intimacy when she'd nestled so closely in his arms. The particular smell of his cologne and the thud of his heart as her cheek had rested on his broad chest were still strong in her mind. She wondered what he was doing now, whether he had been as affected as she herself by their physical closeness, which was all the more piquant for being so public. As her thoughts wandered, gradually the pain in her head lessened. She closed her eyes and tried to recapture yet again the sense of his presence, so close to her and yet, because of the social difference between them, so far.

She longed for a man like him who would be all her own, hers to love and cherish and to be loved and cherished by. No wonder girls were always talking and reading about romance. Now she understood why. If Robert Gascoine were hers, she would never want anything more to make her life complete. In that twilight state between sleeping and waking, she once again imagined vividly the feel of his arms enclosing her, the sensation of his warm breath on her hair, the strong shapely hands at her waist as he lifted her down from her horse . . . The tears started in her eyes.

This was stupid! Part of an impossible dream. Why should a man like Robert Gascoine wish to concern himself with a girl like me? she thought. A slum child from a low family in Ireland. A girl who had never worn shoes until she was ten and then had been given them by Miss Gibson so she could attend Sunday school.

The helpless tears squeezed themselves out from underneath her eyelids and she began to awake from her reverie, feeling sadder than she'd ever done in her whole life. Even when the Baines boys had tormented her, she'd had some pride in trying not to give way and weep. Now, she was ready to sob out loud, and all for the love of a man who was so cool and contained that he would never notice her in that way. She sat up wearily and bleakly acknowledged to herself that this was what made her so sad and lachrymose.

She was so in love with Robert Gascoine. Could anything be more terrible? She must take good care never to reveal this fact to anyone, especially Robert himself. If he suspected how she felt, it would mean at best contempt and at worst instant dismissal.

Slowly and stiffly, she got up from the bed and washed carefully, trying not to move suddenly and disturb her throbbing head again. She resolutely put all thoughts of Robert Gascoine from her mind. Susanna had been sent up by Lady Gascoine to see how she did and Elizabeth asked her to assist in getting dressed. The girl was very young, but she was sensitive and gentle, helping Elizabeth to dress without stooping or stretching and taking care with Elizabeth's stiff joints and painful limbs. Elizabeth had chosen yet another evening gown from her time at Miss Hanbury's. It was a deceptively simple, expensive dress of palest blue crêpe, decorated with ruched ribbons of a deeper blue, which matched her eyes perfectly.

Underneath was a silk slip of silver blue satin and round her neck, as usual, were Lady Gascoine's pearls.

Finally she was dressed and Susanna again shyly offered to help her arrange her hair. 'No, thank you,' Elizabeth said. 'If you would be so kind as to brush it out for me, I can do it myself.'

It took twice as long but Elizabeth managed it, resting her arms frequently and finally repairing her face with powder where it was blotched and reddened. And she was ready. Taking heed of Doctor Godfrey's advice, she had another dose of the pain-relieving draught that he had left for her and she walked about the room until her aches and pains subsided a little. She waited for the gong to summon her to Lady Gascoine's small sitting-room.

Here, she received so many kindly enquiries after her health and whether she felt up to the long evening in company that she felt the weak tears begin to prick the back of her eyes. She answered hastily after every enquiry, 'I am much better, I thank you. Yes, I shall be careful not to exert myself too much. No, dear Doctor Godfrey will not need to visit me again. I am merely a little stiff, that is all.'

Throughout these exchanges, only Sir

Frederick remained aloof, frowning somewhat and merely giving her a polite nod before reaching for a glass of wine from the footman's tray.

Entering a little later, Robert was in time to see the normally reticent Miss Gibson giving Elizabeth a fond kiss on the cheek and hear her whispering, 'My darling little Lizzie, I am so pleased you are feeling better, my dear.'

No one could call Miss Baines 'little', he thought. She was as tall as his Aunt Jane and he was intrigued to hear the undemonstrative Jane use the pet name 'Lizzie'.

He strode up to Elizabeth, greeting his mama and brother on the way, nodding to Bradbury and his Aunt Jane as his eyes sought hers. 'We didn't expect you out of your sickbed just yet, Miss Baines. How are you? How is your head?'

'Much improved, I thank you, sir. And I am already impatient at being confined to my chamber.'

She smiled at him and accepted a glass of wine from the footman, while Robert continued to gaze at her admiringly, taking in her straight, slender figure and the simple pearl necklace against her beautiful throat. He continued to gaze without speaking, as she blushed and sipped her wine.

Lady Gascoine, observing this little

158

exchange, said, 'Well, ladies and gentlemen, our carriages await.'

Immediately, he gracefully offered Elizabeth his arm as they made their way to the front door.

Obediently, she placed her fingertips on the smooth sleeve of his immaculate black evening coat. She felt the strength of his muscular arm under the cloth and closed her eyes momentarily as she breathed in once more the faint tang of his cologne. This warm, living, breathing man was now so dear to her that it was a painful joy to feel the vibrant flesh beneath the fabric of his coat.

She tried to let commonsense in as she attempted to rid her mind of all thoughts of Robert as a man. After all, she should not be indulging in sensual thoughts; they were futile and leading nowhere. He could never care for such as she and it would be better if she stopped thinking along those lines.

Instead, she concentrated on walking slowly to the carriage without stumbling or exacerbating her various aches and pains.

When they arrived at the home of the Athertons, both Mr and Mrs Mason renewed their concerns about Elizabeth's health and she reassured them and also had a joke with Isabella. 'I've heard the expression 'head over heels', Miss Mason, but only when it meant the tender passion of love, never an undignified fall from such a mild little mare as Lucinda.'

Isabella gave a wan smile. She was looking very peaky, so Elizabeth determined to chat with her for a little longer to try and make her smile again. Frederick had disappeared to the card room for a game of piquet and Elizabeth gave a quick glance round the room. Lady Gascoine was chatting to Mr and Mrs Atherton and Robert was greeting the Masons. Now would be a good time to get acquainted with Isabella.

'I expect your wedding plans are now well underway, Miss Mason,' she said. 'Your sisters must be so excited at being your attendants on the happy day. Has a date been fixed yet?'

She immediately regretted her question. Isabella Mason looked positively hunted and then, immediately, miserable.

'Not as yet,' she said in a low voice. 'Of course, Papa and Frederick have got to complete the formalities of . . . of . . . the marriage settlement.'

'Well, I expect gentlemen cannot be hurried in these things,' Elizabeth said and then mentally castigated herself.

What do you know about it? she asked herself. Captain Preston's pretence at an

160

engagement was just that — a pretence. No respectable man has ever offered for you and never will, with your pathetic background. Isabella Mason is all that is eligible in a wife and her family have already negotiated the match between her and Sir Frederick. Your own family merely sold you to the highest bidder.

She felt humble and inadequate in the face of Isabella's obvious unhappiness. What could possibly have gone wrong, she wondered, to cause Isabella to feel such misery?

At that moment Sir Frederick emerged from the card room, looking distinctly aggressive and angry, and strode to a far corner of the room, where he grabbed another glass of wine and threw himself down on one of the mahogany chairs. She noticed that Isabella frowned and followed his every movement with anguished eyes. Something must have happened between them, she thought, and she decided to change the subject.

'I have never met Mr and Mrs Atherton before,' she said. 'It was kind of them to invite me. In spite of my accident, I felt very much better as a consequence. I expect that, like your parents, they have lived in Norfolk for a long time.'

'Yes, indeed,' Isabella said, somewhat

wistfully. 'When we were small children, David Atherton and I used to play together and then . . . '

She didn't continue, but frowned again and looked sad, so Elizabeth was at a loss as to how to continue the conversation. Isabella was so patently distressed.

'And then I expect you grew apart as all young childhood friends do,' she said gently. 'I own I had a particular friend at the academy I attended in Bath, and we were full of promises and resolutions to write to each other when we left to go our separate ways. Alas, this didn't happen and my dear friend — Honoria — and I seem to have dried up over our correspondence. Is it the same for you, Miss Mason, or have you kept in touch with David Atherton?'

'Not recently, no, although I hope . . . I hope . . . he will dance at my wedding, whenever it takes place, that is . . . '

So that's it, thought Elizabeth. She thought of a romantic novel which had been widely circulated among the young ladies at the academy. It was entitled, *Lonely Road*, and concerned a young girl who had fallen in love with a handsome man. After a quarrel with her mama, who wished her to marry a dull but wealthy bore, she had run away to her lover and begged him to take her in. Appalled at her indiscretion, he'd gently tried to persuade her to return home, but instead the heroine had despairingly embarked on a life on the road, meeting up with thieves and vagabonds until, finally, she'd died in a gypsy encampment lonely and penniless.

The lack of romantic urgency on the part of the hero in the story was the reason for the heroine's fall from grace and eventual dissolution. She sensed that Miss Isabella Mason was downcast at what she saw as a similar lack of romantic urgency on the part of Sir Frederick, to sweep her into an ideal marriage.

Aloud she said, 'These things have a way of working themselves out and no doubt your forthcoming marriage has caused you to neglect your old friend somewhat. Once you are wed and running your own establishment there are bound to be many opportunities to rekindle old relationships and entertain friends and family.'

She felt she had sounded patronizing and years older than the young lady she was speaking to, but Miss Mason herself appeared not to notice. 'What a kind thought, Miss Baines,' she said, 'and what a friend in need you could be if I were fortunate enough for us to be friends.'

'I do hope we might be,' Elizabeth said,

and they smiled at each other. She meant it. For the first time in her life, she realized that wealth and privilege did not necessarily bring happiness. At that moment, she would not have exchanged with Miss Mason for the world. Especially if it meant being engaged to Frederick Gascoine.

'May I join you, Isabella?'

They both turned at the sound of a soft and pleasant male voice, and standing before them was David Atherton. Isabella's normally pale face flushed with pleasure.

'Why, David! I . . . David, may I present Miss Elizabeth Baines?'

He was of medium height, not a lot taller than Elizabeth was herself. He favoured his father, she decided, with medium brown hair and steady blue eyes. Good features, she thought, but not nearly as spectacularly handsome as Sir Frederick Gascoine. But then who is? she asked herself.

'Your servant, Miss Baines,' he said and bowed, but Elizabeth noticed that his eyes quickly returned to Isabella. 'May I mark your dance card, Isabella, and perhaps request a dance from yourself, Miss Baines?'

The two women fluttered a little as he scribbled on their dance cards and after a few minutes of social chit-chat, excused himself and went to join his parents, who were still greeting latecomers and circulating among their guests. Very gradually, the different groups merged and separated, becoming scattered and then merging again, in a constant kaleidoscope of different colours and scents. Some guests made for the card room while David Atherton's friends made a point of eyeing up the available young ladies and requesting dances.

Once Isabella had excused herself to go and greet the other guests, Elizabeth and Lady Gascoine had barely time to establish themselves in the saloon before Edward and Emma Mason came up to join them. They had Lydia and Caroline in tow. Both girls were pleased to see Elizabeth again and the four of them were affable and charming. It was obvious that any quarrel Frederick and Isabella may have had was not about to be remarked upon by Isabella's parents.

As Edward Mason bowed politely over her hand, he said, 'Miss Baines, I am delighted to see you so much recovered from your accident. Might I hope you will be able to manage a dance with your old codger? The dancing should be starting up soon, I think.'

Elizabeth smiled at him and glanced at Emma Mason, seeking her acquiescence. She nodded pleasantly.

'This elderly gentleman has so looked forward to a dance with you, my dear,' she said jokily.

Elizabeth blushed and turned away to rearrange Lady Gascoine's shawl, which had slipped to the back of her chair.

And thus it was that Robert Gascoine saw her, bending tenderly over his mama and putting the shawl back around her shoulders. She certainly had a lot of care for his mother, he thought, and then when she turned, he smiled at her and said, 'Miss Baines, may I hope that you feel well enough to dance the first waltz with me?'

'I . . . no . . . that is . . . I thought . . . I thought you . . . you didn't wish to dance, sir . . . ' She blushed and stammered like a schoolgirl as he stood there patiently, awaiting her reply.

How was it, Elizabeth thought, that a man who was serious and didn't wish to dance could suddenly dazzle her with this wonderful, irresistible charm?

He was still waiting and, as though in a dream, she let him scribble on her dance card before going to speak to Mrs Mason. A little later, David Atherton came to claim her and they stood up for one of the country dances. Elizabeth liked his fresh open face and manner and gave him a warm friendly smile as they moved into the first figure of the dance.

He smiled back at her with genuine pleasure and said, 'It is always a pleasure to meet someone who is a friend of Isabella.'

Acting purely on instinct, she said, 'You have known Miss Mason for some years then, sir?'

'Yes, indeed, Miss Baines. We played together as children, until I went to Eton.' He hesitated a moment as though he were about to impart a confidence, then he said diffidently, 'In fact, we were childhood sweethearts, until Isabella — Miss Mason, that is — had her come out in London.'

The next figure of the dance parted them for a few moments and Elizabeth had time to digest this information and try frantically to think of a reply. She was intrigued to know whether, if things had been different, David Atherton might have been Isabella's chosen one. Before they met each other once more a little further down the set, she'd thought of another gentle question.

'So you lost contact with each other, while Isabella was in London for the season?'

'Yes. I left Oxford and did the Grand Tour, with my tutor. When I returned, Mama said that Isabella was like to become engaged to Sir Frederick Gascoine. Perhaps it was the

167

title,' he added bitterly. Then he was immediately contrite and drew back as though he'd said too much. 'I do beg your pardon, Miss Baines. That was unforgivable of me. Please forget that I said it.'

'Of course,' she said and smiled at him. 'But it seems, sir, that you still carry a romantic torch for your youthful love.' He didn't reply to this as they parted once more before the final figure of the dance. But David Atherton's words gave her cause for thought. She was certain that Edward and Emma Mason would not have persuaded their daughter to give her hand where she could not give her heart and yet the affianced young couple seemed unhappy and ill at ease with each other. Very strange, she thought, and then she and David joined hands for the final steps of the dance and ended at the bottom of the room. There was no further opportunity to continue their conversation.

'My thanks, Miss Baines,' he said and Elizabeth was pleased to have met such a well-mannered young man, and thought what a pity it was that Isabella could not have returned his love. She went back to Lady Gascoine and David went to seek his next partner.

Elizabeth was not engaged for the next dance, which was a quadrille, but conscious of Doctor Godfrey's advice, she remained standing near to Lady Gascoine's chair, rather than sitting down. She observed that David Atherton and Caroline Mason were in the same set as Isabella and Frederick and although she was too far away to hear what was being said, the overall demeanour of the group appeared to be of polite formality. It was certainly not the picture of youthful enjoyment that might have been expected at a meeting of such old friends.

The next dance was the waltz and Elizabeth's heart pounded most alarmingly as Robert approached her and bent over her hand, requesting the pleasure of the dance. She gazed at him, her stomach turning over and her breathing suddenly difficult. For a moment, she stood frozen with embarrassment, then she put her hand in his. His touch was as cool and firm as she remembered it. She put her hand on his shoulder and felt the warmth of his body through the fine cloth of his evening coat. She was conscious of his hand holding hers firmly as he began to guide her skilfully across the floor.

'I hope the dancing will not bring back the pain of your injuries,' he said.

Elizabeth's reply was rather breathless. 'No . . . indeed . . . not . . . not at all . . . I have taken some of the . . . the medicine left for me by Doctor Godfrey,' she stammered inanely and was immediately furious at herself for being so gauche.

'That's all right, then.' His arm tightened round her waist and his thumb traced a little caress on the palm of her hand, which thrilled her unbearably.

Fortunately, Signor Guiseppe had schooled her so well in the steps and patterns of the waltz that Elizabeth's steps didn't falter for a moment. She recognized that Robert was equally as skilled as his brother at the waltzing technique. Their steps matched perfectly as they glided to the rhythm of the music.

Nevertheless, he seemed conscious of her awkwardness with him and tried with his unfailing courtesy, to put her at ease.

'My mama seems very content with your companionship, Miss Baines. I own that I wondered if she would ever come about when Miss Holmes died so suddenly and yet now it seems you have filled a part in her life which is bringing her some happiness and pleasure. You deserve a medal as big as a chariot wheel for the cheerfulness and kindness you have shown.'

Again, she did not know what to say. She was totally unable to look into those steady eyes and make an answer. She was distracted by the warmth of his hand at her waist. It seemed to be burning through the fabric of her dress, and made her both long for and fear a closer embrace.

She managed, 'It's a pleasure to serve Her Ladyship, sir,' and then with an effort, she changed the subject and tried to make conversation. 'Miss Mason and her sisters are in excellent form tonight and do not lack for partners.'

'True, Miss Baines, but you outshine them all. I know your dance card will be full this evening,' He leaned closer to her ear and said softy, 'You are like a beautiful orchid in a field full of daisies. Cannot you see, my dear girl, that if you wished you could have your pick of all these young men and Mama would soon have to find another companion to attend her?'

She was surprised to find that these words didn't discomfort her. She knew she was blushing hotly, to be sure, but whether the joy of dancing with him or the confidence she'd gained from waltzing with Signor Guiseppe had inspired her she didn't know. All she knew was that for the first time that evening she was looking openly into his eyes. His unusual green-brown eyes, as alive as quicksilver, were looking into her own with an admiring sparkle that made her laugh with sheer enjoyment. She dared to continue looking and tried to read what she saw. Humour? Certainly. Pity for a destitute spinster? No. She would never forgive that. Friendship and affection? She hoped so. Love, even . . . ?

Now she was being stupid. Maybe she'd had too much of the draught from the Doctor. She knew that it could never be. Why would such as he feel that kind of emotion for his mama's companion when he could have any one of these eligible high-born ladies?

Neither of them was inclined to break the spell, but finally Robert Gascoine's practised politeness triumphed and he held her close for the final twirling steps and then thanked her courteously and trusted her headache had not returned as a result of the dancing.

Until the supper interval, the evening was rather a whirl, and in one thing at least Robert was correct. There was no shortage of young men wishing to dance with her and her card could have been filled twice over had she not pleaded to be excused from some of them on account of her accident. Robert appeared before her as she was sitting out the second waltz, just before supper. He bowed and lifted her dance card to look at it more closely.

'Miss Baines, how is your headache?' he said, smiling down at her. 'You are not engaged for this waltz and neither am I. Do you wish to dance with me?'

It was obvious he was funning and his eyes sparkled with laughter. Elizabeth responded equally lightly, 'I thank you, sir. My head is completely better. Alas, only my legs are somewhat rebellious at the thought of another waltz, so I beg you to excuse me.'

He looked at her more keenly, as though trying to decide whether she was merely tired or suffering from the after effects of falling from her horse. 'Very well then, ma'am, I accept defeat. Your legs will not permit you to waltz and I am free to dance with you. It is difficult for a fellow to know what to do.'

Again, there was that delightful intimacy of his teasing her and, throwing caution to the winds, Elizabeth was emboldened to reply in the same vein. 'I think you are the sort of fellow who always knows exactly what to do,' she said softly. 'Indeed, I think that at this moment you have divined that the best thing a fellow could possibly do is keep me company until the supper interval.'

He laughed out loud at her youthful attempt at flirtation and immediately said, 'Very well, on condition you will allow me to procure a glass of champagne for you.'

Elizabeth blushed and smiled again and he returned in a few moments with two crystal flutes of golden liquid. She had rarely tasted champagne before and was aware that he was watching her as she sipped it carefully. She perched somewhat stiffly on the edge of the little gilt sofa, not entirely at ease with the situation or the champagne but determined to enjoy the moment. Robert, meanwhile, observed her reactions. He had removed his gloves and one arm was draped negligently across the back of the sofa, his fingers not quite touching her bare shoulder.

They sipped in silence until Elizabeth gave a somewhat unladylike snort as the bubbles went up her nose. She tried to sneeze and could not. 'I beg your pardon,' she said. 'I . . . I am not used to champagne, sir . . . '

He leaned closer to her until his lips almost touched her cheek, and then very carefully he took the glass from her hand and set it down on a small table and took both her hands in his. Holding her palms upwards, he carefully and deliberately kissed the fingers of each hand in turn, pressing them lightly with his warm lips, so that she felt the pressure of his mouth through her lace mittens.

Elizabeth remained passive, still able to feel the sensation of his kisses, half thrilled and half frightened by this unusual gesture. Very gently he released her hands and gave her back her glass. 'Dear little Lizzie,' he said.

'Don't ever change or become sophisticated about champagne. Stay just as you are.'

She remained silent and after a few minutes he said more briskly, 'There is the supper gong. I expect you will have to attend Mama now. She will expect it.' He gave a polite bow and was gone.

Collecting her wits with difficulty, Elizabeth went to find Lady Gascoine, who declared she fully enjoyed watching the dancing. 'Dear Frederick has had so many partners,' she cooed, 'and he and Isabella danced so becomingly together. If only Robert would find an eligible and charming girl like Miss Mason and settle down, my cup of happiness would be full.'

Elizabeth didn't answer. In spite of the unexpected pain that Lady Gascoine's words caused her, she concentrated on bringing little plates of refreshments and signalling to the footman for a glass of champagne for Her Ladyship. In a secret part of her mind she hugged to herself the experience of Robert's gesture.

The rest of the evening was rather an anti-climax. She danced mechanically, trying not to let the pain in her stiff arms and legs bother her too much, and she didn't see Robert or Frederick at all. She concluded they were in the card room. The one person she did welcome when he came to claim her hand in a dance was Edward Mason. He was always so polite and charming, sufficiently complimentary to a young girl to appear avuncular and gallant but not heavy or patronizing.

They exchanged some lively conversation and then Elizabeth was somewhat perturbed when he said seriously, 'You know, Miss Baines, my old friend Jane Gibson has confided in me somewhat about your previous . . . erm . . . rather unhappy background in Ireland. I would not wish to distress you in any way, my dear, but I am a magistrate and Justice of the Peace. If you agree, I feel it is time some enquiries were made as to the background and causes of your miserable treatment with the Baines family.'

He saw the look of abject terror in Elizabeth's eyes and covered her hand with his own. 'You see, Elizabeth, unless you have papers, a certificate of baptism, perhaps, it will be very difficult for you in the future to claim any inheritance from Mr Baines, or even get married. In short, my dear, to live a free and normal life. What do you say, my dear? Will you allow your old codger, to help you in this?'

Elizabeth's mouth went dry and tears filled

her eyes as a mental picture of Baines came into her mind. That he was her natural father she had never questioned, and the thought of perhaps having to confront him face to face or, worse still, the evil Captain Preston horrified her. Nevertheless, she answered bravely, 'I think . . . I don't know . . . I don't know what . . . But yes, I would like to make some investigation into my origins. I would be very pleased if you could help me, sir.'

Her determination was so obvious that Edward Mason was encouraged to continue. He said gently, 'I'm so glad that you trust me. I will ensure that nothing will harm you or distress you, Elizabeth.'

His sincerity was so obvious that Elizabeth felt she could indeed trust him. Her confidence was tested when they returned to Waringham and Lady Gascoine announced blithely that they would be spending the New Year in Ireland with Miss Gibson and Bradbury. In spite of Edward Mason's support, a cold fear gripped Elizabeth and an icy hand squeezed her heart, until she felt breathless and like to die. It was one thing in theory, searching for one's origins, but she realized she would have to be brave and determined to follow it through.

She managed to retain her composure as the rest of the party chatted over the events of the evening at Mr and Mrs Atherton's and gradually said their good nights and went to bed.

As she climbed wearily into her own bed, Elizabeth was still numb about the proposed visit to Ireland. She wanted to find out her true identity but what if her father and the wicked Molloys were to find out she had returned to the neighbourhood and was making enquiries about them?

She tossed and turned for a few minutes and then there was a tap on the door. 'Who is it?' she asked and sat up fearfully. It was only the well-meaning and reassuring Jane Gibson, in nightdress and peignoir and with soft slippers on her feet, who opened the door and came slowly in.

'Miss Gibson,' she faltered.

'Pray don't be alarmed, Elizabeth,' Jane said. 'I thought you looked a little upset at Lady Gascoine's plans to visit Ireland so I have come to set your mind at rest, my dear. Is it the thought of meeting Captain Preston again which upsets you this evening?'

Elizabeth nodded dumbly.

'But he and his regiment will be long gone, posted to Spain, I shouldn't wonder. You need have no fear of him or anyone else while you are in service to my sister. What is it? Does aught else trouble you, child?'

Elizabeth nodded again, still without speaking.

'Can you not tell me, so that I can help you?'

'My father . . . ' Elizabeth whispered.

'Well, you need not get in touch with him if you don't wish it, but remember, he will have all the medical knowledge of where you were born and your mother's origins. Remember also we are urged to honour our father and our mother . . . but you do not have to see him again if you do not wish it,' she said hastily, as Elizabeth shuddered and went white.

'No . . . I don't wish it,' Elizabeth said. 'But I am determined, with Mr Mason's help, to find out my true origins. It may be that I am not, in fact, the natural child of Mr Baines. I wish to find out. It's just that when you and Miss Bradbury have gone back to Ireland I shall have no one to care for me while I try and find the truth about myself.'

'Nonsense,' Miss Gibson said very gently and she leaned forward and kissed her. 'You will always be our dear little Lizzie. By all means follow Mr Mason's advice if you wish it. If it's important to you to discover your true origins, so be it. But remember, it doesn't matter a jot who you are to those who love you, who or what you are. You will always

179

be our beloved Elizabeth. Lady Gascoine thinks the world of you and when Bradbury and I go back to Ireland we shall see you often. Now that you are a grown woman, my dear, and have a secure position in the Gascoine household, Bradbury and I feel we have done our duty. Good night, Elizabeth. Try and get some sleep now.'

Long after she had gone, Elizabeth still lay awake with her thoughts. Not just Jane Gibson's visit to her room but the riding accident and her growing regard for Robert. Dancing the waltz with him, feeling the closeness of his warm body, the touch of his hands. She wondered for a moment if she had imagined those kisses on her fingers, the laughter in his eyes when he'd teased her. If these pleasures were all she'd ever get from him, she would be content, a veritable beggar in love. But what of the future? Would her own and Edward Mason's enquiries enable George Baines to snatch her newfound happiness away? After all, he was her recognized legal father and in law he owned and had control over her. Exhausted, she gradually fell into an uneasy sleep, beset by hideous dreams of the unhappy past.

8

The next day saw them packing under the strict supervision of Lady Gascoine. Bradbury and Miss Gibson were themselves organizing the maids to press and prepare their clothes for the long journey to Ireland.

'We shall be at Roslaine two days before you arrive, Mary,' Jane Gibson said. 'We'll make sure everything is in readiness for your coming.'

It was agreed that Frederick and Robert would travel on a day later so that all Miss Gibson's guests didn't appear together.

The plan was that over the New Year period, Frederick and Isabella would be guests of honour at the various evening parties and social events organized by his aunt, to meet Miss Gibson's friends among the Irish gentry. Even if the prospective groom seemed to lack any romantic urgency, his mama and his aunt were already setting in motion the neighbourhood groupings that would be an important part of the young couple's future social life.

Elizabeth recognized that this was the way of the world as far as gentlefolk were concerned. She was powerless to prevent the trip to Ireland but it would hopefully make it possible for her to find out more about herself. On the morning after the Athertons' soirée, she was not just stiff, she was hobbling. The bruises on her legs had now turned purple and yellow, and were more painful than when she'd had the accident. She tried to eat breakfast but the food stuck in her throat. However much she told herself that she was going to settle the mystery of her background, Elizabeth was still somewhat anxious at the thought of Roslaine.

Neither Robert nor Frederick appeared at breakfast. Lady Gascoine was having breakfast in her room, so Elizabeth was alone with Bradbury and Jane Gibson. Neither of these two ladies was inclined to talk. Jane noticed Elizabeth's wan face and quiet demeanour and was about to say something but thought better of it. Before long, she whisked her companion back upstairs to help with the packing. The two ladies departed for Liverpool before luncheon and Lady Gascoine was there with Elizabeth to see them off.

'Goodbye, Jane, goodbye, Bradbury, we will see you on Thursday,' they called and both waved until they were out of sight.

For the next two days, Elizabeth had little

time to worry about her own visit to Ireland — in spite of her aches and pains, she was kept far too busy by Lady Gascoine. She had to organize Her Ladyship's writing case and embroidery things, her library books and visiting cards, and then help to supervise the packing. There was a lot of running about to do over the contents of Her Ladyship's refreshment hamper, which was to go with them on the coach. With the addition of Lady Gascoine's abigail, there would only be three of them in the Gascoine carriage so there was ample room for the luggage that they felt was necessary for their journey. Finally, they were ready. There travelling clothes and toilet cases were laid out for morning and cloaks and bonnets brushed and pressed ready for departure.

On the evening before their visit to Ireland, both Lady Gascoine's sons joined them for a quiet evening dinner and Lady Gascoine entertained them with reminiscences of holidays at their Aunt Jane's in days gone by.

'Your dear papa was so fond of Jane,' she said. 'He used to love going to Roslaine for the New Year period and used to say that after a visit to your aunt, spring seemed only just round the corner.' She sighed sentimentally and continued more quietly. 'Your aunt had the reputation of a blue stocking when she was young. She never had that obvious bloom and prettiness of most young girls, and yet, Sir William always declared she was clever enough to be prime minister and kind enough to be a saint. Such a pity she never married. She would have been a wonderful and loving mama . . . '

Robert and Elizabeth listened to this politely, but Sir Frederick moved and shifted in his seat impatiently, not wishing anyone else to speak, least of all his mama. But Elizabeth recognized what Lady Gascoine was saying as the truth. Even taking account of the trend to have the more affluent women educated in certain subjects, Jane Gibson's appreciation of literature, her knowledge of botany, her skill at drawing and painting wildlife were quite outside the talents of most women. That she was humane and deeply religious, Elizabeth already knew. It had never struck her until now just how exceptional Jane Gibson really was. Because she was young, her own needs had seemed paramount and she'd taken Miss Gibson for granted. Now she felt a sudden overwhelming sadness at the thought that their lives were soon going to be separated, perhaps for ever.

It was obvious that Sir Frederick was becoming increasingly annoyed by his mama's reluctance to leave the table. The dessert covers had long been cleared away and yet Lady Gascoine was still inclined to linger and talk of happy days gone by while she sipped her wine. As for Elizabeth, she was content to sit in Robert's presence, saying nothing, just enjoying taking a discreet glance at him occasionally.

Finally, Frederick interrupted his mother rudely to ask Robert, 'Could you sink a glass of port, bruth? If so, I'll get Wilkins to bring some cigars.'

This brought Lady Gascoine back to the present and she said with a smile, 'But how I do run on, my dears. I declare I was quite carried away. Come, Elizabeth, we will leave these two to enjoy their smoking. We shall be in the small saloon when you are ready, gentlemen.' And with that, she and Elizabeth left the room.

When they'd gone, Frederick said sullenly, 'Mama was well down her lane of memories, talking of when Papa was still alive.' He dismissed Wilkins and poured them both a glass of port. Robert stretched himself more comfortably in the chair. He noticed the amount of port in the glass but resolved to drink slowly while he listened to Frederick's long diatribe about the new companion to his mother.

'That cunning little jade encourages Mama

to find her indispensable,' said Frederick pettishly. 'She enjoys all Mama's protection and little luxuries but she don't want to give a fellow anything in return. She'd better look out or she'll get more than she bargained for from me.'

'I think not, Frederick,' Robert said evenly. 'She's no jade, she's a decent, respectable girl, who happens to be poor and in need of the job that Mama offered her. In any case, what would Isabella think? Believe me, Frederick, any playing about with Miss Baines would be sure to come to her notice. Servants are everywhere. They know everything. Nothing escapes the attention of your valet or Mama's abigail. How long would it be before your future wife found out about your little games? I believe she loves you and would be destroyed if you sought a bit of light skirt so near to home. Stick to the muslin company in town, brother. Miss Baines is out of bounds. You are shortly to be married. Why raise complications in your life which might be difficult to resolve?'

'I already have complications,' Frederick snarled. 'Isabella is as toplofty and virtuous as any young lady can be. But you've got your eye on the other ladybird yourself, haven't you? I'm just surprised at you, having inclinations that way. She's not even an ancient statue to add to your collection.'

Robert was appalled at Frederick's knowledge of him. That Frederick had been able to read him like a book and had guessed about his feelings for Elizabeth. He decided to ignore it, but felt that he couldn't ignore Frederick's general unhappiness and frustration. He knew that Frederick was short of money and in debt, but the extent of his bitterness over Edward Mason's refusal to part with any portion of Isabella's dowry was nothing short of sick. It was obvious that there was no love and affection or even commitment to his fiancée. Where was his pride, to want to proceed with a loveless marriage, merely for the sake of Isabella's fortune?

As for himself, he had spent the last few hours trying not to think of Elizabeth Baines, trying to forget the feel of her soft, yielding body when he'd held her in front of him on his horse, trying not to think about her radiant young face as he'd waltzed with her, the slender white fingers when he'd kissed them as they'd sat out the dance and sipped champagne . . . He tried not to think of her at all. At least Frederick was honest — he just wanted a dalliance with a lower-class girl who was vulnerable and would have to give way to the master of the house.

187

He was pleased and relieved when Frederick suddenly flung out of the room with an oath. 'I'm going to the Crown,' he snarled. 'A bit more salubrious company and lively conversation there.'

And Robert was left alone with his thoughts.

Lady Gascoine and Elizabeth didn't stay up late. They had an early start the next day and Elizabeth had only the briefest of words with Robert before they set off.

'God speed,' was all he said to her, as he handed his mama into the carriage. 'Have a safe journey and see you soon,' he said to Elizabeth and then they were off.

In spite of Elizabeth's fears, the journey went well and apart from feeling tired they noticed no ill effects. Jane Gibson had planned a dinner party for the New Year's Eve in Roslaine and they were all to wait up and see in the New Year of 1806. As Elizabeth went to draw her bedroom curtains and get changed for the evening to come, she glanced idly down into the courtyard outside Jane Gibson's house and saw someone standing there, very still, gazing at her window. She drew back and continued to gaze at him without being seen. He was a stranger and very distinctively dressed in a broad-brimmed hat and a red waistcoat. He seemed to be waiting for someone and looked around him all the time.

She stayed in the shadows for some moments, wondering who the mysterious stranger was, and felt quite relieved when Miss Gibson's servant came in to light more candles and see if she wanted anything.

Pretending a nonchalance she didn't feel, Elizabeth said casually, 'Who is that man down there in the yard, Sal?'

The maid looked without any curiosity. 'Him's a redbreast, so he is. He's after some bad 'un, I shouldn't wonder.' She closed the curtains with reassuring finality. 'If there's nothing you want, miss, I'll be off.'

When she went downstairs, Isabella and her parents had already arrived and Elizabeth had another surprise, this time a pleasant one. 'Come, dear,' Miss Gibson said, and drew her further into the room. 'I have someone who is longing to meet you again. Honoria, here is your schoolfriend, Elizabeth.' She smiled at them both as Elizabeth gasped with pleasure and beamed at her former friend, Honoria Wilshaw, who was with her parents.

Honoria was very changed. Gone was the slight and enchanting girl with the tireless physical energy that Elizabeth remembered. There in front of her stood a statuesque beauty with raven hair, elegantly dressed in a gown of peach silk, which set off her vivid good looks to perfection.

Elizabeth extended both her hands warmly and proffered her cheek for a kiss. 'Honoria! What a pleasure. It's wonderful to see you.' She smiled with the utmost friendliness. She was very surprised when her old friend was rather less than responsive. She was polite enough but Elizabeth sensed a coolness in her, in the way she barely pecked at Elizabeth's cheek and then loosed her hands very quickly. Elizabeth was puzzled but Honoria was possibly a little shy after not seeing her for some time. Perhaps later they would have a chance to talk over their schooldays at Miss Hanbury's and catch up with all the gossip about their other schoolfriends.

Mr and Mrs Wilshaw were soon deep in conversation with Lady Gascoine and Jane Gibson, while Isabella remained on the fringe of the group, beautifully dressed as usual but looking subdued in the presence of someone as striking as Miss Wilshaw and as enchantingly pretty as Elizabeth Baines. Her parents, normally so warm and friendly, also seemed unaccountably reserved and although they moved through the group with their usual confidence and charm, it seemed to Elizabeth

190

that they were subtly altered as though they had finally become aware that all was not well between Isabella and Frederick. It was when Sir Frederick and his brother Robert entered the room that the little tableau sprang to life. Isabella waited only for the introductions and greetings to be completed before going to Frederick and putting a hand on his arm almost humbly, and wishing him good evening.

Honoria Wilshaw, on the other hand, stepped forward confidently with her most warm and winning smile to greet the brothers as they were introduced. It seemed to Elizabeth, watching the little scene in front of her, that Honoria reserved an almost caressing smile for Robert and, as the usual pleasantries were exchanged, she heard her old schoolfriend say laughingly that she was determined to dance with him when she got to the Assembly Rooms and that gentlemen who lurked in the card room would definitely be in her bad books. Lady Gascoine smiled tolerantly at this and Sir Frederick looked at Honoria with more than polite interest. Poor Isabella seemed to shrink and grow somewhat shorter in stature as the company assembled in pairs to walk into the dining-room and she was paired with Sir Frederick.

At the table, though, the conversation was

more than usually animated, with all the young people chatting to each other about their Christmas activities, the presents they'd received and their disappointment that there'd been as yet no ice skating. Why, then, amidst all this gay chatter, should she feel so melancholy, Elizabeth wondered? At that moment, she caught sight of Honoria's flirtatious glance in the direction of Robert Gascoine, and felt more cast down than ever.

Mr Mason mentioned the time three years ago when the lake at Tollyvara had been completely frozen over. People came from miles around to skate on the ice, which was so unusually thick that some of the youths from other villages had lit a bonfire on its surface.

Honoria gasped rather theatrically at this and clapped her hands together, leaning forward to say to Robert, 'I promise you, Mr Gascoine, that should the lake be frozen up during our stay then I shall be delighted to dazzle you with a few of my skating twirls.'

Robert smiled but said nothing, while Frederick beamed at Honoria and said, 'That is a pleasure I shall look forward to, Miss Wilshaw. Tollyvara is noticeably lacking in pretty feminine twirls at this time of year.'

Honoria smiled delightedly at this but Isabella looked even more depressed. It was obvious to Elizabeth that she was trying to be lighthearted when she said, 'Miss Wilshaw, that sounds splendid and you seem to be such a good sport. I own I have no skills at skating but I'm sure I shall be just as admiring of your prowess as if you were a gentleman.'

Elizabeth bit her lip. She knew what an effort that generous compliment had cost Isabella and she herself felt excluded as Honoria continued to flirt playfully with Robert.

Her heart went out to Isabella, who now sat like a ghost at the feast, hardly saying anything and so patently unhappy. Something had happened between them, Elizabeth decided. A lovers' quarrel, perhaps? Sir Frederick was looking perfectly relaxed for once, not scowling but smiling agreeably at his fellow guests and his mama, as though he'd noticed nothing of Isabella's discomfiture. Even Elizabeth herself was allowed to bask in the radiance of his smile. He really was the absolute epitome of the handsome Adonis, she decided, and when he put his mind to it he could be so charming. No wonder Isabella was so in love with him. A pity that she seemed unable to meet her beloved's eyes or return his brilliant smile and left all the flirting to Honoria. A little later,

Elizabeth understood why.

After the fish course, Sir Frederick had partaken of sufficient wine to both oil his tongue and become expansive on his plans for the spring trip to Brighton.

'I shall no doubt unnerve Mama by driving down with some of the fellows from my club,' he said genially. 'We're a small but select band, dedicated to excellence in driving and the natural competition between true Corinthians, who are devoted to sporting prowess.'

There was a little silence after this rather pompous declaration but Isabella raised her eyes beseechingly to her fiancé and Emma Mason gave a soft gasp. Lady Gascoine spoke with mock disapproval, but was still indulgent. 'Why, you foolish boy, you must know that we are all totally against your foolish plans. I only hope that you will not take any silly risks and that you will return in one whole piece to your dear Isabella.'

Mr Mason seemed about to say something, but changed his mind and merely cleared his throat.

It was left to Isabella to exclaim in a low, impassioned voice, 'Frederick, my dear love! How can you contemplate such a venture, when we are so near to our marriage? Have you considered the risks involved? How could I ever live without you, should you have an accident? I beseech you . . . '

She couldn't go on. Her eyes filled with tears and she bit her lower lip hard to prevent herself from sobbing. It was Lady Gascoine who finished her plea for her. For once she seemed neither indulgent nor lenient with her firstborn. In spite of being in company, she spoke to him as though they were alone.

'This seems a foolhardy venture, my darling boy. Could you not reconsider this idea? Defer it for a later date, perhaps? You seem to be upsetting dear Isabella and I own we are all apprehensive at the thought of it.'

She spoke quite lightly but in such a tone that all who heard it knew that she must be obeyed. Frederick shrugged and answered good humouredly that it was all arranged. Wagers had been made and accepted. He was perfectly capable of driving safely and was not going to take unnecessary risks. He glanced round the table, seeking to gain male support. 'After all,' he said, 'this monstrous regiment of women is always going to worry about such things. We men must try our skills in competition with each other. There it is. Nothing ventured, nothing gained.'

Once more, Edward Mason seemed about to say something but changed his mind. Isabella gave her mother an anguished look but then dropped her eyes submissively.

Frederick never even noticed. He remained expansive and began to cheerfully engage Honoria in conversation, asking her about her schooldays at Miss Hanbury's, teasing her about the schoolgirl scrapes she got into and quizzing her about Elizabeth's exploits at the academy. Honoria responded delightedly and seemed not to notice Isabella's mournful expression. In the face of Frederick's lighthearted attention, she was quite disloyal to her erstwhile friend as she recounted a tale of Elizabeth getting stuck in a muddy path as they were sketching in the woods and giggling as she told him of Miss Hanbury's displeasure when they returned. She was blind to Elizabeth's meaningful looks and Isabella's sighs. She was enjoying the attention of this very handsome man, while at the same time casting flirtatious glances in the direction of his brother.

It was Robert who brought this unsuitable situation to an end by enquiring blandly if Miss Wilshaw herself had an interest in sketching from nature. Honoria was interested in anything which would engage Robert's attention and began to prattle happily about the drawing lessons at Miss Hanbury's. This made Robert mention quietly that his Aunt Jane was an exceptional artist and watercolourist. Jane discounted this, of course, and the conversation became more general. Only Elizabeth noticed how skilfully Robert turned the situation around and how pleased and grateful was the look Isabella directed at him, as her intended bridegroom gradually turned towards her and she was able to have more personal conversations with him.

By the time they were ready to depart for the Assembly Rooms, Frederick was in a slightly intoxicated good humour and was being heavily gallant to all three young ladies, watched rather sardonically by Robert.

As always, Elizabeth found a space at the top of the room where Lady Gascoine and the older ladies could watch the dancing or chat to old friends, and she prepared to sit with them herself. Edward Mason and his wife laughingly remonstrated with her.

'Miss Baines,' Emma Mason said, 'you cannot be thinking of sitting with the chaperones this evening. You are far too young and pretty and are in your best looks. What a charming gown. You must not waste it on the dowds who are sitting out.'

'Yes, let me mark your card,' Edward Mason said. 'Remember tonight is the thirty-first of December and we shall be dancing into the early hours of a completely new year. In Norfolk, superstition has it that

197

whatever activity a young lady indulges in on January the first, she will be obliged to repeat for a whole year, so may I hope that you will be having a dance with me?'

Elizabeth was warmed by their laughter and their kindness. 'Come, my dear,' Emma Mason said. 'Life is short, you are young. Join the dancing before you are at your last prayers and unable to find a partner.'

It was obvious that the word 'partner' had a double meaning for Mrs Mason, but Elizabeth didn't care. She longed to join the dancing and looked hopefully at Lady Gascoine, seeking to be allowed.

Lady Gascoine nodded her permission and turned back to her conversation with an elderly friend, who was wearing a very imposing turban and was whispering confidentially to her.

While his wife looked on benignly, Edward Mason claimed the first waltz and immediately asked Honoria to grant him one of the country dances. Both Frederick and Robert were also eager to dance with Honoria and Elizabeth admitted to herself that she felt a pang of jealousy as Robert bent his elegant head over Honoria's hand and asked for the pleasure of the cotillion. From the back, his glossy chestnut hair seemed to have almost reached the black collar of his evening coat. It was newly arranged in the Brutus style and Elizabeth had never seen him look so handsome and relaxed. Perhaps he would request a dance with her. Perhaps he was reverting to his former habit of dancing only rarely. She could not tell. All she knew was she was fiercely willing him to turn round and notice her, to leave Honoria's side and come and talk to her, request a waltz, so that she could feel his arm round her again, feel his breath on her cheek . . .

This seemed highly unlikely. Politeness decreed at least one dance from him but he seemed so enamoured of Honoria, what chance did Elizabeth have?

Gradually, the other young men in the room made a beeline for the three young women, laughing and flirting outrageously, scribbling on their dance cards, introducing them to other young bloods, until even Isabella seemed to have forgotten her recent troubles and had a flush of excitement on her face.

Edward Mason came to claim her in the waltz and Elizabeth once more realized how much she liked and trusted him, as he joked with his wife, 'Farewell, my dear Emma. I am about to go and waltz with the star of Roslaine, the beautiful Miss Baines. I just hope that I may return from this experience, still heart whole and still a respectable married man.'

Emma Mason giggled and seeing the looks they exchanged, it was clear that after twenty-odd years their love was as strong and devoted as ever. It would be her ideal, she thought, to meet with such trust and devotion in her own marriage partner. She wondered soberly if Isabella would be so fortunate with the volatile Sir Frederick Gascoine.

Edward Mason waited until they were in the first steps of the dance before he cleared his throat as a preamble to what he had to say. Elizabeth looked at him enquiringly.

He was strangely diffident. 'I have made some preliminary enquiries about Mr Baines,' he said somewhat abruptly. 'He has continued to live in Tollyvara since you left, but things have not gone well for him in the last year and he is in quite a poor way. His health has utterly broken down. I don't know whether you wish to visit him while you are here, my dear. It must be left to you. My informant is a former Bow Street Runner. He's retired now, but I am employing him on a retainer to make some investigations. I hope you approve of the investigations I am making, Miss Baines. Joseph Grimshaw tells me that your father — Mr Baines, that is — is in fact very ill and is like to die . . . '

Elizabeth had gone very white and was now dancing quite mechanically. 'Die?' she whispered.

'Yes, apparently he has always been bronchial. His dissolute and drunken lifestyle and the recent cold weather have brought on a bout of pleurisy. His lungs are inflamed and his breathing sorely affected . . . '

Elizabeth could not speak for some minutes. Try as she might, she could not bring any affections to bear on George Baines's plight. She felt only pity and regret that he had never felt a father's love and concern. The sort of nurture experienced by Isabella Mason, for instance, who not only knew a mother's tender care but had a kind and happy papa and two sweet sisters. What might she have been like, she thought bitterly, if she too had enjoyed those advantages when young? She was immediately ashamed of these thoughts. It seemed unnatural for a girl not to love her papa and want to go to him in his hour of need and yet the idea that George Baines was her natural father was utterly horrifying to her. In spite of the insistent rhythm of the dance, she felt herself shrink away from Edward Mason, her face expressing the fear and loathing that she felt.

'I do not . . . I do not think it is possible for me . . . to feel a daughter's natural love and affection for such as he . . . I . . . I am still too pained by the unhappy past. Pray excuse me, Mr Mason. The idea is totally repugnant to me.'

He was all concern and without drawing attention to her in any way, skilfully steered her to the edge of the room and walked her gently to an alcove where there was a small gilt sofa. 'Please sit down, Miss Baines,' he said. 'May I get you some *sal volatile*? Would you like me to bring one of the ladies to attend you?'

'No, I thank you,' she said firmly. 'The feeling is passing. It was . . . the shock, that is all.'

They sat in silence for a few more moments and then Mr Mason said, somewhat uncomfortably, 'I have further news to impart to you, Miss Baines, but I do not wish to distress you further . . . if you would prefer . . . '

'No, please,' Elizabeth said. 'Please go on.'

'Well, it is this, my dear. Joseph Grimshaw, the Bow Street Runner, has some firm opinions as to your birth.'

Elizabeth looked at him. 'My . . . my birth?' she managed at last.

'There is some doubt in Mr Grimshaw's mind,' he went on gently, 'as to your actual parentage. Mr Grimshaw is suggesting that you may not in fact be the natural child of George Baines.'

Elizabeth's mind was in a whirl. Not George Baines's child? That would explain a lot of things which had puzzled her over the years. Her sense of alienation. His lack of care or concern for her, which was far more malevolent than mere neglect. Her vague memories of a different but distant life. She wanted to believe that she was no child of George Baines. But then who was she? Who was her real father? Who was her mama?

'I'm not sure that I understand, sir,' she said at last.

'No, I don't expect you do,' Edward Mason said quietly. 'Joseph Grimshaw has been conducting some investigations which lead him to believe that you are not Baines's natural daughter, but we shall not know more until we have followed up various lines of enquiry. Have I your permission to proceed with this, my dear?'

Elizabeth was now in turmoil. One part of her wanted to desist, to leave off such painful investigations and forget the unhappy past, but the other half of her mind wanted to delve more deeply and find out more. She could if she wished try to be happy with her position of companion to Lady Gascoine and her life of comparative luxury in Her

Ladyship's beautiful house. But she was no helpless old maid having to be content with her lot, she was a young strong and educated woman and she wanted to take responsibility for her future.

'You certainly have my permission, Mr Mason, and I am very interested in effecting some enquiries of my own.'

Elizabeth had another fleeting memory of her life with the unloving Baines and his equally unloving partner Kate Molloy. She smelled once more the hideous stench of the ruined hut which was their home, saw her drunken father stumbling across the yard to the privy and shouting curses at her, felt the pain of the Molloy boys tugging at her hair and banging her head on the muddy floor. If she could be free of these horrible memories once and for all, she thought, deny his paternity and feel liberated from the inheritance of such a background, she knew that she would be happier.

Nevertheless, it had come as a great shock to her to have her own suspicions confirmed by a third party.

'Of course I give my permission,' she said. And with that Elizabeth fainted.

When she came round, with the acrid smell of *sal volatile* wafting up her nostrils, Elizabeth opened her eyes to see not one of the ladies attending her but Robert Gascoine himself. He was sitting on the small gilt sofa and was carefully supporting her head tenderly with one hand while he bathed her temples with a little cloth moistened with lavender water. As she struggled to rise, he gently held her down and whispered, 'Miss Baines, please stay where you are. You must have swooned for a moment and Mr Mason has gone to fetch his daughter to attend you.'

In spite of her shocked state, Elizabeth was fully aware that it was against the rules for a single woman not only to be alone with a young man but to be almost lying across his knee. Yet the sensation of his cool gentle fingers on her forehead was utterly delicious. She wanted to prolong it for as long as possible.

At last she spoke in a somewhat husky voice. 'I'm sorry, sir. It was just some grave information that . . . that Mr Mason had for me . . . and . . . I . . . it was rather a shock, you see.'

She had no idea how the mere sight of her, lying there so helpless and so beautiful, affected him. He knew that Mr Mason was following certain lines of enquiry about Elizabeth and there was some doubt as to her origins. He saw the pain in her face and longed with all his heart to soothe it away. It struck him with all the force of a cataclysmic earthquake just how tender and vulnerable she was, open to injury not just from the unspeakable Baines but from any upper-class male predator who might feel inclined to put her in the impossible position of a girl unable to resist his advances and so risk losing her place.

Frederick might still feel tempted to make an assault on her virtue, in spite of his impending marriage to Isabella and Robert's own vigilance. Looking down at her pure young face, he was conscious of a desire to protect and nurture her, to ease all her unhappiness and pain, to lead her safely into the haven of his love and care. Immediately, he was plagued with doubts about the young girl he was holding so tenderly in his arms. Without her pleasure and desire, what satisfaction could he expect from her? She was so young and confused, he was not sure how to possess her . . .

Like most young men who had been on the Grand Tour, Robert was experienced with women who were skilled at entertaining men and received payment for it, nothing more. For the first time since Amanda had died, he had another chance to see what it would be like if he were making love to a warm and loving partner, with no payment on either side.

'Robert?'

It was Isabella Mason's voice which drew him back from these thoughts, and at first he looked at her blankly. 'I do beg your pardon. My mind was wandering. What did you say?'

'Only that if Miss Baines is now feeling a little better, I can go with her to Lady Gascoine,' she said.

He looked at the plump Miss Mason, so different from the tall, delicate Elizabeth, and said in a distracted voice, 'Yes, of course, I am sure that Miss Baines is feeling better now . . . '

Gently, he helped Elizabeth to her feet and watched her walk gingerly with Isabella towards the ladies at the end of the room, thinking how brave the girl was.

9

This was a bitter-sweet time for Elizabeth. Most of the social occasions in Ireland were attended by the aunts and other relations of the Gascoine family, and were opened up to the Wilshaws. Instead of being a cause for celebration, Elizabeth gradually realized that because of her position as servant, she was not made welcome by Honoria. Although no frost had been severe enough to freeze over the lake at Tollyvara, Honoria Wilshaw had continued to try and flirt with Robert, and was obviously casting her bonnet quite shamelessly in his direction. Lady Gascoine had appeared to look on approvingly at Honoria's little ploys, as had Mr and Mrs Wilshaw. Elizabeth knew from overheard gossip among the servants that the Wilshaw family was prosperous and had an impeccable pedigree. It was generally agreed that a younger son would do well to marry an only child who was not only beautiful but in possession of a handsome dowry.

Elizabeth was not aware of what Robert thought of the situation. He seemed to remain his usual cool self, polite to Miss

Wilshaw, considerate of his mama and never betraying any private feelings. Once more, Elizabeth admitted to herself the exasperation that she felt at his seeming disinterest. She was aware, however, that what he had said of his father's own art treasures was nothing but the truth. Often in her quiet moments of leisure, she walked in the different rooms devoted to Sir William's collection of ancient fossils, Bronze Age artefacts, Venetian glass, tapestries and Roman armoury. She spent most of her time, though, in the gallery of classical paintings, many depicting fables from ancient Greece and Rome. She was also fascinated by some of the glass cabinets at the end of the gallery, which were anything but ancient and contained precise models and sketches for the whole village. These were obviously plans which had been dear to Sir William's heart before he died. She wondered if Sir Frederick would develop these projects and remembered Jane Gibson's dismissive words about his lack of interest in the family farms and estates.

She had the opportunity to mention it to Robert one morning, when she happened to visit the gallery and came across him hanging some of Sir William's extra paintings which had been stored in one of the attic rooms. Immediately, Elizabeth made to disappear, hoping he had not noticed her, but she heard his melodious voice greeting her. 'Miss Baines, so you're enjoying the paintings this morning. Do you have a favourite, or have you not had time to look at them yet?'

She paused in her flight, in some confusion. 'Why no, sir . . . I have looked at the farm models and rural sketches more. What foresight if those plans could be executed some day. I expect Sir Frederick will — '

She stopped when she saw the expression on his face. Without realizing it, she had touched a raw nerve. It enraged Robert Gascoine to think that his father's legacy and decent intentions were to be dissipated by his dissolute brother and it had annoyed him even further when he had found Elizabeth struggling with the lecherous heir. That had affected him as nothing else had ever done. Robert had spent years dealing with his brother Frederick in the only way he knew was effective. He never lost his temper, retained always an iron determination to treat each situation with humour and was always seemingly patient and serene. That the young girl he admired so warmly should go straight to the heart of a problem like this was almost unbearable. He tried to speak lightly to disguise his feelings.

'I know what you mean, Elizabeth, but you need have no concern. I can assure you my brother will have all Papa's plans in operation once he is married to Miss Mason. Meanwhile, come and view some of the pictures with me.'

Elizabeth followed him obediently and he led her to a sombre painting of a lady from Genoa on the occasion of her betrothal. It was a languid and melancholy painting. The bride looked to be as unhappy as Isabella Mason, the prospective groom was an austere nobleman. In spite of the artist's virtuosity in his rendering of the voluptuous texture of the lady's dress and the surface of his sitter's skin, the message from the painting seemed to be a sad one. The aristocratic bearing of his subjects and their courtly refinement in no way proclaimed any confidence in happiness and satisfaction in marriage — quite the reverse. The young man had dismounted from his horse and showed a figure of unquestioned authority and high culture, but he was turned away from his intended, almost as if he despised her. The young woman was a vision of matchless elegance and dignity, with all the usual trappings of wealth. Nevertheless, the droop of her mouth and her averted gaze revealed patently her lack of love for him.

Elizabeth studied the picture for a few seconds and immediately saw the resemblance to Frederick and Isabella.

'It is by Van Dyck,' Robert explained. 'He was a famous pupil of Rubens and was much admired by the older artist, but he differed from him in temperament and mood. He was somewhat unhealthy and never expressed the exuberance and joy that characterized the masterpieces of Rubens.'

She was silent, saddened by the sombre representation of the betrothal and not understanding the reason for this silence, he said gently, 'Does the painting not appeal to you, Miss Baines?'

Still thinking of Isabella's unhappy situation, Elizabeth shivered. 'No! I . . . I feel it is in no way a celebration. It is unfeeling and expresses only indifference.'

He said nothing and she continued as though she were alone, quite unaware of how naïve and innocent she sounded. 'It is quite horrible. Oh, how can women sell themselves like that? Why on earth do they want to get married? How can they put up with such arrangements?'

He felt a protective tenderness at her youthful inexperience and said gently, 'But if the lady is willing and the families are supportive, it need not be horrible. Marriage

212

can be a first taste of freedom for some young girls and not all men are as seemingly indifferent as the man in the picture. I am quite sure I would not be myself.'

He remembered the incident at the Assembly Rooms and said, 'And I certainly would not impose my attentions on anyone who is unwilling.'

She looked at him quickly, immediately contrite. She seemed to have offended him. 'I'm so sorry . . . I didn't wish to be rude . . . I didn't mean . . . ' She stopped, too embarrassed to go on, and not daring to say that his attentions would always be welcome to her.

Robert felt a surge of tender amusement at the inexperience and complete innocence in her stammered apology. 'I trust that your disapproval of the arranged marriage will not put you off looking at some of the other pictures,' he said gently.

'No, I thank you, sir. I like to look at the pictures. I am grateful for your kindness.'

She turned to go but he caught one of her hands in his. She seemed to hold his eyes in her gaze, and the hand he was holding in his warm clasp was suddenly trembling. He knew he should let her go to attend his mama, but seemed unable to make the necessary effort of will. Then, although they still trembled, he felt her fingers return the pressure of his hand, and the rather serious expression on her face dissolved in a sweet and deliciously shy little smile. Robert was overcome by an urgent desire to kiss those soft, smiling lips. He tightened his grip on her slim fingers and pulled her gently towards him. She looked up at him with wide, enquiring eyes, her lips parted in gentle surprise, and Robert could resist her no longer. He had to show her what a kiss could be like when it was from a man who understood her needs. He drew her into his arms and covered her soft quivering mouth with his own.

Elizabeth stood silently in front of him, trying to control her emotions. In spite of the hot passionate feelings which were raging through her body, she realized that this episode was an unusual aberration as far as Robert Gascoine was concerned. It signified nothing, merely a little dalliance in the rather dull time after Christmas.

You mean nothing to him, she said to herself. It was just a whim on his part. He wanted to kiss you, that is all. Don't read anything into it. Keep calm. Don't let him see how you feel. If you make any stupid remarks now you could lose your position with Lady Gascoine.

She kept her voice light as she said, 'Please

excuse me, sir, I must attend Her Ladyship.'

Robert was amazed that she should be so calm after what had happened. Then he saw her mouth quivering and the bright unshed tears in her beautiful eyes, making her eyelashes dark and spiky.

He stepped forward as though to say something more. But Elizabeth gave him no chance.

Whispering 'Pray excuse me, sir,' once again, she sped away, while he looked after her, furious with himself for leaving it like that.

In her own room that night, Elizabeth tried to concentrate on occupying her mind with all the thousand and one things that needed to be included in Her Ladyship's trunk and writing case. Lady Gascoine had completed a tapestry for one of the footstools at Hawton House. It must be dampened and stretched, ready for tacking on to the little cushioned stool in the south drawing-room, and it would be most displeasing to Her Ladyship if it were left behind.

But in spite of her wish to concentrate on her duties, Elizabeth couldn't help her fingers straying to her lips as she felt again the pressure of Robert's kiss in the picture gallery. She was sure that it would never happen again. A man of Robert's station in life would never give way to the sensual attraction which sparked between them when they touched. He was destined for higher things — for marriage to a beautiful and eligible girl such as Honoria, not a humble paid companion. She closed her eyes and composed herself for slumber, but tossed and turned sleeplessly for hours, trying not to think of that firm, compelling mouth, pressed so seductively to her own.

10

Twelfth night came and went and it was time for the guests to take their leave. Robert seemed very aloof and Frederick was engaged in thinking about his own problems, which meant that no one else was being burdened with them at the time. Miss Wilshaw had returned home with fulsome promises to meet up with Robert, and merely a cool inclination of the head to Elizabeth.

Gradually the house became quieter, and Lady Gascoine and Elizabeth prepared to depart for England. They would again be travelling with Lady Gascoine's abigail, Maria.

'It will be so delightful to be home again,' Lady Gascoine said. 'It is so nice to go away, but so wonderful to be back.'

Elizabeth nodded. She was still totally bemused at the turn events had taken ever since New Year's Day. At one of Lady Gascoine's festive luncheons, Edward Mason had taken her on one side and informed her gravely of the death of George Baines. 'He died peacefully at the end,' Mr Mason said. 'He was not alone. One of his stepsons, Tom

Molloy, was with him and a village woman who nursed him in his last days. He seemed to want to make his peace with God and asked the priest to listen to his confession, but his speech was garbled and unintelligible, except for one thing. He babbled of the Ridgeway Fair, but none could understand him.'

Once more, the name 'Ridgeway' struck a chord in Elizabeth's mind and she strove yet again to remember why it had such a significance in her memory. She wondered what had prompted Tom Molloy to attend the last hours of George Baines. As far as she could recollect, there had been no closeness between them. George Baines had never been close to anyone, she thought. Except possibly Captain Preston. And wasn't he abroad with his regiment?

She was keenly aware of the help and support Edward Mason was giving her and smiled at him. 'I have a feeling of distant recollection in regard to Ridgeway, Mr Mason. Perhaps when we are back in Norfolk, it would be possible to trace my connections with your help and that of Mr Grimshaw, although at the moment I have no clear memories.'

Edward Mason was delighted with the way that this spirited girl responded. He gazed at her delightedly and said, 'Capital, my dear. Joseph Grimshaw believes that actually you have your origins in the village of Copthorne. If you agree he intends to question various people about the circumstances of George Baines' sudden departure for Ireland, all those years ago.'

Elizabeth was now becoming reconciled to the idea that her kind friend and benefactress Jane Gibson was to remain in her country house at Roslaine and that in future they would only see her on special family occasions. She was also keen to establish her own identity.

'I am agreeable to that, Mr Mason. After all, at least then I can meet with dear Miss Jane and Bradbury as my own true self. I do not know Copthorne. I know no one who lives there.'

'Yes, that is the point,' said Mr Mason. 'Joseph Grimshaw believes that Copthorne is your birthplace and there will still be people who remember you. I am inclined to agree with him. I have spoken to Lady Gascoine about this and she is willing to let you go to Copthorne, if you wish it.'

Elizabeth thought rapidly. It would be in her best interests if in fact it were discovered that her father was not in fact George Baines, and that her true parents lived in Copthorne.

She returned his smile and said, 'I quite understand, Mr Mason. I . . . I . . . shall be readily available should you wish it.'

Her expression as he bowed and departed was more confident than she felt. As she mechanically supervised the packing up for the return journey to England, her thoughts were quite melancholy, as was her expression. Sir Frederick had already departed, his declared intention to travel to London and meet up with the racing fraternity. Robert Gascoine was seemingly avoiding her since the kiss in the picture gallery, and he was going in a coach organized by the Mason family.

The Wilshaws were already well on their way to their London townhouse but Elizabeth still had ringing in her ears the fulsome invitations from Honoria to attend them at their home in Bath, to join friends who would be staying there from the beginning of February.

She had swallowed painfully and drawn back to the shadows as the Wilshaws had lingered in the hall with last-minute invitations and every encouragement for Robert to visit.

'And do not forget, dear Lady Gascoine, that we shall lay on some very special social evenings, should you desire to visit us with dear Robert. Honoria has most pleasing and entertaining young friends who attend her in Bath. You would be most welcome to join us.'

Mrs Wilshaw, looking all of her fifty years in a hat which was an unfortunate shade of green, had kissed Lady Gascoine and pressed Robert's hand as she took her farewells.

Honoria herself had given Robert a brilliant smile and said, 'It would be truly wonderful if you could visit us in Bath, Mr Gascoine.'

She looked almost mocking as she addressed him so formally, as though there had been such an intimacy between them that she was used to calling him 'Robert' and not 'Mr Gascoine'.

All of them were ignoring Elizabeth and she thought of the happy days at school, when Honoria had been her friend. She had turned away, sick at heart, to take yet another pile of pressed and folded linen to Lady Gascoine's trunk. She bit her lip at Honoria's unfriendliness towards her and Robert's seeming indifference.

But as Holmes would say, 'Everything passes, nothing is for ever,' and it seemed no time at all before they were on the boat, and well on their way to Norfolk. Elizabeth wondered once more about her true parentage. She was confident and at the same time nervous about the results of her investigations with Mr Mason and Joseph Grimshaw. Perhaps it would be better to let sleeping dogs lie, she thought. She realized for the first time that Waringham really was 'home' to her now. For the first time in her life, she felt that she belonged somewhere and didn't want to leave. Then she recalled the horrible experiences with the Baines family. It was worth going through all the discomfort and stress of the investigations if she could be assured that they were no kith or kin of hers.

She had plenty to occupy her on the journey and only allowed herself a few fleeting thoughts and memories of Robert Gascoine. When they eventually arrived back at Waringham Hall, she was pleased to be back and able to go thankfully to her room.

It was a few days before the Gascoines were back together as a family and even then it seemed strange to be without Miss Gibson and Bradbury at evening dinner. It was the time of year when country people entertained each other, there being little in the way of outside entertainment in rural Norfolk.

In spite of Sir Frederick's absence, the plans for his and Isabella's wedding were well under way and the marriage settlement was due to be signed on 14 February — St Valentine's day, as Lydia had pointed out to

Elizabeth. The wedding day had been set for 31 March. Once Frederick was back at home, they were frequently in the company of Isabella's family and also, much to Elizabeth's surprise, the Athertons. In early February, Mrs Atherton had one of her famous soirées and in spite of the fact that Robert was otherwise engaged, visiting the Wilshaws in Bath, the evening was a pleasant one. David Atherton seemed to put himself out to entertain all the Mason girls, but as might be expected Isabella in particular seemed to respond easily to his quiet charm. Elizabeth noticed that Frederick disappeared early to the card room, and when the young people suggested dancing, Isabella seemed not to miss Frederick but danced with David and the other young men with obvious enjoyment.

Elizabeth, too, enjoyed the dancing. In particular, she relished David Atherton's well-remembered friendly and open manner. 'Miss Mason is looking particularly well this evening,' was his opening remark to her, followed quickly by, 'And you, Miss Baines, seem in radiant good health.'

Elizabeth smiled at this disarming attempt not to overlook her own charms as he spoke of his former sweetheart. 'Yes, Miss Mason is in fine bloom, sir,' she agreed. 'She is obviously enjoying your mama's entertainment as are her sisters. Being old friends, I expect they are very much at ease with you.'

He looked serious for a moment and then said quietly, 'That is true. How quickly time passes. Isabella was such a loyal companion and quite a noted tomboy when we were children. I went to Eton and for a time before I went I shared a tutor with Isabella. I can tell you, Miss Baines, we shared some notable adventures. Heigh-ho! I sound like one of Mama's elderly companions, reminiscing like that, and I'm only three and twenty.'

He pulled a face of mock horror at this thought and Elizabeth was obliged to smile. 'It is indeed quite difficult to imagine such a time,' she said. 'She is now so . . . so . . . '

'Careworn and responsible,' he supplied sadly. 'One supposes that the commitments of her betrothal and her preparations for her marriage have given her a seriousness that she never had. I mind when we were but little things and fishing for minnows in Waringham beck, Isabella was always daring and removed her shoes and stockings and tucked up her dress, the better to wade into the middle of the water. Her governess was not best pleased, I can tell you, when her shoes floated downstream and were lost for ever.' He gave his attractive open grin. 'But I never let her forget, you know, and even now, if she takes on any missish airs, I can always whisper 'fishing in the beck' to make her dissolve into laughter.'

For an instant Elizabeth had a completely new view of the plain Miss Mason. She saw the love and affection that shone in David Atherton's eyes and thought how much happier Isabella would have been if she had been engaged to him instead of Sir Frederick Gascoine.

When the last dance ended, the young people milled about saying their farewells and waiting for carriages. Sir Frederick appeared and sat beside Isabella for a few moments. Copious glasses of claret had obviously been drunk while he was playing cards but, although his face was flushed, his expression was genial.

'Jack Richards is a noted driver and he tells me that my new curricle is the best he has ever seen,' he bragged. 'And of course, the two bays I bought in Ireland are quite matchless. Even Kelly is impressed. We're going to meet at Southdown Common on Saturday. Then a few of us will take our curricles down to Brighton. Any of you young blades who care to lay a wager can stand to win a substantial sum by betting on Kelly and myself to be there first.'

He noticed his mama's frozen face and the anguished eyes of Isabella Mason and continued airily, 'I shall be back Tuesday, with a purse of guineas in my pocket, no doubt.'

There was an uncomfortable silence after this. Guests still continued to take their leave but Isabella disappeared abruptly so that Frederick had to attend without saying his farewells to his fiancée. Both David Atherton and the Masons looked grim and suddenly the whole evening had a sad and disappointing end.

No one saw Sir Frederick next morning, but Elizabeth was informed by one of the maids that His Lordship breakfasted early and had gone to his mama's room to bid her farewell. 'He drove off straight away, miss,' she said, as she tidied Elizabeth's room and removed the ewer and basin. 'And him soon to be a married man,' the maid sniffed.

Elizabeth said nothing, but continued to dress her hair and prepare to go downstairs.

'Well, that's if there'll be a wedding at all,' the maid said provocatively. 'There's many of us thinks he don't act like a man about to be wed. And there's neither sense nor reason in some of the bets he's makin' . . . And that Miss Mason's so in love with 'im . . . ' She spoke quickly, determined to say all she'd got to say and finished in a rush.

Elizabeth gave her a quelling glance and dismissed her. It didn't do to allow servants to pass on gossip. All the same, it didn't seem like devotion on Frederick's part. Her eyes were troubled as she glanced in the mirror to check her appearance. Perhaps there would be no wedding, she thought, as she left the room and made her way downstairs.

Lady Gascoine seemed very subdued and conversation was difficult for both of them, but Elizabeth determinedly broached the subject of her visit to Copthorne. 'I have arranged to use my free time to visit the village where I feel I might have been born,' she said simply. 'I hope I have your approval in this, ma'am, and will keep you informed when I return.'

Lady Gascoine graciously gave her permission, provided that Elizabeth took suitable steps, by taking her maid and one of the young footmen with her. But as it happened they were totally unnecessary as she was going with the Masons.

There was absolutely no sign of Robert and it was a relief when, later in the morning, Mr and Mrs Mason were announced. They had come in the carriage to take Elizabeth to Copthorne and as they sat in the south drawing-room with wine and refreshments, the talk naturally turned towards the wedding. They were too well bred to bring up the subject of Frederick's curricle racing and gambling, but it was clear that Isabella's parents were anxious about the situation. Try as she might, Lady Gascoine was not able to reassure them convincingly that all was well.

'I expect dear Frederick to be back safe and sound by Tuesday,' she said, sounding more confident than she felt. 'He'll come about, never fear, and then it will be all plain sailing for his wedding plans.'

'We must hope so, ma'am,' Emma Mason said. 'The arrangements are well in hand now and Isabella is to have a first fitting for her wedding gown on Thursday week.'

After more polite chat, the Masons and Elizabeth headed to Copthorne and the parish church of St Paul, where they met with Joseph Grimshaw.

The old priest who had attended Elizabeth's grandfather on his deathbed had long since gone and the present incumbent was a recent appointment. He had no knowledge of the former history of the parish and knew very little about his present flock but he was kind and attentive and took them into the vestry to see the parish registers.

'You see, sir,' Joseph Grimshaw said by way of explanation, 'we knows as this 'ere George Baines, who died recently, was one and the same Baines as disappeared all of a sudden, like, fourteen year ago and either by chance or malice aforethought, a little lass name of Elizabeth Winfield disappeared at the same time.'

The name of George Baines made Elizabeth's heart beat painfully in her chest but the name of Elizabeth Winfield meant nothing and she continued to wait patiently while the Reverend Longwith opened a large leather-bound book and began to look down a list of dates and names.

'Here is recorded the marriage of Thomas Winfield, of Coppice Farm, with Sarah Ann Martin, spinster of this parish. It's dated 16 August 1787 and both parties could sign their own names. See.'

Elizabeth experienced a sudden feeling of curiosity and longing as she gazed at the black spidery writing of the register entry. She said nothing for a minute, but her mind was whirling with all sorts of feelings that she was unable to articulate.

The priest allowed her a few minutes to compose herself and then said gently, 'Here in the register of births is the record of their only daughter Elizabeth Winfield's baptism. She was born on 1 June 1788.'

Elizabeth shivered violently as though someone had walked over her grave. That must be me, she thought. She whispered the name to herself. 'Elizabeth Winfield.'

Not Lizzie Baines. Not even Miss Baines, companion to Lady Mary Gascoine, but a person in her own right; a person with a true name, a person with a birth mother and a birthday.

It was Joseph Grimshaw who broke the silence. 'Aye, that makes sense. The afore-mentioned Elizabeth Winfield were snatched away from her nursemaid when she were four year old. She'd be eighteen now. The nursemaid in question is Susan Harker, as was. Now married these ten year to Jack Benson. She still remembers what happened all those years ago, as if t'were yesterday.'

They thanked the Reverend Longwith and made their way to Jasmine Cottage, where Susan lived with her husband. She had never had any children of her own.

'The child being took from me like that haunted my thoughts day and night for years,' she said simply. 'Maybe it was God's punishment for my carelessness.'

'But everyone as I've talked to, ma'am, say as how you were never careless,' Joseph Grimshaw said gently. 'Quite the opposite. They said as how somebody would have to be very determined indeed to steal young Elizabeth from such a devoted nurse. I've spoken to a few at the Red Lion, who remember Baines ranting and raving that he would take the child, but none believed him, until he did it.'

'I hope so,' Susan whispered. 'I loved her like my own. She were a lovely dainty child, as I recall. It was tragic, her being took like that and her poor parents in their grave afore they was forty.'

'And do you still remember Mr Thomas Winfield, Mrs Benson?'

'I do, sir. Handsome he were, his hair black as jet and nary a single touch of grey until his little daughter were took from him.'

'And what about Mrs Winfield, his lady wife?'

'Oh, sir, she were beautiful and so kind. Why, I mind the bad winter of 1789, she worked her fingers to the bone, cooking broth and taking bread to the cottagers. A lovely lady, she were.'

'And her hair,' persisted Joseph Grimshaw. 'Her hair was ditto, like?'

'Oh no, sir. Mrs Winfield were blonde. Hair like spun gold, she had.'

Mr Grimshaw pulled out a bulbous notebook from his pocket and, opening it at a certain page, showed it to Susan Benson. 'Were these Mr Winfield's parents, ma'am?' he asked.

Susan read the words that were carefully printed in Mr Grimshaw's large firm writing.

SACRED TO THE MEMORY OF
JOSIAH WINFIELD,
WHO DEPARTED THIS LIFE
11 SEPTEMBER 1787,
AGE 58 YEARS
AND ALSO HIS WIFE EMILY
WHO DIED 7 MARCH 1779
R.I.P.

'And what of Mrs Winfield's folk?'

'I don't know, sir. I never met them. I believe Mr and Mrs Martin were from Dersingham way, but I don't ever remember meeting them,' said Susan.

'But you remember Elizabeth Winfield clearly?'

'Oh yes, sir. I can see her as clear as if t'were yesterday. She were such a pretty, happy little thing.' Her eyes filled with tears.

Edward Mason pulled Elizabeth gently forward and said, 'Do you see that girl in front of you now, Susan?'

'I don't know ... I can't be certain ... I ... ' She twisted her fingers in her apron nervously. 'I can't be sure, sir. She is like my little Elizabeth ... but ... I don't know ... '

'Did the little girl have any distinguishing feature, birthmarks and such, apart from her mama's golden hair, that is?'

Susan thought for a while. 'She had a mark on the back of her neck. Stork bites they call 'em in these parts. But they generally fade as the child gets older. Hers looked like a little strawberry.'

'Pardon me, my dear,' Emma Mason said to Elizabeth and stood on tiptoe to lift up the curls at Elizabeth's neck. There was the telltale red mark, faded certainly, but still there all the same.

'That seems pretty conclusive,' Edward Mason said. 'Elizabeth, my dear, may I present your old nursemaid, Susan Benson. Mrs Benson, allow me to introduce Miss Elizabeth Winfield.'

There were more tears as Elizabeth embraced her former nursemaid and asked eager questions about her mama and papa.

Then it was time to go. Elizabeth sat in the Masons' carriage as though she were in a trance. Her thoughts were all about what she had seen and heard this afternoon and she knew her mind would be occupied with her new identity for weeks to come. She looked up to give a grateful smile to the two people who had given her support and helped her with her enquiries and saw that they were looking at her kindly. Elizabeth's eyes filled with tears again.

She thought of Robert Gascoine and wondered what he would say at her newly found identity. Would it have made any difference to their actions when he'd kissed her so seductively and she'd co-operated so eagerly?

She now felt uncomfortable about the whole episode. He would return to the family home eventually. She wondered if he would soon have news of his engagement to Honoria; if so, that shaming episode would still be between them. She felt sure that it would be impossible for her to act naturally with him and difficult to remain friends with Honoria, once they were married.

★   ★   ★

Meanwhile unknown to Elizabeth, Tom Molloy and his brothers had arrived in Liverpool and had arranged a meeting with James Preston. Tom Molloy, the leader of the gang of boys who had made Elizabeth's life a misery in the not so far off days when she was in Baines's house. He was the eldest of the Molloy boys who had been looked after by Mr Baines and their mother, if you could call it that.

11

Robert had accepted the pressing invitation of Honoria's parents and had arrived in Bath for a few days with the Wilshaws. He had spent the whole of the tedious journey trying not to think of his mama's companion and trying to persuade himself that Elizabeth had just responded to a passing fancy on his part and that any feelings he might have for her would quickly die. Especially if he acceded to his mama's wishes and tried to find a beautiful and wealthy bride. All the time, he was trying to ignore the pulse in his brain which beat out Elizabeth's name in time to the horse's hooves throughout the journey and to deny his natural inclination to cancel this courtesy visit and go back home.

But by the time he reached the Wilshaws' manor house, he felt that he had successfully faced the fact that he had been trying to avoid. He had to stop thinking about Elizabeth and try to imagine someone like Honoria as his bride. He was a younger son. There was no future for him without a wealthy wife. His mama was wise enough to recognize that, and with the non-infatuated part of his mind, so did Robert. Perhaps he could propose to Honoria quickly and get it over with before he lost control of his emotions and went straight back to Elizabeth, to beg her to marry him.

He was received with the utmost courtesy by Mr and Mrs Wilshaw. Honoria was all that was gracious and the suite of rooms he was to occupy was certainly luxurious enough to match the grandeur of Hawton House. Here was a family who were very rich. Mr Wilshaw may have made his fortune in commerce, but nevertheless they were refined and respectable, needing only to forge a liaison with an uppercrust family like the Gascoines to be even more successful in polite society.

The other guests included a wealthy landowner from Sussex, a local squire and his lady, a friend of Honoria's, her brother, the vicar, and others in the neighbourhood. All were curious about Robert and intrigued at the rumour of Honoria's betrothal. Mrs Wilshaw had only hinted at this, being far too astute to count her matrimonial chickens at this stage, but by the end of dinner both Honoria and her mama were determined that Robert should be brought up to scratch before he returned to London. Perhaps, thought Mrs Wilshaw fondly, dear Honoria's engagement would be announced publicly at the wedding of his elder brother. She was looking forward with ill-concealed impatience to planning the wedding of her only daughter. True, Robert Gascoine was a younger son, but he belonged to an illustrious family. With the money that Mr Wilshaw heaped on them and Robert Gascoine's background, it was obvious that it meant success for the couple.

By the time she retired to bed, she was well pleased with the progress between the young couple. Honoria had been in her best looks, beautiful and elegant as ever. She had entertained very prettily and Robert had played the pianoforte to accompany her singing. He was all that was handsome and charming and Mrs Wilshaw was delighted at the prospect of welcoming him as a son-in-law.

As she creamed her face and donned her lace nightcap before bed, she thought complacently that perhaps tomorrow, if the young couple had some time to themselves, Robert could be persuaded to make dear Honoria an offer. She said nothing of this to Mr Wilshaw — indeed, she never had anything whatsoever to say to him on any subject under the sun, apart from the money it would cost to see dear Honoria wed into a high-ranking family, or the fact that they would need another servant if they were going to move in exalted circles. Mr Wilshaw was not treated to these topics tonight. He was rarely allowed in Mrs Wilshaw's bed-chamber and only then on sufferance. His husbandly duties were performed strictly in the dark, as speedily as possible and with no response or encouragement from his wife. She tolerated this need in men for sexual activity, but she found it so utterly repulsive that she ensured it occurred as infrequently as possible.

She had hinted delicately to Honoria as the girl was growing up that all men were beasts, but women must be noble and acquiesce in this beastliness if they were to achieve the status of matrimony and fit in with what society expected of them.

But tonight her thoughts were focused on the more romantic aspects of Honoria's development. The wedding gown. The venue. The attendants. The reception. All the thousand and one things she was determined would go towards making the ceremony a successful occasion for her only daughter.

She had taken the opportunity to whisper to Honoria that Robert seemed to enjoy reading and had expressed a desire to explore Mr Wilshaw's library after breakfast the next day.

'Your papa is more than willing, my love, if

Mr Gascoine wishes to pay his addresses. I think you may safely expedite matters if you yourself were to be in the library when Mr Gascoine avails himself of Papa's invitation. It is usually quiet at that time and a gentleman who is rather bashful about his courtship might feel more comfortable if he were sure of not being interrupted.'

There was a short pause and then her mother said carefully, 'Gentlemen sometimes need a little encouragement from a lady and may like to attempt a kiss or an embrace at a time like this. Of course, I trust you not to do anything improper, Honoria, but you may allow a chaste embrace if Mr Gascoine asks you to marry him. I expect you will find such attentions unwelcome, repugnant even — that is quite natural. But remember, you must not reveal your feelings by word or deed. A lady must always do her duty, as I do myself. You would wish Mr Gascoine to think that you will make a dutiful wife, Honoria. That is important if you are to make a good marriage.'

'Yes, Mama. I shall take heed of what you say.'

'Good night then, my dear.'

'Good night, Mama.'

★ ★ ★

Next morning, Honoria breakfasted early in her room and was ready in a gown of yellow silk and matching reticule and simple gold and pearl jewellery, well before Robert had finished his breakfast.

When he entered the library, she was carefully posed on the window seat. She was pretending to read one of Papa's books. Her lovely profile was turned to the ancient mullioned window and the morning sunlight lit up her glossy ringlets.

He had to admit she made an attractive picture. Her face was lovely but it was not Elizabeth's face. Her figure was feminine and statuesque but it was not Elizabeth's figure. He wondered briefly if her mama had suggested this opportunity for a little discussion of their mutual desires. But as he strode across the room in order to examine her father's books, he decided it didn't matter. He had no intention of proposing to Honoria, whatever her mama's expectations.

She stood up, expressing a pretence of surprise. 'Why, Mr Gascoine!' she simpered. 'You have caught me at my favourite indulgence, reading one of Papa's books. This is a nice surprise though. Do you enjoy poetry?'

'Yes, I do,' he said briefly. He was determined to make his escape as gracefully as possible. Without warning, Honoria placed a white hand on his arm and smiled winningly at him.

'Robert, this is an unexpected pleasure for me.'

It was the first time she had used his Christian name, and he was aware she had moved even closer to him, gazing at him all the while, her beautiful shapely brows raised a little. She was so close to him that he could see the fine silky down on her upper lip, common in ladies as dark as Honoria. She raised her lovely face to his and he stepped back a little, pointedly avoiding the tilted chin and pouting red lips. He remained utterly still and passive when she attempted to press her lips to his and, becoming aware that she was getting no response, she stopped, puzzled and confused.

It was at that moment the dowdy little vicar bumbled into the room and she sprang away from Robert, utterly humiliated.

The clerical gentleman beamed round and said vaguely, 'Ah, Honoria, my dear. Mr Gascoine. Good morning. I didn't know ... didn't expect ... I was looking for a commentary on St John's Gospel ... Sorry to intrude ... '

'Not at all,' Robert said politely. 'Pray excuse me, Miss Wilshaw. Excuse me, sir.' He left the room hurriedly, blessing the fortu- itous interruption.

The next morning, Honoria didn't see Robert because he had gone out before breakfast. He'd expressed a desire to go for an early-morning ride and Mr Wilshaw assured him that the groom and stable lads would be on duty from 5.30 onwards and he would have his pick of a suitable mount from the stables. Mrs Wilshaw was busy with the other guests and there wasn't an opportunity for Honoria to see her mama and exchange girlish confidences about Robert. In any case, something happened which was to change forever the way she thought about him. Before she had even finished her morning chocolate, Honoria's maid had brought her a letter from yet another old schoolfriend from Miss Hanbury's Academy. After reading it, she dispensed with breakfast altogether and, dressing herself in clothes warm enough for the crisp February morning, dismissed her maid and set off to walk down the drive. She knew exactly where she would wait for Robert when he returned from his ride and, if necessary, would wait until lunchtime.

But he appeared after only half an hour. She heard the sound of hooves thudding dully on the grassy walk which led to the drive and she stepped forward confidently to place herself in his path and halt his progress towards the house.

Robert was surprised at her sudden appearance but greeted her pleasantly enough, reining in his horse so as not to alarm her. 'Honoria. Good morning. Are you out walking so early?'

'And are you out riding so early sir?' she asked by way of a reply, so that he was at a loss to know how to deal with her.

She stood before him, appearing at ease and confident, a well-brought-up young lady, perfectly in control, but making no effort to let him pass.

He gave his usual pleasant and disarming smile and said with polite friendliness, 'And what can I do for you, Miss Wilshaw?'

'I doubt if there's anything, sir,' she said bitterly. 'Sir Frederick Gascoine has confided to Jack Richards, the brother of my old schoolfriend, that you are so enslaved with that common little Irish trash who is servant to your mama that you cannot keep your hands off her. I gather that half the county set observed your behaviour at the Roslaine Assembly Rooms.'

Robert went first red with anger and then pale with loathing for this woman his mother wished to become his wife.

'My God, Honoria. How dare you speak of

Miss Baines like that? It is the language of the gutter, quite unworthy of a lady in your position.'

Angrily, he turned his horse's head and tried to get past her, but she took his bridle in one elegantly gloved hand. 'Don't go, Robert. As far as I'm concerned, knowing Amelia's love of mischief making, I wouldn't consider such a tale worthy of any note. Providing, of course, that Elizabeth Baines is got rid of, I would still be willing to marry you.'

She raised her chin and glared haughtily at him and Robert was suddenly angrier than he'd ever been in his life. Much angrier than he'd ever been with his foolish and wayward brother. Almost angry enough to strike the woman who stood in front of him and who still stared so sneeringly at him. How dare she refer to the tall, beautiful Elizabeth as 'little Irish trash'? He gave Honoria an icy stare and unceremoniously brushed her hand off the horse's reins.

'Miss Wilshaw,' he said coldly, 'I don't recollect that I have ever made you an offer, so you'll have no occasion to either accept or refuse it.'

He rode past her up to the house, uncivilly leaving her to find her own way back on foot.

Why couldn't it have been his lovely Elizabeth who had been waiting for him like that? He would have taken her up in front of him, held her in his arms, pressed his lips to hers, begged her to marry him.

Unconsciously, he quickened his pace, and when he reached the stables he threw the reins to Job and ran upstairs to snarl at his valet that they were leaving and to pack immediately.

Honoria went at once to seek her mama and tell her all about it. At the end of her tearful tale, Mrs Wilshaw's reaction was one of contemptuous anger. 'And where is Mr Gascoine now?'

'He is preparing to depart, Mama. He has requested that his valet starts the packing . . . and the groom . . . the groom is harnessing the horses.'

'This is unforgivable. Utterly unforgivable. Outrageous,' Mrs Wilshaw hissed. 'Furthermore,' she declared, 'if you show the least inclination to accept an offer from Robert Gascoine after this, your father and I will disown you.'

12

If Frederick felt in any way blameworthy at the way he had upset his mama and his bride-to-be the evening before, it was not apparent next morning. He'd always acknowledged to himself that it was only Isabella's money which had attracted him in the first place. That she so patently adored him had never given him the slightest bit of pleasure or satisfaction. He found her adoration cloying and tedious. After all, there were women far more beautiful than she, who could be just as affectionate and attentive. Frederick despised them all. He was a man's man and was happy to use women merely for his gratification, without complications of affection on either side. He saw his future with Isabella as one of convenience — to himself, that is, not Isabella. She was young and healthy. Once the heir was assured and she had a nest full of young children, he would be quite justified in resuming his single lifestyle. This included his friendships with likeminded gamblers and rakes and his continued liaisons with several regular mistresses.

Frederick had woken up with a head still thick from the effects of heavy drinking. He'd not been best pleased that Isabella had disappeared last night while he was extolling the merits of his new curricle and bays. After several cups of coffee, which had not eased his throbbing head, he'd taken leave of his mama and patiently endured her tearful reproaches before making his escape to the mews yard, where Kelly and his smart new equipage awaited him. They were to stop at the George Hotel at Southdown and meet up with Jack Richards and others before the drive to Brighton.

Kelly was a steadying influence on the volatile Sir Frederick and merely nodded a greeting at his master before stowing the luggage inside the vehicle. Then he sprang nimbly up behind and they set off at a sedate pace on the first leg of their journey.

The next day, Frederick arrived in time to join Jack Richards for a lavish dinner at the George. His headache had now completely disappeared and having washed and changed he felt more than ready to do justice to a rather fine claret which had been produced by his landlord.

The dinner had been set in a private parlour and mine host, having ushered in all the various dishes to please two gentlemen of quality, bowed himself out of the room. When he had gone, with entreaties for them to merely pull on the bell rope if they should want him to bring anything further, the two men lounged at their ease and attacked the food.

Jack Richards carved himself a thick slice of ham and smothered it in onion gravy before he discussed the arrangements for the following day. 'The others are meeting us tomorrow, ten sharp. It's exactly five miles to Brighton, according to the milestone. There are only three of us now that Cartwright's dropped out, but he's coming along to see that all's fair. It's been suggested that we should stagger the start, to give us some equality. Yours is the most up-to-date and the lightest curricle, Gascoine, so yours will be last. Thomas will be second and I'm first.'

Frederick looked at him sourly but he grunted acquiescence.

'Fair's fair, old man,' Jack Richards said. 'Thomas's outfit is a real old boneshaker, not ideal for racing, but Thomas reckons his skill at handling the ribbons means he'll get the prize. My own curricle is much heavier than either of yours, so is it agreed?'

'Agreed,' Frederick said sulkily. 'At least the road across the common is wide and flat. There are like to be no problems until we

248

reach South Hill village. Then the road narrows and we have to take more care.' He helped himself lavishly to more food and wine.

Richards poured himself a generous glass of claret and piled more ham on his plate. 'Anyway,' he said loftily, 'at least the betting will be brisk. Thomas is always game for a wager and can well afford the blunt now that his pa's left him so well heeled. I'm putting five thou' on the table myself.'

Frederick's jaw dropped and he paused for a moment in his eating and drinking. Five thousand was well above his usual stake. Still, nothing ventured, nothing gained. He was bound to win and double or treble his outlay. He laughed scornfully.

'I'm ready to match that,' he said recklessly and raised his glass in a mock toast 'To the drive down to Brighton, then,' he said. 'Good luck to us all for tomorrow.'

The next morning brought Cartwright and Thomas to the George and the three of them solemnly placed their bets with Cartwright, who was to start the race by firing a pistol in the air three times.

The three of them were silent as they prepared to depart. They were completely sober now and in the cold light of the winter's morning, Frederick at least was aware of the enormity of the wager he had undertaken and which he could ill afford.

At the edge of the common, Cartwright looked at all the riders and nodded to Richards, then he immediately fired the pistol in the air. Richards was ready and whipped up his high-stepping blacks and they set off at a cracking pace. Two minutes later, it was the turn of Thomas, who was driving a somewhat outdated vehicle, but which was pulled by a very spirited pair of greys. By the time Cartwright gave Frederick the signal, he was impatient to be off and gave chase to the other two riders as though all the devils in hell were after him. Cartwright was on horseback and took the shortest route, so he could be there to meet them.

It was true about what Frederick had said about the common having a wide road, but in truth it was little more than a cart track. There was heavy rain in December, which had led to the ground being churned up. January had been exceptionally dry, and with the frosts the road was pitted with treacherous ruts. Two miles further on, Thomas drove at a crazy speed through a series of potholes. One of his primrose-yellow curricle wheels came adrift and rolled sideways with almost dreamlike precision across the common, to be chased and captured by two gormless village lads, hoping for a copper or two from the fine gentlemen. Thomas was thrown from his seat, and though not injured was shaken and angry, swearing excessively at the boys and shouting abuse at his little tiger who, foreseeing the accident, had leapt clear.

This incident had not only caused Frederick to swerve badly, barely avoiding an accident himself, but it also unnerved him. His heart beat rapidly and the hands inside the elegant gauntlets were damp with perspiration. He had made up a lot of ground at first and had been within yards of Richards, but this setback made the distance between them further than before. He whipped the bays mercilessly and drove them at a gruelling pace until he could overtake Richards. The road was only just wide enough to allow him to squeeze past his adversary, but Frederick refused to slow down. Instead he slashed at his horses in a frenzy, increasing his speed still more. He passed Richards with only two inches to spare but he didn't care.

He was exultant. The race was his. He'd win both his wagers, as well as the glory of being the first to reach Brighton. He heard the thunder of horses' hoofs behind him, but kept to the middle of the road so that Richards wouldn't be able to overtake him. Only a quarter of a mile to go and they were now in the village of South Hill and the road narrowed much more suddenly than Frederick expected. Richards would never overtake him now. Frederick breathed deeply, sure of his victory. But his elation turned to horror as, lumbering heavily towards him along the narrow track, a farm cart laden with turnips was pulled by a slow-moving carthorse. He cursed and shouted to the yokel who was driving it to get out of the way. But it was useless. Not only was the driver unable to get out of the way but the cart was a massive slow elephant compared to his own swift vehicle.

He was obliged to swerve sideways to avoid it. One of the wheels slipped over the edge of the road and Frederick plunged through a farmer's hedge. The smart new equipage turned over, both wheels spinning in the air.

Kelly, bruised and winded, managed to scramble clear and went to his master's aid, as did the carter. Frederick was a crumpled heap beneath the wreck of his curricle, which was splintered almost to bits. Although the two men lost no time in seeking out the driver, they were too late. Frederick had landed on his head and his neck was broken.

★　★　★

Lady Gascoine and Robert were not informed of the tragedy until after noon on the next day. And naturally Elizabeth was present when the accident was reported to Her Ladyship. Elizabeth informed Frederick's aunt and her companion, who both set off immediately for Lady Gascoine's.

The effect was absolutely devastating. Disbelief was followed by denial, followed by anger and aggressive criticism of Frederick's friends, in a classic pattern of reaction which continued with violent hysterics and weeping, before the doctor came and administered one of his calming draughts. Only then did Lady Gascoine come finally to an anguished acceptance of her eldest son's death. Only then did Elizabeth finally persuade Her Ladyship to lie down in her bedchamber and let the doctor's medication take effect.

All this time, Robert was a tower of strength as Elizabeth knew he would be in a crisis. He organized the removal of Frederick's body from Brighton and saw to the arrangements for its internment in the family vault.

Jane Gibson and Bradbury arrived to find Lady Gascoine still devastated by her loss and all her servants absolutely overcast by the tragedy. Jane immediately took charge of the whole household and worked tirelessly at sending out replies to letters of condolence, organizing Madame Françoise to come to the house and make the mourning clothes and making sure that the flowers were suitably acknowledged and put in containers.

Elizabeth saw little of Robert at this time but she understood from the occasional conversation she overheard between Jane Gibson and her companion that he was busy settling Frederick's rather complicated affairs.

'Now that Robert is the heir,' Jane Gibson said reflectively, 'his mama seems to appreciate him at last. He has been a marvel of calm in all this. Why, he even had the forethought to thank Kelly very graciously for rescuing Frederick's horses and conveying them back to the stables.' She lowered her voice confidentially. 'My sister has no idea of how deeply Frederick was dipped at cards and his other gambling activities.'

Elizabeth continued to work busily at her needlework, keeping her head bowed but very conscious of the fact that Miss Gibson was speaking fondly of her beloved Robert.

After a short silence, Jane Gibson went on. 'No one holds Jack Richards responsible for Frederick's death. According to Mr Cartwright, Frederick was driving so recklessly that an accident was inevitable, but he felt that Frederick was desperate to win the wager and so discharge some of his debts before the wedding.' She lowered her voice even further and continued, 'But even if he had won the race, it seems as if his winnings would have been a drop in the ocean as far as his commitments were concerned. Even now, the money he lost on the wager with Richards and Cartwright remains to be paid and he will have everything on to set his affairs in order.'

In the days immediately following the funeral, Robert remained closeted with the estate manager, sorting through bills, promissory notes, rent and receipts, records of tenancy and land rents, trying to establish some system of accounting where previously there had been none. Lady Gascoine had no idea of her son's debts and even Robert was staggered at the massive sum for which the estate was liable. He disappeared to London for a few days, consulting with a lawyer who went through Frederick's debts trying to see ways of cutting back on expenditure, in particular Frederick's team of expensive horses and the stabling costs for them.

Jane Gibson and Bradbury had brought a much needed sense of serenity and acceptance in the midst of Lady Gascoine's tragic loss, which helped her regain some semblance of dignified calm and stoic endurance of a future without her beloved son. The servants still moved quietly and respectfully about the house and their faces reflected Lady Gascoine's own sad expression. They saw little of Isabella or the Mason family, but with her usual courage and forthright approach, Jane Gibson insisted on visiting them with Bradbury and Elizabeth. They were not accompanied by Lady Gascoine who, it was felt, had too tenuous a grip on her feelings to submit willingly to such an ordeal.

The three women sat in rather a constrained silence in the Masons' drawing-room while Mr and Mrs Mason were informed of their presence. Isabella also appeared, as colourless as usual, and dressed in pallid grey which did nothing for her complexion and mousy hair. The Masons were refined and courteous as always, but nothing could disguise the pall of sadness and disappointment overhanging the whole household. Isabella was encouraged by her parents to take a promenade through the long gallery with Elizabeth as the weather was so inclement and the older people remained where they were, talking in hushed tones, still pained by the turn of events which had led to their daughter's devastating disappointment. Elizabeth was surprised when Isabella drew her into an alcove and sat with her on a little cream and gilt sofa, still holding her arm.

Isabella said without preamble, 'Thank you for your condolences on the sad loss of my fiancé, Elizabeth, but I do assure you that my heart is well on the mend. It has been a painful and difficult lesson for me to learn but I have come about and woken up from my dream of love and romance with Sir Frederick Gascoine.'

'But ... I thought ... I thought it was truly a love match ... And ... and a marriage of equals. Sir Frederick was Sir William Gascoine's heir and inherited vast lands and property — '

'Yes, and he frittered vast amounts on gaming and ... and wenching with his cronies ... If he were alive, Sir William would not have countenanced his goings on ... his debts ... his drinking ... Lady Gascoine hasn't a notion how much ... '

She bowed her head as though she would weep and Elizabeth said tentatively, 'But you seemed so fond of him. Your parents obviously welcomed the engagement. It seemed likely to be successful. Many wealthy men in society have ... have ... other interests ... '

Isabella gave a dry, humourless laugh. 'I'm sure they do,' she said bitterly. 'As for a love match,' she went on, 'surely you cannot believe that Frederick loved anyone, even for a moment, except himself, of course ...

That I was so stupid as to be taken in by one so vain and selfish, so shallow and self-seeking, to be carried along by such a reckless foolish dream of love and romance . . . ' Her voice caught on a sob and she struggled to gain her composure, but continued in a steadier voice. 'I promise you that I have known for some time that my idol, the love of my life, had feet of clay. He flattered me outrageously until . . . until . . . my heart was engaged, but it was just a game to him. He wanted only my fortune, you see,' she ended simply, and that acknowledgment of the futility of her love for Frederick tore at Elizabeth's heart strings as no amount of sobs and tears could have done.

On an impulse, she clasped her friend to her closely and tried to comfort her. Elizabeth had never had a sister but at that moment she felt a sisterly affection for Isabella Mason — that she felt would last throughout life.

'You'll find love again Miss Mason . . . Isabella,' she said. 'Next time it will be with someone more worthy of your qualities, who . . . who can love you for yourself alone. Until then, count on me as your friend. Take comfort from your wonderful family and your dear sisters.' Isabella pressed her hand, too emotional to say any more, and they went to join Mr and Mrs Mason.

In keeping with the general air of melancholy which surrounded the families of Frederick and Isabella, spring was late that year. Captain Preston, for a consideration to the Molloy boys, not in any way as generous as the one which he had passed to Mr Baines, had finally agreed to track down Elizabeth. When they caught up with her, he could wreak his revenge.

The weather turned bitterly cold and the country roads were almost impassable. It was difficult to visit neighbours even for brief courtesy calls, but life went on all around them. Elizabeth saw the boys from the village with homemade sledges on the snowy roads. Even the lake at Tollyvara must be frozen by now, she thought, although Honoria had long returned to Bath and so would not be dazzling the company with her ice-skating twirls or figure of eights. Elizabeth wondered fleetingly what had happened when Robert had gone to Bath to stay with the family. It was rumoured among the kitchen staff that Robert had gone to plight his troth with Honoria, but nothing more had been heard of it so either he had done it and been refused or he had not made an offer for Elizabeth's former friend from Miss Hanbury's Academy.

Lady Gascoine's social life was now so narrowed because of her mourning for her eldest son, Elizabeth found she had a lot of time on her hands and indulged in long periods of quiet reflection. Robert seemed to be spending more and more time in London and although Jane Gibson and Bradbury spoke of him frequently, she never joined in these conversations. Instead she remained busy at her sewing, head bent but conscious of every hint and nuance of their discussion of her beloved.

Lady Gascoine spent much of her time on her day bed with the curtains drawn at the window, lace handkerchief clutched between her fingers and a draught of laudanum and water on the table at her side.

As the doctor was a regular visitor at this time it seemed natural, once he had left the house, for Jane and Bradbury to discuss Lady Gascoine's situation, and the advice he had given her.

'He's warned her against repining on her bed all day,' Jane Gibson said in a low voice. 'Instead, he's advised her to take up the threads of her life again, not large social gatherings, you understand, but some discreet entertaining among her friends and acquaintances, as would ease her back into the world once more.'

Bradbury spoke equally quietly. 'It would

seem to me good counsel, if only for her second son, to whom she still owes some responsibility of care.'

Jane now lowered her voice almost to a whisper. 'Mary told me yesterday that she hopes Robert will do his duty and choose a suitable bride, just as soon as is decently possible.'

'Poor Robert. He is in for a difficult time,' Bradbury murmured.

'Yes and the poor young man has never seriously looked at any young lady of his acquaintance in that way. Not since Miss Andrews' untimely death, anyway. He is most obsessively dedicated to his collections and treasures. No young female could compete with those interests.'

Bradbury paused before replying and shot a glance at Elizabeth, who as usual kept her eyes firmly fixed on the petticoat she was hemming. 'I thought . . . I wondered . . . that is to say . . . did not Miss Wilshaw make a favourable impression on your sister, ma'am?'

'Yes. Yes, to be sure she did. But she resides in Bath and besides, the family fortunes have been much depleted by Frederick's extravagant lifestyle. On the other hand, Miss Isabella Mason is well known and well liked by my sister. Mary has hinted lately that after the mourning period is over . . . Who knows

. . . Robert could do worse . . . '

Startled, Elizabeth glanced at Jane Gibson and was further shocked to see that Jane Gibson was looking at her intently.

She knows I was listening, Elizabeth thought, and bit her lip. Shortly afterwards, she excused herself and went to sit on her own in the small saloon.

She sat idle for a few moments, her sewing forgotten. She saw the future mapped out for her, growing old and withered in the service of an elderly gentlewoman, to end her life with a small stipend when Lady Gascoine died, or to be kept on by Robert and his bride, a liability they had to support charitably until the end of her life. Worse still, if she were not so fortunate as this she could look forward to the humiliation and harshness of the poorhouse and a lonely death as a parish pauper. With her hands clasped idly in her lap, she closed her eyes and let the bitter tears fall unheeded.

13

Robert's days were taken up with consulting the estate manager over sale of land and various properties, but he had been able to retain the two family houses and the dower house. Spinks, the estate manager, was an honest and astute man who had been frustrated with Frederick's neglectful style of ownership.

He was delighted with Robert's quiet consideration and attention to detail. Most of all, he was relieved to find he was dealing with a thoughtful and intelligent master who knew how to practise stringent economies without destroying rural communities and poor labourers. They were of the same mind almost immediately and Robert was confident that Spinks would organize not only the sale of the land and property, but valuable trees for timber, for which there was a ready market.

Over the weeks since Frederick's death, Robert, who had never had to consider money before, had come to realize that if Frederick had continued the life that he was leading there would be precious little of the family fortune left to salvage. He wondered briefly if his brother would have run through Isabella's fortune so rapidly. He was finally aware of his father's foresight in leaving Robert comparatively well off — 'in order to extend my collections,' were his father's words and Robert had reason to be glad of his father's thoughtfulness.

When things finally seemed to be in order, he returned home. It was early March and the weather, though still cold, was fine and dry. The pale sun glinted on the snow which still lingered on the roads and fields, giving a picturesque appearance to the badly rutted cart tracks and mud-encrusted country pathways.

It seemed an age since he'd had the opportunity to enjoy the late winter sun and he longed for a country ramble. One morning after he had changed and had some refreshments, he decided to go for a brisk walk. Lady Gascoine was confined to her bed with a cold and his Aunt Jane and Bradbury were out in the village, doing good to the cottagers, taking them food and clothes to help them through a hard winter.

He found Elizabeth half an hour later, in the small saloon, as usual with her needlework, and his heart skipped a beat when he saw how pale she had become, while he had been so preoccupied with the funeral, lands and property. He felt a sense of shock at the sight of her face, drained of its usual attractive animation, and her eyes, which seemed to have lost their former sparkle.

'Miss Baines ... Elizabeth ... Miss Winfield ... ' he began. 'I must become used to calling you by your correct name.' He smiled down at her with the quiet charm she remembered so well, but her own expression remained sombre.

'I have just been to see my mama,' he went on. 'She seems to be recovering slowly, but is still unfit to go out. It must be tedious for you when your own activities are so restricted in this way.'

When she still didn't reply, he stepped closer to her and noticed a solitary tear which was still glinting on her cheek. Impulsively, he grasped her shoulders with both of his hands. 'Are you happy here, Elizabeth?'

She registered the use of her Christian name, but she remained calm and answered in a colourless voice, 'Yes, I am happy. As happy as my situation allows.'

She looked nervous, as though she expected him to say something critical of her. Robert realized that he had made her feel wary of him by kissing her and then keeping her at a distance while offering no explanations for his actions. There were so many things that he regretted — going to see Honoria, for instance.

'I have been very distracted of late, having to deal with my brother's financial affairs, but hopefully things are so much more settled now.'

'That must be a relief to you, sir,' she replied drily.

Uncharacteristically, his mouth twisted in annoyance. 'I beg your pardon, I have no wish to bore you with my concerns. Obviously, you have no interest in the family estate.'

'I was not aware that I was supposed to have any.'

'I deserved that, I suppose. We have all taken you for granted and yet your care and companionship of my mama have been exemplary.'

She eyed him coolly. 'It is what I am employed to do. I am a paid companion to Her Ladyship.'

A sense of dread weighed down Elizabeth's spirit and she had a sinking feeling in the pit of her stomach. Was he going to tell her that she was no longer required and that her employment was at an end? It would be too cruel.

'Do you mean Lady Gascoine doesn't

need me any more?'

He caught her chin and made her look at him. 'No, you silly goose. I don't mean that. We all need you, Elizabeth, in our different ways. But come,' he said, more briskly, and he released her abruptly. 'We could both do with a good long walk in the fresh air. Would you care to join me?' He looked at her, smiling with his eyes and once more she was overcome with shyness.

'Yes, sir . . . very well . . . ' She sped upstairs to change into her warmest clothes.

'I shall wait for you in the hall,' he called after her.

She was glad to make her escape from the silent house and the tedious needlework which had occupied her since Frederick's funeral and had been boring her for days. When she came into the hall, he was waiting for her, dressed not in his elegant clothes but in a country gentleman's nankeen jacket and breeches, with stout leather boots. A footman hovered, waiting to help him into his greatcoat, then opened the door for them.

He took her hand and tucked it warmly in his arm, leading her down the long drive. Elizabeth was acutely conscious of the nearness of him and walked sedately, desperately trying to think of some topic of conversation. It was Robert who finally broke the silence.

'While I was in London, my Aunt Jane wrote and told me what a great help and support you have been to my mother,' he said. He was smiling down on her again in the old charming way. It was as though Honoria Wilshaw had never happened.

'I only did what it was my duty to do,' she said modestly.

'But it's the way you do it,' he said. 'Such a kind and willing companion. No wonder Mama is feeling so much better.' He pressed the hand that was in the crook of his arm and Elizabeth blushed. She was glad when they were at the gate and were away from prying eyes. They turned along the cart track which led to the village.

In spite of the bitter cold, there were already signs of spring. Once or twice they passed little clumps of primroses which were thrusting their pale green leaves through the grassy bank at the side of the path. Further on, near a little stream, they saw the tight buds of the catkins on the overhanging willow. All around them small birds flew in and out of trees, marking their territory, gathering nesting materials and singing to attract a mate. Even his brother's tragic death was not able to dim the bright morning sunshine, and his happiness at being with Elizabeth again. He had spent the last couple of weeks trying not to think about her. Trying to muffle the voice in his brain which murmured her name over and over to him. Trying to persuade himself that it was just the passing fancy of a young man for a young and pretty girl. And once he was married to someone suitable, what he felt for his mother's companion would be just a memory.

Gradually, however, he realized that Elizabeth would never be a distant memory. His heart was pounding because of her nearness. His body was increasingly aware of Elizabeth's hand nestling in the crook of his arm. He need only to turn his head and her mouth would be within kissing distance of his own. He remembered the delicious sensation when he'd claimed those lips for the first time and she'd surrendered so sweetly and completely. What an innocent she was. How soft and yielding . . . Oh God! *Stop thinking about it!*

He tried instead to think of some harmless, polite remark, but none came to him. He glanced carefully at her. She seemed solemn, engrossed in her own thoughts.

Neither of them was prepared for an unusually deep rut in the muddied cart track, hidden by a sprinkling of snow and much deeper than it appeared. Elizabeth tripped and her fall seemed inevitable as she sank up to her ankles in soft snow.

Robert's immediate reaction was to clasp an arm round her waist, as she held on to his arm, then to hold her up as she desperately tried to regain her balance. She reached up to him with her other arm and clung to his shoulder, trying to steady herself. She managed to stay on her feet, enjoying his warm clasp, but to her surprise Robert didn't release her. He looked deep into her eyes and raised the hand he was holding to his lips.

Her eyes were wide with apprehension and he could feel her shaking a little. Robert wondered briefly if she had any idea of how that wide-eyed look of hers shattered his resolve into little fragments. She held his gaze with his own, staring up at him, her lips slightly parted as she unconsciously relaxed against him. And Robert was lost. He knew he should let go of her at once but instead he threw all good intentions to one side and drew her closer still, absolutely overwhelmed by the temptation of those soft lips. Her arms still clung to him and she responded to the seductive pressure of his mouth instantly. Her lips opened like a flower unfolding and artlessly she pressed herself against him, striving to get even closer to his body.

He felt unsteady with the passion which was consuming him as he plunged his tongue into her soft, willing mouth, caressing it with sensual strokes. His desire rose uncontrollably at the pressure of her breasts through her clothes. He slipped his hands inside her cloak and began to fondle her body. He heard her groan as he began to stroke her with more intimacy.

Elizabeth was now completely lost in the pleasure of the moment and her body's responses to the sensations of his lovemaking, rejoicing in the pressure of his hard body and the compelling hands which pulled her ever closer and moved over her so sensually. He was no longer gentle and considerate but had become more strongly possessive and still she allowed herself to respond, even if it did set her trembling.

Robert had now almost reached the point of no return. He was aflame with a desire stronger than any he had ever known before. He was burning with the need to make love to her properly, to kiss and caress her until he had satisfied her completely. His own body was crying out with the need for fulfilment, his loins screaming to possess her and relieve his own pent-up passion.

With a groan of frustration, he let her go and looked down at her flushed face and red lips. They stood silently, facing each other, both of them too shaken to speak.

Elizabeth had been so lost in the passion of the moment that insanely, she wanted to declare her love for him. The words were pounding in her mind with every beat of her hasty heart: *'My dear love, I love you. Darling Robert, I love you . . . .'* She felt as though her brain would burst with the emotion she was not allowed to declare. She knew that if he had continued to make love to her like that, she would have surrendered to any demand he cared to make of her, would have given herself without a struggle, she wanted him so much. She stood, silent and shaken. She loved him. He would seduce first her body then her mind. He would break her heart and never marry her. He was destined to marry a wealthy girl, not such as she. Her cheeks burned and she averted her gaze. She stared out at the bleak countryside, noticing as though in a trance the Gascoine carriage returning along the road, taking Jane Gibson and Bradbury back home.

Robert, still bowled over by the strength of his own emotions, took a deep breath and said, 'Elizabeth, I . . . I never intended . . . You must know how much I love you. I'm sorry that I . . . gave way like that . . . I meant no insult. I love you very much.' His voice grew hoarse as the coach carrying his aunt and Bradbury drew nearer and the coachman slowed to give the ladies an opportunity to greet Sir Robert and Miss Winfield.

'I think I know what you intended, Sir Robert,' Elizabeth said bitterly, her voice shaking a little. 'A little romp with your mother's companion to while away an idle hour. I quite understand.'

Then the carriage stopped. 'Damn!' he said loudly. 'Elizabeth, please. Please let me . . . ' But no one heard as the coach stopped and the steps were lowered to take them up, and the ladies were full of polite conversation. Robert looked at her, willing her to look at him, but she pressed her lips together so that she wouldn't humiliate herself by crying and turned away, gazing out of the window until they arrived home.

Robert was outwardly calm but seething inwardly with frustration and thwarted desire. Why didn't he mention how he felt about her first? He had never felt this insane passion in the whole of his life. His whole body ached with the pent-up emotions of love and sexual longing. He wondered if he dare beg her pardon again for losing control like that. His only saving grace was that he wanted to marry her and care for her for the rest of his life. He looked across at her and saw the pain in her eyes. He realized with a pang that when he had pressed kisses on her this afternoon he hadn't mentioned marriage. She must think him a swine, a hardened rake who just wanted to take advantage of her, just like his late lamented brother, Frederick. He was a crass fool, that he was. He'd never even asked her. He must set this right at once.

But they were already at the house and his Aunt Jane and Bradbury were still murmuring platitudes about the villagers and the new babies who had been born since they last visited. They were met by the usual servants and he watched while Elizabeth hurried upstairs to her room. He was powerless to stop her without making the devil of a scene in front of his aunt and her companion. He strode into the study and threw himself into a chair, clenching his fists in anger over his inept wooing.

Elizabeth, meanwhile, had reached her room and taken off her bonnet and cloak and crouched to warm her hands at the fire, her mind still racing. If only he would . . . If only he would what? Seduce her? Make an offer for her? He would never do that. Her face flamed as she acknowledged to herself how little effort it would take on his part to get her to be his mistress. A little more wooing and a few words of love and she would have been his, with or without marriage. She asked the maid to bring her supper to her room. She couldn't eat any of it, but merely drank a little of the lemonade and then removed her clothes and washed herself all over, as though to remove any taint of the emotions she'd felt for Robert Gascoine.

14

The next day brought a visit that would change Elizabeth's life for ever. It all started mundanely enough when she'd woken heavy eyed after a restless night. She had preserved her usual helpful courtesy with her employer, however, when she went to receive her orders for the day. Lady Gascoine was feeling much better and desired Elizabeth to attend her on a visit to Mr and Mrs Atherton. It was a courtesy call, and a small step on the journey to some sort of recovery for Lady Gascoine. Jane Gibson and Bradbury were in attendance and, as they were ushered into Emma Atherton's drawing-room, Elizabeth noticed with some interest that Isabella Mason was also present.

She was as always dressed with restraint in a dove-grey watered silk dress which had a very modest neckline and long sleeves. But it was Isabella's general demeanour which Elizabeth found so arresting. Gone was the haunted, sad expression and the drooping shoulders of the profoundly depressed young woman she had seen at the funeral. Instead, Isabella stood as tall as her five foot four allowed. She was not beaming in any unseemly way but was calm and composed and was accompanied by her cousin Georgiana and David Atherton. It seemed to Elizabeth that David Atherton was behaving very circumspectly, attentive to all his mama's guests and only betraying by the most subtle of signs his special interest in his former childhood companion.

Lady Gascoine was made much of as befitted her station and was very gracious in return to Mr and Mrs Atherton. She made an effort to be affable to Isabella, although Elizabeth was aware what it must cost her to act so calmly towards the young woman who was to have been her daughter-in-law. As for Georgiana, she greeted Lady Gascoine naturally in spite of the other woman's recent bereavement.

'How do you do, Lady Gascoine, and how are you bearing up with the weather as cold as it is? Shall we be seeing the spring soon, do you think, or must we shiver until next June?'

Everyone smiled at this and Lady Gascoine, who had been very solemn to start with, responded to the young woman's charm and began to relax somewhat. Elizabeth noticed the look of relief on Mrs Atherton's face and the way that David now stepped forward to welcome the visitors, and attend to

Lady Gascoine's comfort.

The talk now became pretty general and they started to discuss the celebrations for Lydia's sixteenth birthday. 'It will be a fairly quiet affair,' Isabella said. 'I know Mama is hoping you won't find it unsuitable to attend, dear ma'am.'

Lady Gascoine was admirably well composed and merely said, 'We shall see, my dear. Life must go on and a birthday is important to a girl of sixteen.'

Everyone smiled politely at this and the conversation turned once more to the unusual inclement spring weather and the effect it might have on crops and cattle. Under cover of the general buzz of conversation, Isabella Mason whispered shyly, 'Elizabeth, I know you truly wish to be my friend, so I am going to confide my secret in you.'

Elizabeth looked at her questioningly. For the first time since she had met her, she felt Isabella Mason looked young and happy.

'David . . . Mr Atherton and I . . . that is . . .'

'Oh, Isabella.'

'Yes, he has asked Papa if we may become engaged, after we've observed six months of mourning for Frederick, of course, and Papa has consented.'

'Oh, Isabella, I'm so happy for you.'

Elizabeth knew that Isabella would eventually find happiness with David Atherton.

Just as the Gascoine family were about to take their leave, Mr and Mrs Mason were announced. Elizabeth observed the flicker of embarrassment from Lady Gascoine as they entered the room, but this was quickly forgotten as Edward Mason strode up to her and said in a low voice, 'Elizabeth, my dear, has Joseph Grimshaw been in touch with you yet?'

'Why, no, sir.'

'Well, I'm sure he will. There has been a development in the George Baines affair, which you should know about.'

Intriguingly, that was all he would say about the matter. Elizabeth left with Lady Gascoine, Jane Gibson and Bradbury, and the coachman quickly conveyed them home.

Elizabeth was confused by her conflicting emotions. One half of her was still determined to find out more of her true identity. The other half was still consumed with emotion at her last meeting with Robert. What game was he playing? What did he want? He seemed so genuinely attracted to her as she was to him yet . . . In any case, she was a fool to think that a man in his position would feel emotional ties to such as herself. He probably considered her only fit for a casual affair, a swift tumble before his real life started as a married man with a suitably well-connected young woman.

But all thoughts of Robert were driven from her mind half an hour later, as she sat sewing with Lady Gascoine in the south drawing-room. Luncheon was over and Jane Gibson and Bradbury had retired to their rooms, leaving the house unnaturally empty. A young footman came in to enquire whether Lady Gascoine would permit him to admit a tradesman of the lower orders, who carried a message for Miss Elizabeth Baines. He coughed and begged pardon.

'Miss Winfield, ma'am, that is,' he corrected himself.

Lady Gascoine exchanged glances with Elizabeth. 'Read your note, Elizabeth and decide for yourself if you wish to see this person,' she said.

As she took the note from the silver salver, Elizabeth thought of Mr Mason and his rather cryptic message, and was surprised to find she was trembling.

If Miss Elizabeth Winfield, last heard of at Tollyvara in Ireland, would contact Messrs Abbot, Laing and Jordan, Church St Norwich, she will hear something to her advantage.

It was the firm of solicitors who had acted for Sarah Ann Winfield all those years ago. Silently, she passed the note to Lady Gascoine, who read it and nodded to the footman to give permission to show in Joseph Grimshaw.

He was dressed neatly as always though today he was not in uniform, but still carried his stout stick and bowed politely to Her Ladyship and to Elizabeth.

'As you know, ladies,' he began very deferentially, 'I have been making enquiries as to the whereabouts of a certain little child, as disappeared wi' no trace at the Ridgeway Goose Fair, fourteen years ago to be exac'.'

Elizabeth looked at him more closely. After Susan Benson's recollections the name 'Ridgeway' now meant very much more to her. Elizabeth only had a hazy memory of the fateful visit to the fair with her nursemaid, but suddenly and excitingly she felt this man was going to impart something terribly important to her.

'I'm looking at your hair, miss.'

'My hair?'

'Yes, the colour, miss. My enquiries showed it to be the self same colour as that of Sarah Ann Martin, as married your pa in 1787. But his hair was the opposite, as you know. Black as coal.'

'Black as coal?'

'Yes, miss and so was your Grandpa Martin's.'

'Grandpa Martin's?' she echoed again.

'Yes, Miss Winfield. Sarah Ann Martin. Your Mama was not an orphan as most people supposed. She was a respectable, gently born girl who refused to marry the man her parents had chosen for her and she ran away. She ended up as the dressmaker and seamstress in the village of Copthorne. She settled down there and met your pa, Thomas Winfield, and love bloomed as they say.'

'But . . . but . . . George Baines?'

'He also loved your ma, miss. Disappointed he were when she upped and married your pa. His revenge was to bide his time and then at the right opportunity, kidnap you and spirit you away to Ireland.'

Elizabeth sat motionless, her head bowed. That explained so many things. She had no feelings of self-pity for the abuse which had blighted her childhood, only a tremendous sadness at the loss of her parents. Try as she might, she could remember very little of them, except for that haunting shadowy memory of the sensation of a soft touch and a sense of sweet perfume, wafting fleetingly over her.

'And this letter?' she asked quietly. 'What does it mean?'

'It means, Miss, as they solicitors, Abbot, Laing and Jordan, have already been in touch with your Grandpa Martin and wish you to pay a visit to their offices in Norwich. It's about a legacy as I understand it.'

Elizabeth was too bemused to take in what Mr Grimshaw was saying, but Lady Gascoine understood perfectly and suddenly threw off the lethargy which had affected her since Frederick's death, and became very brisk.

'This is most fascinating, Elizabeth. Of course you must go and see Abbot, Laing and the other one, my dear. Fortunately, I am not in shock now and I cannot be a weak straw. There is only one person I could trust to see you safely to the lawyers and that is, myself. No,' she said imperiously, as Elizabeth opened her mouth to protest. 'No, it is only right and seemly. Robert is very busy today. I have no husband and you have no father or brother. It is my duty to ensure that any legal matters are explained to you and should you have been fortunate enough to have come into a modest legacy, I shall get my own man of business to advise you about putting it in a bank account, against some rainy day in the future.'

She noticed Joseph Grimshaw smiling at

283

her as the other ladies crowded round to add their hearty best wishes to Lady Gascoine's, as she stood bemused and unbelieving. As if in a dream, she got through the morning and after luncheon she went to her room to prepare herself for the visit.

Lady Gascoine's abigail was to accompany them and the coach was brought round straight after luncheon. They spoke little on the way to the law firm, but Elizabeth's thoughts were whirling chaotically round in her head.

'Would you wish me to accompany you for the interview?' Lady Gascoine asked, when they arrived at the offices in Church Street. 'If not, Maria and I will go to the book shop and return for you at about four o'clock.'

'Thank you, ma'am . . . I feel I can manage . . . on my own but I thank you.'

Lady Gascoine nodded approvingly and Elizabeth was set down on the same imposing steps where Thomas Winfield had stood all those years ago.

Old Tobias Cobham was long since deceased but Mr Abbot, now the senior partner with the firm, was all that was affable as he greeted her very courteously and begged her to be seated. He indicated Mr Grimshaw, whom she nodded to.

'First, my dear young lady,' he began

somewhat pompously, 'I have in the next room a person who wishes to be reunited with you. None other than . . . ' He paused for dramatic effect. 'None other than your grandfather, Mr Andrew Martin, who has never seen you.'

Elizabeth stared at him in total bewilderment, but Mr Abbot, like a conjuror producing a rabbit from a top hat, opened the door with a flourish and bade Mr Martin to 'step in, please'.

The elderly gentleman was tall and distinguished looking. He still had a good head of hair, which had once been black but was now heavily streaked with silver. In his hand he carried a small picture wrapped in oiled cloth. His side whiskers gleamed against the soft pink of his skin and the eyes beneath the craggy silver brows were a bright, almost piercing blue. Elizabeth was not prepared for what was coming next.

For when he came face to face with her, he gave a startled exclamation and stepped back suddenly, grabbing the edge of Mr Abbot's desk with his free hand to steady himself.

'Lord have mercy on us,' he whispered hoarsely. 'She is my Sar'ann to the life.'

While Elizabeth continued to gaze at him he stepped forward again, unwrapped the picture carefully and held it up at the side of

Elizabeth's face. 'She's the image of her dear mother, God rest her,' he exclaimed and his bright blue eyes looked as though they would fill with tears. Silently, he handed her the picture and Elizabeth studied it curiously. It was a likeness of a young woman of roughly the same age, with a fresh open face and bright golden hair. For an instant it almost seemed as if her heart had stopped and she suddenly felt faint. The girl in the picture really was herself. Apart from the clothes, which were somewhat old-fashioned and countrified, this girl really could be Elizabeth Winfield.

'Sir, I don't know what to say,' she faltered.

'No need to say anything, child. This picture says it all.' The tears which had threatened earlier now began to appear in earnest. He bowed his head, overcome by strong emotion, and wiped the back of his hand across his eyes.

'No need to say anything. This is the final proof if proof were needed,' Joseph Grimshaw said to Mr Abbot. 'This young woman is Sarah Ann Martin's only child and the only surviving heir of Sarah and her husband, Thomas, both now deceased.'

'Please be seated, Miss Winfield, and you, gentlemen,' Mr Abbot said to the assembled company. 'This young lady is indeed your long-lost granddaughter, and I'm sure you will want to get more closely acquainted. All in good time. First, I have further news to impart to Miss Winfield.' He turned to Elizabeth. 'Shortly after she married your father, Sarah Ann Winfield came into a substantial amount of money from her Great Aunt Elizabeth. During their married life together, Thomas Winfield used the money sensibly. He paid off all his father's debt to Lord Maversham and worked hard to make the farm prosperous again. When he died he left a fortune of twenty thousand pounds, which has been deposited with this firm since his death. With prudent investments in consols, his original capital, with interest accrued, has grown to thirty-four thousand to be exact.'

He made a castle with his fingers. 'This will ensure you are very comfortably off, my dear. This should mean an income of at least a thousand a year. Yes, at least a thousand,' he repeated, and looked at Elizabeth to note her reaction, but she was too numb to take it in.

'In addition, there is a comfortable and substantial property, which is also bequeathed to you,' he said. 'Now, my dear, you will need time to digest these facts and possibly become better acquainted with your grand-papa.' Mr Abbot smiled approvingly as the silver-haired gentleman rose from his seat and went to give Elizabeth a hug. Both were too emotional for speech, and remained in each other's arms for several seconds, before Lady Gascoine knocked on the door and came to claim Elizabeth for the journey home.

If Elizabeth had been fairly quiet on the way to Norwich, she was totally silent on the way back to Waringham. There had been more tears when she had parted from Andrew Martin, but he was lodging in Norwich and would be accompanying her to Copthorne, as soon as Lady Gascoine was gracious enough to arrange it. Elizabeth huddled wearily in a corner of the carriage, too overwrought to discuss the sudden change in her fortunes. After a few attempts to get her to talk, and making no headway at all, Her Ladyship laughed and said, 'Good gracious, Elizabeth, this is as difficult as drawing teeth. Can you really be so blasé as to have no comment to make on the momentous happenings of this afternoon?'

Elizabeth was obliged to smile at this, but it was still hard for her to explain her own confused emotions. The shock and sadness at seeing a picture of her dead mother and the obvious delight and affection of her newly acquired grandfather had literally rendered her speechless and Lady Gascoine had to contain her soul in patience. It was only later, in the comparative calm of the south drawing-room, that with many hesitations and emotional pauses Elizabeth managed to relate all that had happened at her interview with Mr Abbot. Once Her Ladyship knew the whole story, she was at first excited and then thoughtful at Elizabeth's good fortune.

She said very little except, 'I realize now that you were too surprised to say very much and, in any case, it wouldn't do to let Maria or any of the servants know about your private business. We must give some thought to your future, though. The life of a lady's companion for a young lady of substance is perhaps not very suitable.' She looked askance at Elizabeth and smiled kindly at her.

'I . . . I don't know, ma'am. That is, I . . . I'm not sure of what I will do.'

'Suffice it for now that we will plan to go to Copthorne and take a look at the home you have inherited. If you will allow me, my dear, I should very much like to go with you. You may need a supportive friend and I could do with a little excursion.'

'How kind you are, ma'am. I didn't expect . . . I . . . Thank you.'

'That's settled then,' Lady Gascoine said briskly. 'We've been somewhat quiet of late . . . since Frederick . . . since the funeral

. . . It will be good for us to have a diversion. It should be an adventure, in fact.'

That evening, Lady Gascoine was to attend a quiet dinner with the Masons but Elizabeth pleaded a bad headache and begged to be excused. Lady Gascoine was in an exceptionally good mood and laughed, saying, 'We ladies and our headaches, Elizabeth. Where would we be without such an excuse?'

But it was not merely an excuse. Elizabeth lay on her bed with a real headache, the sort that seemed to thump with the rhythm of her heart, and in spite of the momentous events of the day she found herself in low spirits. The house was unaccountably empty when Lady Gascoine had departed and after she had been served with a light supper and some wine, the servants had disappeared. She sat alone in the small breakfast room, pushing the food around her plate, until it was cold. Then she sipped her claret. Everything outside was still. The garden was dark and there were no natural sounds. Not wanting to disturb the servants, she decided not to ring for a footman to mend the fire but instead crouched down and stirred the coals into a more cheerful blaze.

She was startled by a sound from the hall, and suddenly Robert entered the room.

'You,' he said. 'Where is Mama?'

She curtsyed and said. 'Her Ladyship is dining with Mr and Mrs Mason.'

He looked puzzled and said, 'You do not attend Mama, then.'

'No, sir, I have the headache and feel . . . out of sorts. I shall go to my room directly.'

He looked at her more closely then and bowed. 'I'm sorry to hear it,' was all he said and he went to stand by the fire.

He was dressed in the height of fashion this evening, in a blue superfine coat and buff-coloured pantaloons, with ruffled shirt and high collar. His cravat was tied exquisitely and he looked for all the world a complete dandy. Had Elizabeth not known better, she would have thought him a complete fashion plate. The clear grey eyes studying her were, however, too intelligent and observant for a mere fop.

They continued to gaze at each other until Elizabeth began to feel uncomfortable and said, 'Lady Gascoine was not expecting you to dine at home this evening, sir.'

'No, but it is of no moment.'

Elizabeth continued to look at him without speaking. His eyes took in the table set with the uneaten supper.

Elizabeth stood up. 'If you will excuse me, Sir Robert, I shall retire to my room.'

She made for the door, but he caught her arm.

'Please don't go yet. I want to talk to you.'

She faced him angrily, the thumping in her head much worse. 'But I have nothing to say to you, sir.'

'Then please grant me the opportunity to say something to *you*,' he said pleasantly. 'Please sit down and hear me out.'

She sat down but turned away and stared fixedly at the fire grate, her lips pressed together, her eyes opened as wide as possible to try and stop herself from showing any emotion.

He gazed at her averted profile and said evenly, 'Please don't quarrel with me, Elizabeth. When you first came to Hawton House with my Aunt Jane I knew that you were a special type of girl. I tried — clumsily, I admit — to beg you not to be spoilt by the vapid missish airs so common in young ladies who are educated in establishments like that of Miss Hanbury's. I wanted you to remain the shy girlish beauty with the soft brogue as you had at our first meeting.' He smiled at her and attempted to take her hand but Elizabeth sprang to her feet and answered angrily.

'Honoria Wilshaw was educated at Miss Hanbury's. There is nothing shy about her, and yet . . . and yet . . . ' Tears filled her eyes and threatened to spill over. She floundered to a halt, silenced by the expression in his eyes.

His hand fell uselessly by his side and he continued more gently. 'I knew when I fastened that pearl necklace for you that I was in danger of falling in love with you. I, a second son, who needed to fulfil Mama's ambition for me to make an advantageous match with a wealthy young lady, fell for a poor but adorable lady's companion. I have tried to follow the path of common sense and fall in with the conventions of society, but I cannot let you go Elizabeth. You are the one I want to be my wife. No one else will do.'

Elizabeth, still smouldering over the affront she had felt at Honoria's interest in him, burst out, 'Now you dare speak to me of marriage, but only because of Sir Frederick's death. You've realized you must offer more than a carte blanche in order to have your way with the humble lady's maid. But you can afford it now, can you not? You can afford to buy anything you want, including 'the shy girlish beauty' from the bogs of Ireland. But this is not entirely my background.' She turned and looked at him fully, the blood pounding through her head. 'I tell you, sir, I wouldn't have you for the world. I'd refuse you even if you were the Angel Gabriel himself, so I would.' Her mounting fury caused Elizabeth to momentarily drop Arabella Hanbury's elocution rules in favour of Kate Molloy's mode of speech.

Even though he smiled inwardly at this, Robert was hurt and humiliated by her instant rejection of him.

'You obviously have no opinion of my love, or of me,' he said. Wounded pride made his voice austere. The warmth of his proposal was now dissipated and he reverted to the kind of ascetic cold voice that was entirely his own. They were now facing each other, and he said, 'We have spoken plainly. I will wish you a good evening.' At the door he turned and said with the ghost of a smile, 'And I hope your headache is soon better.'

He left the room and Elizabeth went up to bed. She lay unable to sleep. Her head still pounded and throbbed. The events of the day still crowded and jostled together as she tried to empty her mind. First Sir Robert's proposal. It seemed inadequate and out of character. She thought of other more romantic episodes and sighed.

Nevertheless, she was forced to recognize that it *was* a proposal. Probably a ploy to get her into bed. No. She was ashamed of this thought. No. She believed that Robert was honourable and a gentleman. How then to explain his dalliance with Honoria?

Hot tears pricked at her eyelids and she closed her eyes tightly, determined to think of something else. But it was no use. Her thoughts kept returning to the spring walk they had taken together, when he had kissed her so passionately. Then she thought of his obvious pain and humiliation when she had so summarily rejected him this evening. Well, at least she could now take herself off and never see him again. She owed sufficient loyalty to Lady Gascoine and Jane Gibson to wait long enough for a replacement companion to be installed, but after that she had the legacy and the house at Copthorne. They would open up a new life of freedom and independence. She choked on a sob as she thought of life without Robert. Did she want independence and freedom if it meant never seeing him again? She was being ridiculous. Why should she fret over a man? After all, she told herself, you may be sure he doesn't fret over you.

She deliberately willed her thoughts to the journey to Copthorne with Lady Gascoine where she was to meet with her grandpapa again. Her Ladyship said it was bound to be an adventure. How much of one she had no way of telling.

15

There was no sign of Robert at breakfast the next morning, which was understandable because he was already out looking at the fences in the oldest field with a view to having them renewed. After breakfast the two women sat discussing the legacy and their visit to Copthorne. Lady Gascoine said that there were two men of rather dubious appearance asking the whereabouts of the village of Copthorne when she had visited the church on Sunday. They had mentioned the public ale house at Ridgeway. She dismissed them out of hand. They were only innocent travellers who had lost their way. She had no fears for their journey but looked on it as a delightful experience.

'We shall go when the coach is ready, and be back in the same day,' said Lady Gascoine.

Elizabeth was surprised at Lady Gascoine's much more relaxed approach, to what she saw as a threat to herself, as well as the intolerable burden of her loss. She was pleased that her excitement at the legacy seemed to have infected Lady Gascoine as well as herself.

The March weather was fine but blustery as the women went out to enter the coach. Maria, Lady Gascoine's abigail and her experience of chatting with her employer was a novelty which Elizabeth enjoyed thoroughly. The experience did much to rouse Elizabeth from her melancholy feelings and for the first time she almost felt like Lady Gascoine's social equal. This must be the result of suddenly becoming a woman of substance, she thought wryly.

She discovered a side to Lady Gascoine which was quite different from the more usual one of a kind and dignified employer, or fond mama, mourning her eldest son. For a few hours, Mary Gascoine became more like a charming and humorous aunt and, for the first time, seemed to relax in Elizabeth's company as though they were friends. Maria was by the window busily knitting and Lady Gascoine regaled Elizabeth with reminiscences of her youth and her life with Sir William.

'Ours was not an obvious love match, Elizabeth. Young people are so fortunate nowadays. Parents look with favour on a child's desire to marry for love, but it has not always been so. My parents chose Sir William for me and of course in those days one would never dream of flouting one's parents' wishes.'

Elizabeth said nothing, thinking of Robert and his Mama's wish to see him wed to Honoria. No doubt he would do as she wished, she thought bitterly. Aloud she said, 'But Miss Gibson has never wed, has she, ma'am?'

There was a pause, and Lady Gascoine lowered her voice somewhat. 'Jane was the rebel of the family, my dear. She refused to have anything to do with the marriage mart and ambitious mamas who sought out eligible husbands for their daughters, at any cost to the girl's happiness. 'Meat market', Jane called it, and would have none of it, although . . . '

'Although?'

Lady Gascoine sighed and gave a little smile. 'Although I always felt that she had a soft spot for William.' She gave herself a little shake. 'But in any case, ours turned out to be a love match in the end. My parents chose wisely for me, Elizabeth, and my husband and I had nearly thirty years of happiness before he was so sadly taken from me.'

Elizabeth thought it time to change to a more cheerful subject and mentioned how much she was looking forward to seeing the farmhouse at Copthorne.

'I have no memory of it, ma'am, but I shall delight in exploring the house and the area round the village.'

'Well, I am sure we shall be at our destination about mid-afternoon, but you are young my dear. You have all the time in the world to explore to your heart's content. It would be wrong of me to envy you your vitality and freshness. I am utterly delighted at your good fortune and I am sure that once you have settled down in your own establishment, you will not lack for suitors. You will be able to have your pick of all the decent eligible young men in Norfolk.' She sighed, regretfully. 'If only Robert would get on with choosing a bride for himself and starting up his own nursery. I long to be a grandmama, my dear, and I had hoped that he and Honoria . . . but . . . but he is as obstinate as his Aunt Jane . . . Determined on nothing less than a love match, foolish boy.'

Elizabeth said nothing and Maria kept her head down studiously over her knitting. Although her mind was in a whirl at this, there seemed nothing more to say. The brief interlude of closeness with Lady Gascoine was now over and the three women retreated into their own thoughts and settled down to an uneventful ride. The Gascoine carriage was well upholstered and comfortable.

Gradually, as they travelled the light became duller. No doubt the darkness would be early today. The coachman saw the lights of Copthorne gleaming ahead and whipped up the horses for the last leg of their journey. The weather had turned distinctly colder and the coach was full of the sound of strong wind and the creaking of the horses' harnesses. Unable to see in the dim light of the carriage, Maria had put her knitting to one side, sensing they were near their journey's end. Elizabeth roused herself and sat up straighter, trying to see through the gloom. Ridgeway Hill was but a short way from Copthorne now, and she had only just gathered herself together when there was a loud inarticulate shout and the coach juddered and swerved. There was the sound of creaking wood put under intolerable strain by the coachman as he suddenly jerked the horses to a halt.

He had the presence of mind to yell 'Foot-pads, my lady!' before one of the black-cloaked felons knocked him to the ground.

'Get the bags out,' one of the louts ordered him and gave him a vicious kick as he went to do as he was told. The luggage was ransacked and Lady Gascoine's good scarf was got out with a grunt of triumph. Lady Gascoine clutched at her throat when the highwaymen wrenched open the carriage door and thrust their faces inside. From somewhere at the side of the road a wild animal slithered through the undergrowth and one of the men turned quickly to look and turned back again. In that split second Elizabeth was able to make a rapid assessment of the assailants. In spite of the rapid and businesslike way that the highwaymen had been able to take the rings and brooches off Lady Gascoine and any money she carried, these were not professional highwaymen, she was sure of that. There were two of them. One had a makeshift disguise made out of a bandanna tied round the lower part of his face, while the other was wearing a soft grey hat pulled well over his face.

The one with the bandanna thrust his ugly unshaven face towards Lady Gascoine's. 'Outside, you,' he said and gestured with his gun, an old-fashioned pellet gun used by farmers to shoot crows. Trembling visibly, she did as she was told, closely followed by Maria, who crossed herself and whispered her prayers. Then it was Elizabeth's turn.

'Now you,' he ordered. His companion was armed only with a stout stick and also carried a hessian bag, which had obviously once contained flour. As she obeyed, Elizabeth's mind was racing. These weren't local lads. Their accents were rough Irish, reminiscent of the local tinkers that she remembered from her youth. Reminiscent of the Molloy brothers, in fact. She felt a sudden flash of recognition for the one with the bandanna. It could be . . . it *must be* . . . Tom Molloy. The two of them looked scared underneath their show of brutality, and she stood quietly by as Lady Gascoine removed her diamond ear-rings and pulled off her rings.

'In the bag,' Tom Molloy snarled, and immediately Lady Gascoine dropped them in, her face agonized as she pulled off Sir William's betrothal and wedding rings. Then he waved his gun at them and barked, 'Raise your 'ands, all of yer, or yer'll be for it.' The plan, devised by James Preston, had not involved robbery, merely the abduction of the Baines' girl and the smuggling of her back to Ireland, but Molloy was an opportunist.

Obediently, the coachman and the three women raised their hands. 'Now get back in the coach,' he growled and they did as they were told. 'Now you take us to the Black Lion on the Ridgeway road.' He gestured with his gun and the coachman had to obey.

The Black Lion was less than three miles from Copthorne, yet it could have been on the other side of the world for all Elizabeth knew. It stood on a desolate and isolated stretch of road and was the haunt of thieves and whores. If indeed she had any inkling of its existence, Lady Gascoine had no knowledge of its reputation as a low-lived flash house, where the landlord received and processed stolen goods. The bag of jewels was drawn tightly closed and given to the youngest boy to look after. He was also given the gun and left to guard the coachman while the other one pushed the women inside the inn. Judging by the noise and the rabble in the bar, the landlord was doing good business this evening, but no one looked round at all as the three women were shoved into the private parlour to be met by none other than James Preston.

Elizabeth shivered with cold and fear as she recognized him. He still wore the customary uniform, in accordance with his rank, but he was unkempt and unshaven as though he had been awake all night. His neck cloth hung untied beneath his stubbled chin, and he scowled at her with the utmost hatred. He thrust his leering face near to hers and she could smell the rank breath of him. She looked at his eyes, which were blank with the vicious lewdness of his character. All the pent-up hatred and aggression which as a refined young lady she had to stifle and deny rose up within her like bile and with no thought of danger, she launched herself towards the door.

He grabbed her from behind and held her arms to her sides, almost suffocating her. Elizabeth struggled and thrust her foot backwards, trying to kick him in the groin and make him double up with pain. But it was no use. He merely swore and tightened his grip, while he glared at Lady Gascoine and Maria and cursed his accomplices.

'What's the meaning of this, Molloy?' he snarled. 'Who told you to bring in this crowd? It was only the little beauty I wanted. Get rid of the others.'

Molloy scowled and shuffled his feet. 'Get rid of them where?' he muttered. He hadn't been paid for his part in the kidnap yet; still, he had the jewels and Preston didn't know that.

'Outside,' Preston snarled. 'Keep them away from here. These old birds aren't going to fly anywhere.'

He smiled evilly as Molloy pushed the two women out of the room. Both women resisted, casting anguished glances towards Elizabeth, trying to stay for her sake and protect her. It was impossible. They were taken back to the coach and held prisoner with the driver. Tom Molloy took the opportunity to leave the hostages and he went to join the rabble in the taproom, hoping to meet a competent fence.

Preston turned his attention to Elizabeth. 'Now for our unfinished business. First, I shall pour us some wine.' He poured two from the almost empty bottle and handed one to her. Immediately, Elizabeth put it down.

'What do you mean?'

He'd released her, but he stood between her and the door. She was trapped.

'I mean I'm entitled to my dues,' he snarled.

'Your dues?'

Elizabeth didn't understand what he meant. She thought of the jewels Tom Molloy had taken from Lady Gascoine. 'Do you mean Her Ladyship's jewels?'

'NO! You bitch!' Preston lunged towards her and cracked her head against the wall, leaving her breathless and weak.

She gasped and struggled to breathe, inhaled the filthy smell of his stale breath and tried ineffectively to turn her head away. Preston cursed loudly and slammed her head against the wall again. Her eyes filled with tears of pain.

'No, you filthy little Irish whore, I mean my bride price. The money I paid to that bastard, Baines. It's time to receive full value for the money I paid him and by God, I'm going to have it.'

'I . . . I don't know what you mean.'

'You soon will.' He moved his hand to caress her throat, sensually and obscenely. 'We have all night. I shall have every last penny of my money's worth from your white bitch's body.'

'No, you won't!' With a tremendous effort of will Elizabeth forgot the pain in her head and flung him off, picked up the empty wine bottle and made for the door. She wrenched open the door and he staggered backwards, making a wild bid to catch at a table to steady himself. She was through the pub and out of the building by the time he had regained his balance. He cursed and scrambled after her but Elizabeth was off and across the yard towards the coach. It was now pitch dark but she had the advantage of knowing exactly where it was and which way led to safety.

As she got nearer to Lady Gascoine's carriage, some instinct warned her to go forward very quietly. With the carelessness of youth, Tom Molloy lingered in the taproom of the Black Lion, hoping to meet someone who would give him a fair price for the jewels his younger brother was guarding for him. The younger Molloy boy was just inside the coach, supposedly keeping an eye on the coachman and the two women.

With the advantage of surprise, Elizabeth

used the bottle to fetch the youngest Molloy boy a cracking blow to his shoulder, which momentarily stunned him. The coachman, seeing his chance, now sprang from his perch and seized the gun. The younger Molloy boy leaped out of the carriage and punched Elizabeth in the face. The blow made her gasp for breath and she saw coloured lights as she sank to the ground at the coachman's feet. The younger Molloy boy, feeling outnumbered, ran with all haste to tell his brother and henchman all about it. The two women were bundled unceremoniously into the coach, and the coachman hurriedly threw the bag of jewels towards Lady Gascoine and they were off.

Elizabeth's legs shook, and she raised a tentative hand to her split mouth, feeling the warm blood against her cold fingers. Her burning tears dripped down her cheeks to sting her torn lips as Lady Gascoine and Maria carefully wrapped a cloak around her. Her ears were singing as she went from near fainting to terror as she thought of Captain Prestons' hateful presence.

When they finally reached the haven of Coppice Farm, it was to find Elizabeth's grandfather waiting for them. He had already organized a team of village women to clean the house for him until it shone and a good supper had been prepared for them. He was about to ask them if they'd had a good journey, but the question died on his lips and his blue eyes misted over at the sight of Elizabeth's injured face.

'Who ... has done this to you?' he managed. His shoulders sagged and his face drooped. Suddenly, he looked like an old man.

'We met with footpads, Grandpapa.' Elizabeth forced the words through her chattering teeth and split lip. She had time to tell her grandpapa of the Molloys and Captain Preston and then promptly fainted, and Maria chose that moment to have a fit of the vapours and had to be given *sal volatile*.

At the end of the evening only Her Ladyship had partaken of the excellent supper. Andrew Martin sat in the downstairs sitting-room with Lady Gascoine and the maid. He was shocked and horrified at the events that had unfolded and which had been relayed to him by the Bow Street Runner. He remembered his daughter vividly. He had learned his lesson at a hard school. He realized now that it was too late, how stiff-necked his pride had been. To let his only child be robbed of his grandchild and then the grandchild be in danger did not bear thinking about. He informed the still rattled coachman that he was to ride to Waringham and tell his master, Sir Robert Gascoine, that he must come to Coppice Farm without delay.

★   ★   ★

Robert had spent the day riding round various farms which the farm manager felt might need an input of money and resource to make them viable. After a busy day, it was usually a pleasure to eat dinner at home but the absence of both Elizabeth and his mama meant he had no company this evening, unless he was prepared to go and seek it elsewhere. He wandered aimlessly round the drawing-room. His thoughts were all of Elizabeth and he remembered how taken she'd been with the statue of Diana the Huntress when she'd first seen it. He remembered her open and naïve expression as she said that it was an ideal of womanly beauty. Elizabeth herself had that same brave, open spirit and physical loveliness, he thought. He missed her presence and longed so much for her to be back. He knew she had gone with his mother to Copthorne but was unclear as to why. Sighing, he took the note his mama had left him out of his pocket.

My dear Robert
Tomorrow we travel to Copthorne and
will be gone before you read this. Miss
Winfield has received further news of her
parents and family, who it has been
discovered hailed originally from Cop-
pice Farm. I am determined to help her
pursue this connection and achieve her
inheritance. We shall be back in time for
supper this evening. Meanwhile I remain
your ever loving Mama.

Robert wondered idly what Elizabeth's
'inheritance' could be. He was only vaguely
aware of Edward Mason's enquiries about his
mama's companion and wished he'd paid
more attention when it was being discussed.
One thing was for sure, he thought as he
thrust the note back into his pocket, he
couldn't get Elizabeth out of his mind.

The time passed in a sort of limbo; he was
unable to concentrate on a book or read
seriously the sheaf of accounts left him by the
farm manager. He cursed himself for allowing
Elizabeth to quarrel with him. She must think
him a complete oaf. As soon as she returned
he would set matters to rights. As it grew later
still, the absence of Elizabeth and his mama
became more worrying.

At 6.30, Wilkins served him dinner. With

absolutely no appetite, he pushed his food about and left it. Even the fine claret laid down by Sir William and brought to the table by the butler was unable to tempt him. He had half a glass and then sat staring at the ruby-coloured liquid, brooding over his inexcusable folly in letting her go like that.

In the kitchen, Wilkins the butler was preparing to entertain a lady. He'd helped himself to a nice platter of cold roast beef and a side of home-cured ham. Mrs Ruddock was a tidy little widow woman and Wilkins had high hopes she would say she was willing. Especially if he could prime her with a drop of Sir Robert's claret, he thought. He took a peek into the dining-room. Sir Robert sat alone at the long mahogany dining-table, gazing gloomily at his wine, swirling it aimlessly round and round in the glass.

What he needs is the love of a good woman, Wilkins thought, smug at the prospect of his own good fortune. 'Will there be anything else, sir?' he said and bowed, his eyes on the almost full bottle of claret.

'No, you may clear now. I'm afraid Her Ladyship and Miss Winfield must be dining out — '

They were both startled to hear a furious knocking on the door and, when it was opened, the sight of the normally stolid coachman stumbling in with a frantic expression on his face and the news of the attack on his mama and her companions.

Robert raced down the steps to mount his horse, leaving his groom to seek rest and refreshment in the kitchen.

16

Robert would never forget that journey as long as he lived. Barely pausing long enough to give orders to the coachman to get a good supper from the kitchen and a good night's sleep before he rejoined them, he ordered the horse to be saddled and without more ado he set off in the darkness to ride to Coppice Farm. Wilkins, when informed of the decision, never let his expression slip for a moment: with a 'very good, my Lord', he said goodbye to the proposed dalliance with the merry widow.

As Robert drove through the darkness he wondered what Elizabeth's family were like. He had understood that she was alone in the world now that her stepfather Mr Baines had died. In any case, he thought, his Aunt Jane had proved more than willing to take on responsibility of such a lovely orphan, and perhaps she was not alone in the world, after all. It certainly seemed that she had a house in Copthorne. It was futile to speculate, after all, he would be seeing her soon. Just for now, he must concentrate on making the best speed he could.

The coachman had given few details, merely that they'd been detained at the Black Lion. Robert had also stopped at the Black Lion, but not for rest and refreshment. He wanted to try and obtain information about the attempted robbery, and attack on Miss Winfield. He got nowhere with his enquiries. Both the landlord and the rabble in the tap room were determined to know nothing. He was soon off again on his way to Coppice Farm. With any luck he should reach them very quickly. Pray God Elizabeth was all right.

Dusty and anxious, he arrived at the farmhouse to find all the lights blazing and Andrew Martin, opening the door himself. He greeted Robert worriedly in the hallway, before introducing himself as Elizabeth's grandfather.

'Your servant sir,' Robert said politely as they shook hands, then more urgently, 'what has happened? Where is Elizabeth?'

'Her Ladyship was set upon by ruffians who were in the pay of Captain Preston, on the way here, and my granddaughter is even now with the doctor. She has sustained some injuries to her head. He has recommended a decent woman from the village, to help with her nursing care.'

Andrew Martin tried to speak calmly, but

his voice cracked and broke as he told Robert the story. The usually smart and youthful looking man was grey and drawn, his hair untidy and his face unshaven. 'The felons were from Ireland and were in the employ of a Captain Preston of the 47th foot. They are known by the sergeant at the Ridgeway Watch House and will be apprehended as soon as possible. It will be the end of James Preston's army career.'

'Ah, here is the doctor now,' Robert said with some relief.

Her Ladyship ushered the doctor down the stairs and he entered the hall, carrying his leather case and clamping on his soft wide brimmed hat.

Robert gazed at the small grey-haired doctor. 'How is she?' he demanded.

'Comfortable for now. She has been bled and she is now resting.'

'Bled do you say?' He thought of that slender pale girl and wondered how it could be possible to bleed one who looked so delicate.

Looking into the two anxious faces, the doctor said in a gruff tone, 'It is usual to bleed a patient who has head injuries. There can be a risk of fever you see. She has bruising and contusions on her face and bruising on her back where she fell heavily.

But her skull is not cracked, sir, and she will soon be on the mend.' With a reassuring smile, he called for his horse and set off for home. This reassurance was not enough for Robert who reflected that his mother and his beloved had been through a very stressful ordeal.

So, there was no way that Robert could see Elizabeth until the morning. After the first exchange of anxious greetings they went into the sitting-room and sat rather stiffly, saying little and thinking their own thoughts.

He was surprised to hear about Elizabeth's legacy and the discovery of her long lost grandfather, but it was his mother who surprised Robert the most. Once she had got over the shock and horror of the attack, she was an absolute whirlwind, organizing the sick room, helping Elizabeth with warm soothing baths and running up and down stairs to make sure the kitchen woman was preparing and cooking the meals as specified.

When the coachman came the next day, he brought with him a packhorse and saddle bags, filled with the best in poultry, with eggs and wines, and bags of linen and clothes for Her Ladyship and Maria. Andrew Martin was looking at least ten years younger now that he had Lady Gascoine's help and the whole village seemed to be streaming up Ridgeway

Hill, to pay their respects to the new young lady at Coppice Farm, who had so bravely rescued Lady Gascoine from footpads. Baskets of early spring flowers, preserves and eggs and handsome sides of bacon were left with Andrew or the industrious Maria whose needles clicked constantly when she wasn't in the sick room. Both she and Lady Gascoigne blossomed under the responsibility of having an invalid to care for. Jane and Bradbury were sent for and set off promptly, in spite of the farm guestrooms being somewhat difficult to organize.

The only person not involved in nursing care or housekeeping was Sir Robert Gascoine, and he was forced to hang about uselessly while every one bustled round him. Robert's frustration grew by the minute as he received the same response to his requests.

'Miss Winfield is not well enough to receive visitors, sir.'

This was the message that was relayed to Robert every time he made a request to see her or to speak to her and after two days, he could stand it no longer. He waited till Mama was in deep conversation with the cook and Elizabeth was being attended to by Maria, then he ran up the stairs two at a time and knocked on her door. He strode into the room and motioned to the maid to be gone.

The maid scuttled away obediently, throwing a glance of terror towards Elizabeth who had just stepped out of the bath and was standing with her back to him, wrapped in a towel. Not expecting him, she turned carefully when she heard the door, mindful of her sore head and bruised back, but stepped back quickly, drawing the towel more closely round her slim body, as he stepped into the room. She looked round desperately for the maid, and blinked at Robert's haggard profile and distraught expression. The main impression that she gave was one of embarrassed pleasure. She tried to speak but no words came. She wanted to tell him that it was not the action of a gentleman, unworthy of a man in his position. She stood unable to move; trembling violently as he strode across the room, towards her.

'What are you about, Elizabeth, to deny me access to you, when you must know I'm beside myself with anxiety for you?' His despairing words were accompanied with a firm grip on her naked shoulders, swinging her round to the light so that he could see her face the more clearly.

As she looked up at him Elizabeth felt an overwhelming sense of relief. And joy. A shuddering sob escaped her and she fell against him clutching at his familiar, wide chest, breathing in the perfume of him, and ruining with her hot, copious tears the fine fabric of his fashionable jacket.

He drew back a little and secured her face, slippery with tears, between his hands, tilting it gently to his. He was about to say something, but her injured mouth and bruised eyes made that too difficult.

Elizabeth sensed his hands consciously becoming gentler, his grip less firm as he saw the extent of her cruel bruises. She looked up through spiky lashes, drenched in tears as his eyes searched her face, and she watched his anguish as he whispered her name and silently, gently, stroked the still-swollen purple lip, and the yellow and blue bruise on her cheek with a careful finger.

'Is this what the brutes did to you?' he asked quietly.

'It was my own foolishness,' she faltered, 'but I was so angry when he threw Lady Gascoine's jewel box into the sack and when he . . . he . . . ' She hiccupped with the strong emotion of her recollection of the evil, grasping Captain Preston.

'Hush,' he soothed her and pulled her close to him, his fingers winding through her damp golden curls, his lips ceaselessly caressing her so gently as not to hurt her bruised skin.

'Here, let me dry your hair,' he said and

took a spare towel to press out the water from her ringlets and smooth the wayward curls away from her brow. His hands slipped to her shoulders and held her warm body through the damp fabric of the towel. Elizabeth began to feel the strangest excitement gripping her.

Instead of protesting, 'Oh no, Sir Robert I am quite able to dry myself,' she was welcoming the feel of his hands. Worse still, the closeness of his body to hers, which should have had her recoiling in disgust, felt oddly comforting. She artlessly wound her arms round his neck and he bent to kiss her, very carefully. The upper end of the towel, which had been wound firmly above her breasts, was now in danger of slipping and destroying what small modesty she had left, and she hastily lowered one hand to clutch it to her. His lips at last found hers and his tongue tip gently caressed her silky, painful lips. Just as her breathing quickened and her lips parted in response, there was the sound of footsteps on the stairs and Lady Gascoine entered suddenly with Jane Gibson.

'Why, Robert,' his mother said calmly. 'What can you be thinking of to disturb Miss Winfield like this? She is under doctor's orders to take her sleeping draught and be in bed by nine o'clock.'

She bustled up to Elizabeth and said,

'Come, my dear, let me get you back to bed. If you are feeling better tomorrow, you may get up for an hour or two. Look, here's my sister and Bradbury to see how you are. Shoo, Robert. You are most indelicate to intrude in a lady's bedchamber like this. Go away at once.'

'No,' he said. 'I won't go, Elizabeth, until you tell me that you love me.' He approached Elizabeth again. 'Say you love me, or I won't go.'

She cast an anguished look at Lady Gascoine. Miss Gibson and Bradbury remained frozen in the doorway, gazing fixedly at her, awaiting her response.

'Say it,' he growled with his eyes upon her.

'I . . . I love you,' she acknowledged, with an anguished wail.

'Say you want me as much as I want you. Say it.' He held her.

The three women watched with bated breath.

'Yes, I want you,' she said at last.

'And that you'll marry me.'

'Yes. I'll marry you, whenever you want.'

With his honour satisfied, he kissed her again and allowed the three women to make way for him as he carried her to bed.

We do hope that you have enjoyed reading this large print book.

Did you know that all of our titles are available for purchase?

We publish a wide range of high quality large print books including:
Romances, Mysteries, Classics
General Fiction
Non Fiction and Westerns

Special interest titles available in large print are:
The Little Oxford Dictionary
Music Book
Song Book
Hymn Book
Service Book

Also available from us courtesy of Oxford University Press:
Young Readers' Dictionary
(large print edition)
Young Readers' Thesaurus
(large print edition)

For further information or a free brochure, please contact us at:
Ulverscroft Large Print Books Ltd.,
The Green, Bradgate Road, Anstey,
Leicester, LE7 7FU, England.
Tel: (00 44) 0116 236 4325
Fax: (00 44) 0116 234 0205

Other titles published by
The House of Ulverscroft:

A PARTICULAR CIRCUMSTANCE

Shirley Smith

Charlotte Grayson and her sister Kitty are living with their widowed mother at Westbury Hall, which they are renting from the wealthy Sir Benjamin Westbury. During a violent thunderstorm, part of the library panelling is broken away, revealing a gruesome skeleton. The man had obviously been murdered — but who is he and how did he get there? To make matters worse, Sir Benjamin returns home unexpectedly, bringing with him his handsome great-nephew, Hugo, who demands that they leave the Hall forthwith. As this gripping story unfolds, past family tensions are revealed and Charlotte puts herself in mortal danger.

TANGLED DESTINY

Shirley Smith

Beautiful heiress Sophia Winterton runs away on her wedding day, defying her Aunt Harriet and her fiancé, Lord Devenish. Still in her wedding gown, Sophia takes the stagecoach to London to seek sanctuary with her godmother. Walking to the Eight Bells coaching inn, she meets the attractive Sir Paul Maunders, who is reputed to be a rake. He escorts Sophia to her godmother's house in Islington. But Sophia's troubles have barely begun. Harriet is bent on revenge and Sir Paul is determined to have his own way. Sophia has a testing path to follow before finding happiness.

DANGEROUS LEGACY

Shirley Smith

When Sir Thomas Capley inherits a fortune from his great-uncle, he returns to Wintham determined to restore the family seat to its former glory. In somewhat unusual circumstances, he meets the proud and beautiful heiress, Miss Helena Steer, who has decided never to marry and, instead, devotes herself to her widowed father and her two young sisters. However, aided by Thomas's mischievous grandmother, the couple fall in love. There are many dangerous adventures for both of them, but will Helena find happiness with the passionate Sir Thomas?

DEAR MISS GREY

Shirley Smith

When beautiful Lucy Grey and her brother, William, become orphans, their futures are organized by hard-nosed Aunt Esther. Whilst Will is sent to Oxford University, Lucy is found a post in London as governess to Lord Hallburgh's two motherless children. However, Lucy soon senses a strange and threatening atmosphere in the household, run by Edmund Hallburgh's much older sister, the autocratic Honourable Caroline Hallburgh, who is physically disabled. She sees the growing friendship between Lucy and Edmund as a threat to her own position and is determined to break Lucy Grey . . .

A COUNTRY COTILLION

Sandra Heath

Beautiful Elizabeth French learns both the pleasure and pain of love as the bride of James French. But when the irresistible and infamous libertine dies, Elizabeth chooses to wed a handsome lord, as different from James as day is from night: Sir Alexander Norrington is dark, where James had been so fiercely exciting. Elizabeth assures herself that this is for the best. Then she meets Marcus Sheridan, the Duke of Arlington, who, like James, sets Elizabeth's pulse racing — even as she desperately tries not to fall prey again to a man who would win her heart only to break it.

THE DASHING MISS FAIRCHILD

Emily Hendrickson

Rich and beautiful, Clare Fairchild decides to travel to Bath but, prior to her departure from a Marlborough inn, someone abandons an infant in her carriage. No parents or nanny can be discovered . . . Once in Bath, however, Richard Talbot, an old friend, offers to help solve the mystery. But after they confront the suspected villain, their lives are put in mortal danger. Clare discovers Richard's strength most comforting, whilst Richard, finding Clare ever more enchanting, longs to make her his own. Between the gossips of Bath and the danger of their quest, will they survive to make this possible?